JACK'S GIFT

JACK'S GIFT

Two families, an ocean apart,
changed in ways never imagined

DORINE ANDREWS

AUTHOR'S NOTE

The inspiration for this story sprang from a single incident in my family's past: the death of an uncle at twenty-two, two years before I was born. I asked myself, "Suppose that when he died, he left behind a relationship that would have changed the course of my family's history?"

The details of the B-17 bomber's midair collision are historically accurate, based on accounts of the incident documented in War Department correspondence and letters of eyewitnesses.

In all other aspects, this novel is a work of fiction. Names, characters, places, and incidents are either the product of the author's imagination or used fictitiously, and any resemblance to actual persons, living or dead, and to events or locales are entirely coincidental.

For my mother, Marion Andrews,
from whom I inherited the letters and materials that
inspired this story.

TABLE OF CONTENTS

PROLOGUE

The three B-17 bombers were exposed that day in November 1944, ghostly flying shadows as they broke through a dark steel sky, skating 500 feet above the ink-black sea off the Dutch coast. Whitecaps exploded off the twenty-foot waves. The planes' captains, all Blue Chip pilots, held their positions in the trio despite the buffeting wind and piercing rain that blurred Jack's view out the plane's ball turret nose.

He was confident that his navigation skills and his captain's prowess would get Arf & Arf to its Glatton Airfield home through the muck. But confidence and skills were not enough. In a slit second, something sliced through the plane's fuselage, splitting it in two, pitching the pieces out of the sky into the sea.

PART I—AMAHLI

CHAPTER 1

Rain beat against the window as Amahli opened her eyes to a colorless dawn. Every bone in her body ached, numbed by the horrid weather and the wretched train ride from London to Glatton the day before. She expected the Christmas holiday to be an easy, pleasant break from the pressures of Glatton, but it wasn't. She compelled herself to keep the secret from her parents. She never did that before, and the result this morning was a throbbing head.

That and her anxiety over Jack missing in action combined to create a toxic brew twisting in her gut, putting her to bed, wishing she had never come to Glatton to work in the first place. It took all the fight out of her, leaving her a ragdoll, a tattered, torn mess. New Year's celebrations were for the others. Only buried in the in the oblivion of sleep did she finally escape the painful fog.

An unceasing banging on the door finally made Amahli drag her tall frame out of her disheveled cocoon, pitching off the comforter her mother gave her when she left for Glatton.

"All right! Who is it? I'm coming," Amahli bellowed. The room's cold air bit at her skin. She grabbed her dressing gown from the back of the chair, haphazardly swinging it around her body, and propelled her feet into worn slippers.

"Buggers. I'm coming!" Amahli whacked her hand against the metal headboard. Dizzy and nauseated, she steadied herself, then tramped across the room to the door. Slamming the lock back and turning the knob hard, the door flew open, nearly hitting her in the face.

"I'm knackered, narky, and messy. What's so important?" Amahli's voice squawked like crow.

She gasped. Patricia, one of her two close mates at Glatton, stood before her, dripping, damp, and breathless. "Sorry. I don't seem to have my wits about me."

"I guess not and I forgive you, sweetie. But I've news about Arf & Arf that can't wait. I'm freezing— let me in, will you?"

"Of course." Amahli moved aside like a dutiful servant to let Patricia into her boardinghouse room. She was two heads shorter and plainer than Amahli, with clipped, unruly light-brown hair and round features, but her voice carried a tone, an assuredness, a presence that filled any room she entered. In stark contrast to Patricia, Amahli's appearance was one of striking comeliness: long black hair draped in soft curls at the shoulders, fine high cheekbones, and soft dark-brown eyes that could cool any temper.

Patricia kicked off her muddied wellies and yanked off her damp woolen hat and rain-streaked mackintosh. After handing them to Amahli, she gave her friend a look-over and frowned. Plopping into the saggy seat of the secondhand upholstered chair in the bay window, she announced in her most serious voice, "I've got news to tell you. You've got to hear it."

"Take a minute and let me wake up. How about I put the kettle on for a cuppa?"

Amahli regained her emotional footing. When someone else was upset, she knew to take the opposite tack. She calmed, transforming herself into a soothing friend.

"You're spot on. Both of us need some tea," said Patricia.

Amahli pushed aside the dizziness and stomach upset as she put the dinged but serviceable black kettle on the hotplate and set out two cups on her only tray. She reached for the milk sitting on the cold window ledge, poured tea and milk into each cup, and laced the saucers with shortbread biscuits from an open box she found in the back of the cupboard. Being British counts for something, Amahli reminded herself as she added spoons and brought the tray to the small drop-leaf table lodged in front of the bay window.

Pulling her robe under her, she sat in the straight-backed chair, straining its prewar cheap caning. "I think I'm awake now, so tell me what is urgent this early. It's New Year's Day, right? Why aren't you still tucked into bed sleeping off last night's celebration?"

Patricia inhaled as if priming to slam a medicine ball to the floor. "You mean the celebration you missed? I couldn't sleep after what I learned—I tossed around for a while, so got up and came here."

"I've never known you to not be able to sleep." Amahli thought about the times they shared together. "Anyway, go on. I'm all ears."

"You know my Bill was flying in Dragon Girl that day when Jack was in Arf & Arf."

"Yes, I remember. Tommy was in Bad Time and BJ was in Dragon Girl. Why? They told me that everyone on Arf & Arf was declared missing in action, and everything's been classified."

"They may be just rumors, but I doubt it. Bill got pissed last night—so completely off his trolley in fact that several of his mates had to carry him back to the barracks, but not before he told me about the crash."

Amahli carefully placed her cup back on its saucer and sat motionless, fixing her gaze on Patricia as the words shot through the air.

"He said Bad Time hit Arf & Arf's prop wash. It flung the plane up, then threw it straight down into Arf & Arf, breaking it apart. He said the Arf & Arf boys didn't have a chance. Bad Time recovered, only losing an engine, and Dragon Girl wasn't damaged at all."

"Rubbish! How can you believe a word of it?"

"Because you can't disappear into the North Sea and survive in a storm like that day. And as you said, BJ and Tommy wouldn't tell you anything."

Amahli sat in silence for what seemed like an hour, but was only a minute or two. She exploded in a mournful wail and pitched forward, catching her head in her hands. She gagged then grabbed the waste bin next to the table, spewing vomit. Bits caught on the bin's metal sides and sour liquid splashed on the bottom. Patricia reached for the tea towel, tossed it into her friend's hands, and ran to the sink for water.

"Here, rinse your mouth and spit it in the bin." She handed Amahli the water glass. "Get that foul bile taste out of your mouth, love."

Amahli did exactly as told but remained anchored over the bin. Patricia soothed her, pulling her hair away from her face, and softened her voice to a whisper, her face brushing up against her friend's. "It was an accident, Amahli. He said it was just an awful accident."

Amahli turned, struggling to decipher if the words could be true. She sat back in her chair, speechless, gulping air and more sips of water.

"How in the hell did the pilot let that happen? Did he fall asleep?"

Tears reddened her cheeks. At her side again, Patricia embraced her, letting her fall into emptiness, saying nothing. No words could express what Amahli felt. She'd joined the ranks of hundreds upon thousands of women who endured such anguish, their young lives ripped apart by the folly of war and the men who fight it. Amahli had seen more than enough of it, but at that moment, she was the only one that mattered. Both women were quiet. After a time Patricia broke the embrace to look directly at her.

"I know how impossible the future must look right now. But in time, the vinegar of your pain will evaporate, leaving behind the cleansing scent of cherished memories. When my sister lost her husband in '41, I saw his death try to rip her apart, but now, three years later, she's on the mend because time itself heals, and you will too. We'll survive this damn war. You, of all people, will make yourself whole again. You're not nothing without him—you may even love again if you don't let bitterness stop you."

Amahli grabbed her head. A monster was growing inside, threatening to devour her. Patricia was right: she had to stop it. She inhaled deeply again and again until her pulse calmed. After a time, she took a small cloth, poured warm water from the kettle on it, and cleansed her face of grief, if only temporarily. She stood erect, effecting a restored condition. "I didn't mean to scream like that. I'm a mess. I know you're only the messenger."

She fell into Patricia again, resting her head on her friend's shoulder. "I know eventually I may feel differently, but right now, I just don't see how I am capable of happiness ever again. On top of everything, I'm just completely flummoxed that BJ and Tommy didn't trust me with the truth when I asked them about Jack's disappearance."

Patricia released herself and went to pull on her wellies, now dry. "You may be confused, but quite frankly, I'm livid that none of the men told any of us. Only survivor's guilt and alcohol finally opened Bill up. I bet the airmen's families haven't been told the truth either. I'm going to make sure they are."

"I admire your strength and passion to act. I feel very helpless, disappointed, and let down," said Amahli, then helped Patricia on with her coat, her only protection against the morning's freezing rain that continued to muddy the roads.

"You'll feel stronger. Give yourself time. Remember, I didn't have a genteel upbringing like you. I had no time to be naïve about my future. University was never an option, even in my wildest dreams. I got my passion, my hot temper, by fighting, by taking care of myself. I was the only girl in a poor family of five boys, and we lived among the tenements near the docks. My mum was my only champion—she wasn't strong enough to protect me physically, but she taught me how to take care of myself. She was driven to make sure I would have more than what she settled for."

Patricia paused in buttoning her coat. "She might have looked like just another mousy, ill-clad woman, but she made sure that I learned not to buckle, to wipe my nose and get back in the fray. She taught me to fight with my brains. How do you think I ended up a nurse instead of getting knocked up at seventeen, or working in some filthy factory job? You need to put one step in front of the other, and don't let your emotions get the best of you."

"Well, my friend, I will try. I never knew how much you endured growing up. You inspire me, but do you really think writing the crews' parents is the best thing to do right now?"

"I know I shouldn't, but I must. Bill knows the Arf & Arf's copilot's father—met him back in the States before they came over. I'll write to him. No one should be left in the dark as to how they died that day. They need closure."

Amahli fastened her arms snuggly around Patricia, so close that she felt the other woman's heart beating. After a time Patricia left, closing the door behind her. Amahli dove back into her bed, constructing a cave with her comforter and pillows, and buried herself. Patricia's news confirmed what she sensed when she learned the plane was lost that first week in November. Now she knew there was no hope. Patricia inspired her, but what was the point to a life without Jack, genteel upbringing with university education or not?

Amahli slept for a solid ten hours and into the night after tea and a bite to eat. When she peered out from under the covers before dawn on Monday morning, the rain had stopped, suggesting a better day. Amahli was now restless. Work would rescue her from grief, but it was the nauseating odor from the bin that forced her out of bed.

She held her nose, taking the bin down the hall to the toilet for a washout. In her room, she gathered her clothes and returned, this time for a shower while her room aired. Instead of dressing in her normal work skirt and blouse, she opted for hiking clothes—loose black slacks, sturdy brown hiking boots, and a forest-green knit sweater. Not very ladylike, but she felt stronger and protected in these clothes.

As she tidied up, Amahli chastised herself for not telling her mother and father about Jack on her holiday visit. But she had done everything possible to avoid a confrontation—hence, the secrets. If only she had kept her distance from the GIs that first day in the pub, she wouldn't be suffering now. But she didn't listen to her mother's warnings. She felt like a child again, over protected and unprepared for what was coming. She feared her mother's reaction when she confessed.

Those thoughts were obliterated before she could finish her toast and tea. Her stomach churned and she puked again into the bin.

CHAPTER 2

Amahli tramped the gravel road to the village's main corner, kicking at the bigger stones with the tip of her boots like a frustrated footballer. Her stomach finally settled. Mulling over what few options she could think of, she skipped the local bus that would drop her at the base on its rounds across the countryside surrounding the village. Instead, she set out to walk the two miles to the base. The January air was crisp and the temperature a bit milder. The hike would help clear her mind.

As she walked the road, dodging trucks and carts, her thoughts turned to BJ and Tommy, her other protectors. She was more angry than confused at their distrust. Why hadn't they told her about seeing Jack die? The lame excuse that the plane's downing was classified until after the war wasn't sufficient, because the men knew she had top-secret clearance. She wanted to confirm Patricia's news, and BJ and Tommy were going to be her sources. She was tired of being shut out, of being treated like a victim or some fragile lady.

***

The workday sped by, like it did normally, as Amahli immersed herself in the dozens of communications that needed translating. The work successfully blocked out everything else. Grief awakened only once during the day, at a midday meeting when she glanced up at the big board in the ops room and saw Arf & Arf on the "classified as missing" list.

As the day descended into darkness, she looked up at the wall clock with its red secondhand dashing methodically around its track. She was going to be late if she didn't leave immediately and she couldn't cancel. Her morning note to BJ and Tommy made it clear that they should meet her at the pub. She heaved herself back from her desk, pulled on her coat, and raced to catch the bus.

Wrapped in woolen layers, braced against the now cold, blowy opaque air, Amahli plodded through the slush from the bus stop to Glatton's Addison Arms pub. The road was dark, lit only by her torchlight. She pushed the pub door open, plunging herself into the main room with its aged wood walls, polished bar, low beamed ceiling, and the scattering of tables and benches.

But unlike last autumn, the room was hushed this January evening. The war dragged on, the number of unaccounted for planes increased and the pub grew quiet like a hospital room with people waiting for news. Despite the knowledge that the Third Reich was being pushed back, the pub's inhabitants mourned. Airmen in muffled conversation stood drinking pints at the bar. Others, mostly locals, gathered in small groups, drinking and smoking sitting on benches, a few at tables. Others played darts. Amahli gathered her thoughts while she surveyed the room.

BJ and Tommy huddled in the corner of the pub's back room by the fire at the same table where she and

Jack became engaged the night before the fatal mission two months ago.

"BJ, Tommy!" she called as she strode toward them, her long legs eating the distance between them. These men didn't look like warriors, but rather like boys masquerading as men: cornered, feet nervously tapping the floor as if they had been called to the headmaster's office. No longer the smartly dressed USA airmen who came to save Britain and the world from oblivion just months before, their leather bomber jackets were now scratched, tattered with rips, oil, and sweat stains. Shirt collars, now loose at the neck, were ringed with sweat, and the hands holding cigarettes trembled at times.

War took its toll, swiftly aging their bodies and wounding the men's minds with experiences they could not talk about. Maybe it was easier for those who died because they no longer had memories to haunt them at night.

***

BJ considered Amahli a very classy woman. As she approached the table, her wet boots, wrinkled slacks, pea coat, wool warmer around her neck, and wooly cap—her raven hair pushing out from underneath—couldn't hide her appeal. But today, instead of a glowing smile and bedazzling eyes, BJ gazed upon her deeply furrowed brow and sternly set lips and caught a weariness in the way she held her body. As she pulled off her cap and inhaled deeply, he nudged Tommy to stand up and pay attention, and he braced himself.

"Sit down." The men obeyed.

"Can I get you a pint? I was just going for refills for me and BJ," Tommy said, watching Amahli as she settled into her chair.

"No. I'll just have a tea." She sat silently, staring at the floor, until Tommy returned.

Amahli took a drink of the tea; its warm milky smoothness seemed to relax her some. She took aim at her two friends.

"Is it true what happened to Arf & Arf? That it split in half and fell into the ocean? That it was hit by one of our own planes?"

Before either man could answer, more words spit from her mouth with a voice that had new strength. "Why didn't you tell me when I asked you about it? Why did I have to hear it secondhand two months later from Patricia, whose drunken boyfriend was flying in Dragon Lady?" Her voice slapped at them across the table.

BJ sat upright, rolling back his shoulders to buy time. "Amahli, it's deplorable what happened, but we couldn't tell you—you know that—and that made it all the more awful. Losing Jack was anguish for me as well." He reached for her hands but she withdrew them, putting her hands around her mug. BJ kept talking.

"Bill broke military secrecy. He could go to jail for it. We did not and would not do what he did. I'm deeply sorry, Amahli."

"But did he tell the truth?"

"It's been a living hell for both Tommy and me since it happened. I couldn't even write to Jack's parents about it."

Tommy looked down at his shoes. His hands were shaking, almost spilling his beer. "I didn't write his parents and the others about it either."

Amahli repeated herself. "I'm sure you're sorry, but I am asking you, did he tell the truth about what happened? Was the plane hit by one of our own, causing it to crash into the sea?"

BJ confessed, "Yes. I saw Bad Time hit Arf & Arf and watched it break in half and fall into the water."

"Was it an unavoidable accident or carelessness by the pilot that killed Jack?"

BJ and Tommy looked at each other in silence, hesitating, looking into their beers, avoiding eye contact with Amahli.

"Answer me! Was Jack a war hero or collateral damage because of someone's stupidity?"

Neither man answered her.

"You both know Jack and I would be married right now if he were alive. I have every right to know every bloody detail of what happened, and why it happened. Do you understand?"

BJ saw the terrified look on his buddy's face, watching Tommy gather his courage and speak through his terror. "We've lost a best friend. We are suffering like you are, Amahli."

"You have no conception of what suffering I am going through. I'm pregnant and Jack is dead. You know everything and I know nothing." Tears ran down her face while Tommy and BJ sat in stunned silence.

Pregnant? A baby? The words flashed through BJ's mind.

"Look, I understand that you both tried to protect me. But I need the truth more than I need protection."

Amahli turned Jack's ring around and around on her finger as she spoke.

"We… I'm going to have a baby. It's all I have left of Jack: that and this ring he gave me the night before he died. What I need now is to know what happened." Amahli sat, arms crossed, waiting for the men to speak.

BJ was still unable to speak, suffering in his own anguish. He'd always kept his feelings about Jack secreted away, knowing Jack couldn't love him the same way back, or in the way he loved Amahli. But now, to save his friendship with Amahli and hopefully bring her some peace, he risked it all.

"Amahli, listen to me. I utterly understand what you're going through because I loved Jack as you did. You are not alone in your grief." His head hung down toward the floor.

Amahli reached for his hands and held them tight. "You don't have to tell me, BJ. Your affection for him whenever I saw you two together made it clear to me. Jack would never have rejected you. You know as well as I do that he always took people as they are, not as the world wants them to be. He knew that you loved him and was sad that he couldn't return that love."

The two mourners held hands in silence, sharing their grief. Tommy, bewildered, said nothing and listened to a conversation he obviously did not understand.

"What I can't grasp, BJ, is why you, of all people, wouldn't tell me about Jack and that plane?"

"I know—I should have, and it was an accident, not pilot error. The weather over the North Sea was worse than here at Glatton. We were in a tight formation. The prop wash from Arf & Arf was like a wind shear, shooting Bad Time up and then slamming her down into Arf & Arf.

"Don't blame the pilot because he's a great pilot who did everything he could. It's a miracle that he got his own plane back to the base. It could have been my plane, but we were lucky to only lose one—not two, or all of us."

Amahli hung on his every word, her face frozen.

"We were in the air for over twelve hours. The stress was incredible, out there all alone with no support: just three planes, naked without the whole squadron. Everyone else was called back to base at the start of the mission. Our planes had the lead, too far ahead for radio contact. Without a good dose of Benzedrine keeping him alert, Bad Time's pilot might have been too slow or confused to react quickly."

"What?"

"The War Department issues it—we're not supposed to fall asleep during a mission. Some guys take it all the time, some never."

BJ paused, digging through his mind for what to say next. "Listen, I don't know if the pilot took it or not, but he reacted quickly, saving his plane and ours, the lives of many men. The whole thing was just a tragic, horrible accident."

The mourners sat silently for a time.

"Can we ask you about the baby?" BJ spoke softly, scanning her face. She nodded.

"What will you do?" Tommy blurted out. BJ shot him a look that would have killed him if it were a bullet. But that didn't stop Tommy from letting his naïve, conservative Nebraska churchgoing beliefs push him onward.

"Amahli, you're in big trouble, from what I know. I can only guess what will happen to your reputation. Do your parents know? Will they accept it? You can keep the child a secret, give it up for adoption, you know."

Amahli gently smiled at Tommy's outburst. "Good questions. My parents don't know anything about Jack, his death, or the baby. My father won't judge me and will support my decision to keep the baby because he will welcome his first grandchild. My guess is that my mother will be hysterical and carry on about me being an unwed mother of an American GI's child—which she warned me against. I am counting on the fact that her desire to be a grandmother will win her over. Eventually, she'll let me out of Naraka and I won't have a minute to myself."

"What's Naraka?" Tommy was again bewildered.

"It's Hindu purgatory, where you wait after you die until your fate is decided. Once she accepts the baby, she'll take over. My mother is a very strong woman, like your General Eisenhower. That I'll have to endure, but it's an exceedingly small burden to bear to have a child that is not only loved by her mother, but also cherished by grandparents."

BJ smiled. "That's my mate—brilliant, such strength. You'll have challenges, but like me, you'll find a way. Living outside of what people expect gives one a broader perspective on what is important to cherish."

"But what about Jack's family? What are you going to do about them?" asked Tommy.

"Nothing. What would you say if your twenty-two-year-old son fathered a bastard halfway around the world with a mixed-race, five-foot-ten Amazon of a woman? And that she was four years older than him and he only knew her for five months?"

"Uh, if you put it that way." Tommy blushed.

"They'd call me a slut out to snag an American husband. That's what they'd say." BJ and Tommy had never heard a woman speak roughly, especially a British woman. They both sat up, like being called to attention in a roll call.

"I'm not throwing unneeded emotional damage on the child. She'll have her family right here in England to protect her and keep her safe."

BJ's eyes met hers. "I see where you're going, but eventually the child will want to know about her father and his family."

He was about to say something else, but she said, "I'll cross that bridge when I come to it, BJ. My world has just gone upside down. It's all I can handle right now."

Her abruptness pierced the air between them. The three sat silently, the men looking down at their beers again, their faces full of worry.

***

Amahli sat at the table, her frustration having exhausted itself like air from a burst balloon. She remembered how kind and inclusive the two men had been since Jack's disappearance.

"Look, my friends, I may appear shipwrecked, adrift in a leaky lifeboat, but I know I will survive, so don't worry. I have a patch kit in my pocket and I won't bodge it up. I'll keep myself afloat…I'll make it with my child."

Amahli longed to believe what she just declared. If she said it enough times, maybe it would be true. The three friends stood, turned together arm in arm, and left the pub, heading back to play their roles in the bloody war.

The night was surprisingly warm and clear, a waxing moon lighting the way. The men walked back to the base, leaving Amahli to amble home by herself. She wanted to be alone for a bit and so took the path across the grassy and tree-lined town square. It was quiet, the air still. Blackout rules kept the village dark, but she didn't need her torchlight. She gazed at billions of stars that filled the sky and the moon that lit her path. Seeing the Milky Way galaxy overhead reminded her of just how inconsequential humans are in the greater scheme of the universe. Whether that was reassuring or frightening, Amahli wasn't sure because she felt both.

She put up a strong front for BJ and Tommy, but waves of conflicting thoughts and piercing fears now knotted her brain as they crashed against her skull. It all felt very raw…with sharp edges. She fought to keep panic at bay, knowing that her situation couldn't get much worse. She could destroy everything—the relationship with her parents and her hopes for a career and independent life—if she stumbled about like a belligerent bull, breaking everything in its violent path. But reality was reality.

Instinct told her that the priority was the health and well-being of her child. Her bones told her it was a girl who must thrive. Amahli needed her parents. The family had resources, unlike the families of many unmarried and pregnant women her age. In the end, her parents would not throw her into the streets to survive alone. Or will they? No matter what was to come, she must heed Patricia's advice to fight for what she wanted and stop herself from becoming a victim of circumstances.

The brilliant moonlight now overpowered the night sky. It glinted off Jack's silver locket ring. She pulled it off her finger, opened the compartment, and held it out in front of her.

"Well, Jack Jackson. What have we done? How I wish you were here with me." Amahli would never again hear his voice, feel his touch on her body, or share the joy of this child. "I will always wear this ring, and our daughter will be everything she can be." Amahli smiled, her hair falling softly on her shoulders, hiding her face as she snapped the locket closed with renewed strength and returned it to her finger.

In the morning she posted a letter to her parents, after speaking with the base commander about leaving in April. That would give her time to establish life with her parents and prepare for the baby. She still grieved for Jack and it hurt like hell, but she was going to create a path to the future, whatever the consequences might be.

Dearest Maa and Papa:

I hope you are both safe and well despite the dreary winter weather and continued bombings. I worry sometimes that London is too dangerous for you. I have good news. I'll be coming home in less than four months—April, I expect. My work will end soon now that the war is winding down. The Nazis are taking a beating from our American friends. They can't hold out for many more months.

It has been good working here at the airbase. The Americans are swell…"brilliant" as we say. I've learned much and believe that I've made a difference, but it is time to come home.

I will let you know about my train arrival as soon as firm plans are in place.
Your loving daughter, Amahli

CHAPTER 3

Amahli cozied herself into the window corner of the train's compartment bench facing south, toward London, and watched the April English countryside pass by. Pleased that she was the sole occupant, she let her mind ramble as she listened to the hum of the wheels on the track. Spring growth carpeted the fields. Roads were framed with green hedge rows and flowers. In the villages, people once again were walking about, freed from the winter's cold. She yearned for her parents to welcome her today as they did when she arrived for the December holiday four months earlier. She had first spotted them standing back from the edge on the cold platform as the train pulled into Paddington, its steel and glass roof cocooning the multitude of track platforms. A cacophony and blurred movements greeted her—people scurrying, shouting, and waving at trains; steam engines wheezing, bells ringing, whistles piercing; and trainmen yelling instructions. The jammed platform hadn't stopped Papa as he boldly pushed through the crowd, clearing a path for her mother to greet her at the compartment door.

Amahli pulled her case from the overhead shelf, thinking how fine it was to be tall in circumstances like these. Glancing at her hand, she spied Jack's ring. She quickly pulled it off and stuffed it into her purse. She couldn't fathom how to tell her parents about him. She was afraid they wouldn't understand their relationship, his tragic death, or the resulting pregnancy—one that did not yet show. "Thank heaven for small favors," she whispered to herself.

The train ride didn't muss her suit, which straightened nicely when she stretched to pull her case down. The green serge fabric offset her olive complexion and dark hair perfectly. Her mother's pearl necklace and earrings, a gift when she left London for Glatton in the summer of 1943, framed her neck. Her deep-burgundy–leather heeled shoes, resoled and polished, complemented the suit…but not perfectly. Black shoes would have been better, but it was the only good pair at hand. The skirt, shortened instead of being replaced, highlighted her long legs, the narrow black belt emphasized her small waist, and the dramatic cut of the lapels pointed to her strong square shoulders. Like many women during the war, she learned to mend what she had, unable to acquire new clothes and accessories due to rationing.

After smoothing her hair, she donned her black swing coat and matching hat, balancing herself as the train jerked to a stop with one final blast of steam just past where her parents were standing on the platform below. Stepping from the train compartment, Amahli saw the small sprig of holly with a red ribbon pinned to the lapel of her mother's coat, which her father always gave at Christmas. Underneath that deep-brown frayed cashmere overcoat was the bright yellow and gold sari Maa wore only for celebrations.

Papa looked distinguished and well dressed as always, his hair just beginning to gray at the edges with a single silver streak arching over the top of his head. His face was clean-shaven with a well-trimmed mustache, and his Scottish blue eyes sparkled behind gold-rimmed glasses. He wasn't stout, but certainly no longer as slim as when she was a child. In every way, she considered him a perfect father.

With open arms, Amahli's happiness at being home again bubbled over. "Not being with you on this Christmas holiday would have been unbearable. It feels good to be home."

Papa stretched to his full height, looking like the diplomat he was. He faced her, pinned a beribboned holly sprig on her coat, and whispered, "You have come back to us. Thank you." He stepped back ushering his wife forward.

Amahli admired her father for giving way to her mother, Amita, gracefully, but always close at hand if she and Maa got into a dustup.

Amahli smiled as her mother said in Hindi, "Oh, my dear, it's good to see you again. Safe. All in one piece. But my, you look very sharp in your suit." Maa clucked, kissing her again. "You do look a bit weary… Was the train journey difficult?"

"No, Maa. But I have been working extra hours so I could come for the holiday as early as possible. Don't worry—it's just tiredness from work. My spirits are lifted now that I'm home."

"You will come home to a fine dinner. We saved our ration coupons for your return to eat just as we did before the war. I've made all your favorite dishes." Maa was a brilliant and proud chef. "We'll start with papdi chaat, then murg makani, kaali dall, tikka masala, and jeera rice. And of course there's kaju katli for pudding."

Amahli's mind raced as her mother ran through the menu. The curry and masala distinctive spice aromas always awakened her senses. The cardamom, ginger, cumin, nutmeg, cinnamon, cloves, saffron, coriander, mace, and turmeric—earthy fragrances—were intoxicating, filling her memories. Of course, the cashew pudding didn't smell as much as tingle her tongue with its fabulously sweet, nutty flavor.

"Maa, you must have been cooking for days. We can't possibly eat all of it."

"It doesn't matter, my child. I will take some to the feeding center near the hospital if need be. Besides, you look like you've not eaten in days. Is something wrong?" Maa lovingly nagged.

"There's not much Indian food in Glatton Village, I'm sorry to say. There I eat to live, not live to eat." Her mother, shorter than her daughter, hugged Amahli, resting her head on her child's chest.

Papa picked up Amahli's case and guided his women down the platform and out of the station, following others who came to welcome home their loved ones. Maa, arm in arm with their beloved offspring, followed her husband as they walked to the slushy curb where a line of black cabs queued. Papa opened the first cab's back door, ushered them into the vehicle, and loaded the luggage. He stepped in, taking the hinged seat behind the driver to face backward in the cab.

Amahli was not shocked to see a woman driving the cab. The war had pulled most able-bodied men into service, leaving it to the women to keep transportation alive, along with many other infrastructure necessities.

The family slid back and forth on the leather seats as the cab careened through the city, dodging building debris in the street.

"Sorry 'bout that, my dears," the driver said as she swerved around a pile of wreckage. The cab's hand straps saved them from crashing into each other. "Bombs landed in this area last night. Luckily, only a few were injured now that the attack sirens and radar are working. People have time to get to shelters."

Amahli looked at her parents with a serious frown. "The bombing has not eased?"

"We've learned how to handle it. Not to worry." Her father always had a way of not exactly answering her questions. "The radar and American antiaircraft guns are making a significant difference. We're safer now. The heaviest bombing is on the other side of London Bridge, near the docks and in the southern manufacturing boroughs."

The cab pulled up in front of their home on the north side of London. Their townhouse was still intact, three stories with large blackout-cloth–draped windows. The exterior needed some repairs to its sandstone skin, protective black and gold appointed iron gate, and the small columned portico.

Papa caught Amahli gazing at up at the building. "We still have utilities, and renters on the third floor now. People need housing, so we offered it to a genuinely nice family. Don't worry—the house is safe and all is functioning here…at least, most of the time."

Although her father's voice was full of joking, Amahli knew he was serious about the intermittent outages. No one escaped the war. Not even Papa, a diplomat. "When the war is over, it'll all be repaired."

"Papa, you never change, do you? Always full of facts, practical actions, and a positive outlook." She took his arm as they walked up to the house.

Maa's dinner was delicious, extravagant, and colorful, perfect for the homecoming celebration of their only child. Amahli had forgotten how unashamedly this food warmed her soul, the aromas soaking deep into her senses. The tastes quieted her worries. She indulged in her parents, reflecting back their warmth and caring, telling them stories about her work at Glatton, the Americans, and their unusual ways. She made them roar with laughter.

Papa updated her about the Foreign Office, which was now focused on war support and, as it was since 1939, secret and not discussed. Maa chattered about how she was still practicing medicine, attending the wounded at the hospital and in the streets, doing triage after raids. She told stories about her circle of Hindu women friends with whom she organized food centers and shelters.

Life was not idyllic, but Amahli saw that her parents felt useful and dedicated, helping as many people as they could to get through the war alive. She admired and was grateful for Papa and Maa, even though Maa's traditional ways sometimes encroached on Amahli's modern sensibilities. Amahli knew that her mother's love was deep and boundless.

The holiday week flew by. Amahli slept late, spent hours by the fire with her parents, shopped with mother, and visited the hospital where she was working. She accompanied her father to his office, where Papa boasted proudly of her work at Glatton as he introduced her to some of his colleagues, including

Sir Williams, another section head at the War Department. But when a rocket bombing happened just two days before she was to return to Glatton, Amahli realized that the risks to her parents were still enormous, despite what her father said.

It was close to ten at night when the sirens started to blare. Her father calmly said, "Amahli, get your coat and come to the shelter with us. The rockets can be deadly, but luckily the radar alerts give us ten minutes, enough time to move to the shelter."

Amahli followed her parents, who easily organized themselves as they had done dozens of times before. "It's much safer in the shelter than huddled in the pantry here in the house. The V2 unmanned rockets are more deadly than the Luftwaffe's bombs."

The family left the house, joining throngs of neighbors who scurried down the street to the Tube entrance. Standing on the underground platform, leaning against the back wall, Amahli listened to rockets exploding. It was both thrilling and frightening. The whole experience reminded her of the German folktale of the Pied Piper who ridded the town Hamelin of a rat manifestation with the lure of his lute. When they emerged an hour later after the "all clear" blast, they found that their street was not severely damaged, but several blocks away she saw smoke and sandstone dust rising in the air. She thought herself lucky that Glatton was too far north to be bombed.

Her parents were unflappable. The next day, life continued as if the air raid was just another event whose results needed attending to. Her father went to the office for several hours and she accompanied her mother to the hospital to help out where she could.

Maa prepared her favorite food once again for dinner on the last night. Amahli thought the visit would end as smoothly as it began, but as they sat drinking tea while finishing the rice pudding, Maa asked cautiously, "Amahli, have you thought about marriage after this war is over?"

"Maa, we've talked about this before. I'm really not ready to get married."

"I know, but you should start to think about it. You're twenty-six now. You don't want to spend your life alone, do you?"

"Maa, please." Amahli was not amused, but knew not interrupt her mother…yet.

"I know several young men who would make a handsome partner for you." Amita's eyes twinkled as she persisted. "All from good Hindu families, with strong ties to London, public school educations, and solid government positions to work in afterward.

"Don't you agree, Thomas, that we should make plans? With the Americans now in the war, I believe we'll have Amahli back by summer."

Maa looked at her husband, anticipating a supportive response. Amahli also looked expectantly at Papa, begging for an argument against it.

"Amita, my dear, I think we'd better wait for such plans until we truly know the war is over. Perhaps Amahli would like to finish university and work first. And remember, our daughter is half British, so an arranged marriage might not be quite right for her."

"Yes, yes. I understand, but I do want grandchildren. Don't you?"

"Maa, please. I know you mean well for me, but I do prefer the path that Papa lays out. I will marry in time and I will give you grandchildren—at least one, I promise."

Amahli held her breath, knowing that the last half of her statement had already come true.

"Maa, consider what an advantage I will have if I delay marriage for a while. Whether he be English or Scottish or Hindu, no professional man will want an uneducated wife."

Amita's face lost its expression as the words she didn't want to hear were spoken. Amahli had to turn the conversation before there was an argument. "And I would much prefer to meet someone by myself, like you did when you met Papa. I want to be like you."

Her father closed his eyes for a minute. Maa ignored her statement, deflecting attention from her own story. "This war has changed you, and many young people. All our traditions are being thrown out the window, whether they're British or Hindu."

She was now pleading with her daughter. "Promise me that whoever he may be, he comes from a good family with a good education, has a decent place for you to live, and a good job in London. I want a proper engagement and wedding. And please, no running off to America. Their men are brave, but I'm not sure about their manners and casual ways."

"Maa, I won't run off to America. You can trust me on that. But remember, you're not exactly a traditional woman yourself."

"Yes and no. But that was a different time and place," Amita said, deflecting again.

Papa comprehended the web his wife was weaving. "Now, Amita, Amahli is a modern woman who will know when she is ready to be married. For now, she's working for the war effort and doing quite well. All that you talk about is just too far into the future." Papa winked at Amahli.

"Maa, please don't worry. As we say, at times like these we must breathe deeply and keep calm." She laughed, hoping her mother understood the humor. Taking her mother's hand, Amahli asked, "Now, how about serving up that last bit of the kaju katli before I go to bed?"

***

Now the train's whistle announcing its arrival into Paddington brought Amahli out of her reverie. Instead of dressing smartly, as she did in December, she looked down at the shapeless hand-me-down print housedress and light cotton twill coat she borrowed from Patricia's older sister. They hung loosely, providing breathing room for her swelling belly and much-needed camouflage. Instead of stuffing Jack's airman's ring into the bottom of her purse, she held out her hand to admire it. She was weary, but ready to be home and ready to be honest with her parents. Unfortunately, her stomach churned and sweat formed around her hairline as she contemplated the afternoon that lay ahead.

As she opened the compartment door and struggled with her bag, she almost fell into her parents' arms. Her mother's brow was furrowed as she greeted her, but it quickly became a painted-on smile.

"What has happened to you? Why are you dressing like an old flower woman?" Maa asked, hugging her daughter. Her forehead wrinkled again as Amahli's protruding abdomen pressed against her body. "What's wrong?"

Amahli opened her mouth, but before she could say a word, Papa said, "Amita, let's just get Amahli home. She can tell us all about everything once she's settled."

She thanked her father with her eyes as the three walked together to the cab stand, this time in April's garden-fresh, sun-drenched air, not cold winter rain. Amahli's face warmed and she lost herself to the spring breeze for the moment.

Like before, a black cab driven by a woman swiftly delivered them home. Once inside the house, Thomas and his daughter settled in the front room while Amita went to prepare tea, leaving them alone.

"Papa, my life has changed. I don't know if Maa is going to understand, because it isn't going to be easy when I tell her what has happened. More than anything right now, I need your support."

Amahli caught her father gazing at the ring and the shape of her dress. He didn't ask any questions. She realized that the afternoon was going to be more difficult than she expected. Whatever was going to happen, she would have to deal with her mother herself. She was a grown woman now, and Patricia was right—it was time to wipe her nose and take on her own struggles.

"I love you. I love your mother. You must trust me to support you in my own way and in my own time, but today you must tell your mother the whole story," was all that he said. They waited together in silence for Maa to come with the tea.

Amita joined them carrying a large tray of tea, small crustless cucumber sandwiches, and delicately iced petit four cakes. The meticulously prepared creations reminded Amahli of her mother's love of English tradition. Now here she was, breaking all tradition.

Amahli tried to stand to help her mother, but her body no longer balanced as it should and she dropped back into her chair before she careened across the front room floor. Thomas was quickly at Amita's side, blocking her view, easing the tray from her hands and gently placing it on the table.

As the sun began to recline in the afternoon sky and mild dry air filled the room from the open windows, the unraveling began.

"Maa and Papa, it is time to tell you what has happened. Last Christmas I kept secrets from you."

Amita put down her tea, her gaze focused on Amahli. She said nothing.

Carefully choosing her words, Amahli recounted the past year: Jack, how they met, fell in love, and how he unexpectedly died in a tragic bomber accident. She showed them her ring, told the story of why it was not a diamond, and opened the locket to share their photo, telling them about his marriage proposal, as well as his kindness and humanity. She ended with an apology.

"Maa, I know I did not heed your warnings. I should have taken them more seriously, but please, please forgive me. Jack was everything I wanted in a husband. His kindness and caring, his strength, and his love of life brought me joy."

Amahli bowed her head, her eyes glistening as tears dropped to the napkin still on her lap. Her mother's every breath echoed off the walls in the now silent room.

***

Maa sat with her eyes closed, absorbing what her daughter just told them. Loss is always difficult, but the loss of someone you truly love is a tragedy. Amita turned to her husband, reaching for his hand, unable to fathom what it would be like without him at her side. She was not going to punish her daughter, but she was not pleased either.

"I'm sorry for you, but perhaps it is for the best. The difficulties after the war would have been insurmountable: having to choose between London and someplace in the middle of America, for instance, unable to be near us. We'd all be miserable with you far away."

Maa looked down, raised her head, and spoke softly but firmly to her daughter.

"It is difficult to imagine, but I believe that what happened to Jack is all for the best, my dear. He's gone now—it's over and you're home. With rest and some decent food, you'll mend and be able to move forward with your life.

"You were correct in your letter. The war's nearly over. The bombings have slowed to a trickle, people are returning to London. You can look forward to finishing university, find a job, if you wish, and in time make a marriage with someone more like us, more accustomed to our way of life."

Amahli swallowed, gasping for air. "Maa, blaming Jack for being an American isn't fair. That is neither here nor there, is it?"

"No, I don't suppose it is fair, but it is the truth and it is over."

"Maa, no, it isn't." She stood, boldly displaying her pregnancy, pacing the room as she prepared to speak.

Her mother now recognized the situation and sat on the edge of her chair as if a lioness, set to pounce. Thomas sat back, his arms casually draped on the arms of his chair.

Amahli spoke. "Jack and I were going to be married in November. The night before he died… Well, we had a night together. As you can see, I'm pregnant with his child. Jack never knew." She collapsed into the sofa instead of the chair.

The softening orange and yellow sunset and fresh air didn't come close to extinguishing Amita's blistering reaction. Some mothers might have given in to the dramatic hysterics typically attributed to women's fragile female emotional states. Not Amita: she had never fainted in her life. Instead, she unloaded controlled barrages of accusations, blame, and hurt onto her daughter. She knew her words were like bullets shooting into Amahli's body.

Amahli said nothing for the longest time, not defending herself or Jack, or yelling back at her mother. She did not cry, nor attempt to ask her mother's forgiveness.

Amita finally exhausted herself, stopped her pacing and folded herself in the cushion next to Amahli on the sofa. She knew she overreacted. The fact that Amahli didn't dissolve into tears impressed her, and Amita's disappointment and frustration gradually subsided: she did want a grandchild.

Amita took her daughter's hand and spoke again, this time calmly. "You have stained our family, Amahli. Your father and I will survive, but I fear desperately for you." Her words fell flat in the room. "The path you have set for yourself is arduous and perilous. You'll face rejection at every turn, especially when you attempt to join a social group. Do you have any idea what you're up against?"

Amita pulled out a handkerchief to wipe her wet eyes. "My child, my dear sweet innocent Amahli, I fear for your future and that of the child."

There was nothing more to say as they retreated from a battle which neither would win. Thomas gave Amahli's hand a squeeze as he left the room. Mother and daughter walked in their own aloneness with a gaping distance between them. Each slowly climbed the stairs, caught in their own separate anguish.

***

In her room, Amahli clambered into bed. Maa had given her crisply ironed sheets, a fluffed and fragrant with lavender comforter, and pillows carefully sheathed in lace-trimmed cases. She tried to luxuriate in the bedding, but she couldn't settle with her increasingly cumbersome body making movement difficult.

Amahli was at war with herself, simultaneously despondent, hopeful, and anxious. Her mother's words scattered about her brain, creating chaos that made sleep impossible. Would her mother force her from their home? Would she take the baby away?

Amahli now realized the extent of her crisis if she were left alone with no help from her parents. The baby was unplanned, here and not going away. Above all, the baby must be kept safe and she would give up everything for her child. She shifted from side to side as she listened to the loud whispers coming from her parents' room across the hall. Finally the buzzing faded into the background and she fell into a fitful sleep.

For the next three days, Maa did not speak to Amahli. If she came into the sitting room, Amita would retreat to the office, firmly closing the door behind her, refusing to acknowledge Amahli's presence. She cooked meals but did not eat with Thomas or her daughter in the dining room.

It was a brooding torment to be in the house. During the day, Amahli escaped for walks, going to the library to sit and read in a space where no one would judge her. At night in bed, she listened to her parents' muffled talk. On the fourth night, she heard nothing.

CHAPTER 4

Amita walked into her daughter's room, pulled back the blackout curtains, releasing streaks of sunshine into Amahli's room and awakening her, despite her efforts to hide under the comforter. She set a breakfast tray full of Amahli's favorite pastries and tea on the bed.

Amahli sat up and Amita asked one question. "When is the baby due?"

"The doctor said the first week in August." Amahli scooted back toward the headboard to sit more comfortably.

Amita put her hands together as if praying and said, "We must prepare for her arrival."

"Maa, where is your wall of silence? What happened?"

"I realize that your innocence in this situation—and, quite frankly, your stupidity—are defects your father and I brought upon ourselves. We protected you too fiercely, so you went to Glatton without the proper armor."

"All right, but I don't think that's actually the case, Maa."

Maa changed the subject like flipping a page in a good book. "It'll take time to create a nursery because this room must work for the both of you. We need to paint and decorate. Supplies and furniture will be hard to come by, so we need to start sorting it out today.

And clothes… We need clothes for you and baby clothes for the sweet little girl you will have."

"Maa, how do you know it is going to be a girl?"

"How do I know? How do I know?" her mother sang. "I know because of the god Krishna—you know, the embodiment of love and divine joy and destroyer of pain and sins. I have meditated and prayed to him since you came home. He answered my prayers, telling me that all that is good would come to me and bring me joy because I am your mother. You will give birth to my granddaughter and we will raise her together, the three of us."

"Really? What about all the discussions with Papa these last nights?"

"Well, it was both Krishna and your father." Amita blushed. "He helped me interpret the insights that Krishna gave to me."

Amahli grinned like a Cheshire cat. Here was a highly educated woman, a medical doctor, who fell back on her religious beliefs in crisis. Maybe there was something precious in having such faith.

"And what makes you sure your grandchild will be a girl?"

"Mark my words. You will have a daughter." Maa was adamant, clapping her hands again in the air as if sprinkling fairy dust throughout the room. "What if your circumstances are less than traditional? I'm fine with it now that your father has reminded me of some parallels in our lives. And like I said before, the war has changed everything. If I don't accept the situation, I will lose you and my granddaughter, and that cannot happen. We can't look back, only forward and together. We have a new family member to take care of and I have some catching up to do!" Her face glowed.

Amahli reached out, taking her mother's hands. "Maa, every time I think I have you figured out, you surprise me. Is there something I should know about your past that you never told me about?"

Maa hesitated before answering. "Some time I will tell you about it, but now's not the time. Eat your breakfast. You need decent clothes, good food, and joy in your life from now on."

Amahli fell into her mother's arms, welcoming the smothering. Papa stood in the doorway, a look of approval on his face. Amahli wondered if she would ever love someone as much as her father loved them.

42

CHAPTER 5

One evening later that month, with preparations well underway, Thomas retreated to bed before ten. The house was quiet. Amahli sat on the sofa reading in her mother's study. On the side table, an antique lamp with a mica shade cast a warm glow in the room. Amita was finishing paperwork at her desk on the opposite side of the room. Amahli laid down her book.

"Maa, you never told me much about your life before Papa. I know you were the daughter of a raja and that you met Papa when you were going to medical school in England, but nothing else. Why did you move to London? How did you obtain your parents' approval? Wasn't it against tradition for Hindu upper-class women in the 1920s to marry outside the religion and work for a living?"

Maa pushed aside her paperwork on her desk and moved to the cushioned sofa to sit next to her daughter. She nestled comfortably into the sofa's softness.

"I never told you about my life in India because I wanted you to be proud of me. I wanted you to have a normal upbringing. What happened to me brought me shame."

"But didn't being the daughter of a raja protect you? Were you abused?"

"In a manner of speaking. I learned that nothing protects a woman. I did something against tradition because I had no other choice if I were to survive. Although we're happy for you and the baby, you'll not escape the shame. Have you thought about that?"

"Yes, Maa. I realize that now. I'm an unwed mother and my daughter never had a legal father."

"Good. I am pleased that you've gotten beyond the denial of your situation."

"I don't care what people might say of me, but I am concerned of what they may say about my daughter, you, and Papa because of my actions. I'll protect you all, I promise. How do I do that? I'm not sure yet."

"You'll start by letting us help you because you can't do this alone; we'll work together to protect the baby. Your father and I will be fine." Maa wrapped her arm around Amahli's shoulder. "Now, sit back and let your worries go. I'll tell you my story.

"I was twelve when my mother started to plan for me to marry a handsome man of means in three years. Once married, I would quickly make her a worthy grandmother by having many children to extend the family lineage. And because father was a raja of some stature in our district, I was sent to the best schools he could afford, a new and rare opportunity for Hindu women. This, my mother believed, would create competition for my hand, so she encouraged my education. I agreed. Accepting what she wanted for me as was the tradition…until the accident.

"Our family was invited to attend a grand exhibition built by the maharaja of our state, a forward-thinking man for his time. The event was on the grounds of his palace. It was fabulous, with glass- and metal-framed buildings reaching several stories into the sky filled with farming, communications and new business technologies, art, weaving, foods, and such—not only from India, but from around the British Empire, and even China. We were thoroughly enjoying it, each of us concentrating on our own interests as we wandered through the exhibits. I wanted to escape from my brother, who was supposed to be chaperoning me, so I quietly ducked out behind a garden display, leaving my family inside."

Amahli interjected, "Why didn't your brother run after you? Why didn't he tell your father?"

"Because he didn't want to get in trouble. I believe he thought that I would find my way back to them when I was ready, and anyway, everything was extremely exciting. He didn't want to leave the building.

"Once outside I explored the outer smaller buildings until I came upon one named Library of the Future at the edge of the grounds. I always loved books and went in, even though I was by myself." Maa stopped talking and stared out the window into the night.

"Maa, whatever you tell me, I will keep it with me. No one else will know."

Maa turned to face her daughter, and with misty eyes said, "Please don't be ashamed of me. What I'm about to tell you must never be shared with anyone. Only your father knows."

"What could be terrible?"

"As I said, I wasn't supposed to be alone, but I was—a young, curious girl. I got lost in the books, paging through one after another for some time.

Realizing my family might be looking for me, I started to leave, but my way was blocked by an older man, probably in his thirties. He was elegantly dressed in a traditional, colorfully embroidered and gold trimmed satin suit…and I didn't know that he was the maharaja himself.

"At first I was scared, thinking he might attack me, but he didn't. Instead, he asked, 'Young girl, why do you read these books?' I told him that I loved to read and learn new things. He was intrigued. I don't think he ever met a twelve-year-old girl who spoke directly and enthusiastically about learning. We talked. I was enjoying his company—he was warm, almost flirting with me. I was naïve and flattered so I let it go on and lost track of time again.

"Suddenly we heard people yelling FIRE! and we ran toward the flames engulfing the main hall. People were running everywhere trying to escape, but the fire blocked all but one exit. Some were carrying buckets of water and rugs, hoping to put out the flames. Everyone was colliding with each other, creating chaos of the worst sort. The building collapsed, sending steel and glass down on the people. It's difficult to talk about it, even today.

"I screamed for my mother and father and for my brother. I couldn't find anyone and panicked. If I had returned sooner, we'd have left before the fire started. They were lost in the fire and it was all my fault—"

Amahli interrupted, "Or you could have died in the fire with them."

"I didn't believe that for many years. Through my young eyes, it was my fault that my family was still in the building. I was inconsolable. The maharaja ordered me to go to his home. I was scared… I didn't know what to do, so I did as he commanded.

"In the end, their bodies were found in the middle of the collapsed scaffolding. My family was gone. I had distant relatives in the north, but I didn't want to go to them because they were poor farmers and I never met them. I lied, telling the maharaja that I was now an orphan and would be lost to the streets if he didn't help me. He was an enormously powerful man who could have found a guardian for me. And at the time, I didn't know that I had inherited money. I knew nothing about such things and naïvely believed he would never discover who my family was.

"The situation opened an opportunity for him. You see, he liked me, so I let him charm me and became a member of his household. By the time I was sixteen, our relationship had to be hidden, a dangerous secret because he wasn't like a father anymore. I was special to him, even though he had a wife. The arrangement was simple: be his mistress and I'd be taken care of, and allowed stay or leave when I turned twenty-one. I agreed.

"I was nineteen when I found the field of medicine. Women were beginning to be accepted into medical schools. Without a profession, a way to make my own living, I would've had to remain totally dependent on his kindness, authority, and power. It was also clear that he had found my family's money and kept it, claiming that he was my guardian. I didn't know I might have rights. I was young and naïve, with no other support.

"There were also suspicions among his family members about my special role. The maharaja agreed to send me to university in England for medical training. It was advantageous for both of us. It was there I met your father in my first year at medical school. We dated and I became pregnant with you. You see, I know even experienced women can make mistakes."

Amita cast a solemn expression. "I was devasted to find myself, once again, unmarried with a man older than myself.

"When I told your father about you, he was very good to me. He was in love with me and asked me to marry him immediately. I liked him, but wasn't sure I was in love with him the way he was with me. I had no choice but to accept his proposal. I also decided that I couldn't keep my past a secret from him. I believed that if I didn't tell him and he discovered the truth, I was risking not only my future, but more importantly, yours. I was frightened, but I told your father everything, thinking he would walk away."

"What happened?"

"He didn't reject me. I was taken with his strength and kindness, and the respect he showed me. It was in that very moment I fell deeply and forever in love with your father. We married the next week in a small private ceremony, a mixed-race and mixed-religion couple. We knew the challenges in front of us, but we were committed to make it work and raise you together."

"Did the maharaja come after you?"

"He said to stay in England when I told him I had married Thomas. He wasn't an unkind man. However, he did stop all support and demanded that I never return to Delhi or get in contact with him or anyone in his household. He said my name would never be spoken in his home again but wished me well."

"There is a happy ending?"

"Actually, there is more to the story. You see, your father and I agreed not only to marry, but also to create a partnership. He consented to supporting my medical education and ensuring that I could practice medicine. I promised to stay by his side wherever he was sent for his work. Together, we would raise you. Our partnership provided careers for both of us."

"Maa, what an amazing journey! Is life always like that: a journey with no known end?"

"My dear child, the twists and turns of life will take you in directions you could never imagine or control. You can't let yourself be a victim of circumstances. Turn a situation into a new path, a journey through which you take risks when most don't dare. There is no going back to before—move forward to face what's around the corner… Or in my case, around the library door." Amita laughed.

"Based on what you just told me," Amahli said, tongue in cheek, "you'll not be saying anything more about an arranged marriage with the right Hindu man?"

"No, my dear daughter, I will not. But there must be no secrets between us. Promise?"

"I promise, Maa." They fell into each other's arms.

***

Thomas, Amita, and Amahli Simmons danced with their neighbors on the announcement of victory over Europe on May 8, 1945. Amahli, then seven months pregnant, didn't dance as so much as sway in her father's arms. The war was over. Life could and would move forward.

On August 8, 1945, in the predawn morning, Amahli's water broke, waking her from an unsettled sleep. Within an hour the midwife arrived, noting that everything was at the ready thanks to Amita's perfectionist planning. The three women began the birth ritual on the bed where Amita gave birth to Amahli. Amita soothed her daughter, coached her breathing, and told her when to push as the midwife guided the baby down the birth canal into the world. After an earth-shattering yell at 10:00 a.m., Amahli gave birth to a delightfully large and healthy 8 lb. 6 oz. girl, who announced herself with a ferocious scream to celebrate her freedom. After a bit of cleanup, weighing, and wrapping, the baby girl lay quietly in her mother's safe arms. Papa was called in, joining Maa and Amahli in welcoming their granddaughter.

There were many discussions about the baby's name. Maa wanted Amahli to honor her Hindu heritage. Amahli did that, formally naming her daughter Jaya for the Hindu god of victory, pleasing Amita no end. But Amahli insisted that they honor the baby's father, so everyone agreed to a middle name of Jack and an informal name, JJ, which always reminded them of the love that created her.

JJ was immediately the center of the Simmons family. Although she had her father's gentle nature and big laugh, JJ also had her mother's lungs, which she generously exercised. There was the memorable time when eighteen-month-old JJ was discovered standing in her crib after a nap, swinging her wet nappy over her head and yelling, "Wet! Wet!"

JJ was a playful child with no fear, engaging with people from the moment she met them, along with robust energy. Always pushing boundaries to get what she wanted and screaming at what she would not tolerate. Luckily she liked most food—except kidney pie and aubergine—making dinners an endurable experience for the adults.

On the other hand, once she started walking, she seldom allowed herself to be carried. This led to several embarrassing screaming sessions on Oxford Street. A stroller was the best answer to quell the resistance to being carried, because it seemed it was the looking forward JJ craved more than the walking itself. For Amahli, all of this brought her joyful delight, allowing the grief of losing Jack to ebb away. Happiness returned in full force. Like Patricia told her, time heals.

Maa insisted on taking JJ under her wing, teaching the little girl to call her Nani, the Hindu name for a maternal grandmother. Nani assumed the responsibility of JJ's daily routine, as Thomas was working more than full time in the Foreign Office and Amahli was at university every day finishing her studies. Both Amahli and her father knew they had no choice in the matter. Nani would ensure that JJ learned to eat Indian food, would be immersed in playful learning at all times, and would be read stories until she fell asleep on nights when Amahli was studying late. Nani created a classroom for JJ for her third birthday, determined that her granddaughter learn to read and write in French, Hindi, and English as early as possible. The Simmons family was content, and JJ thrived.

Amahli, however, was concerned for her mother. Although Maa continued to practice medicine several days a week at the hospital, Amahli noticed she was spending little time with her circle of Hindu women friends. One evening after her father had retired and they were once again together in her mother's study, she asked her about it.

"It's no worry," Maa replied. "Between work and the baby, I'm very busy."

Amahli heard something in her voice and was not satisfied with the answer. "But it's not like you to abandon your social life. What happened to your weekly lunches? They must be pleased you're a grandmother. Is it because I'm not married?"

Her mother sighed. "My dear Amahli, you were too young, and it took a long time for them to accept that I'm a doctor. I didn't fit what they thought I should be. The same has happened now that I'm a grandmother. They expected me and your father to find you a husband—any husband—to keep up appearances in the community, or for you to give the child up for adoption. When I told them neither would be possible, that you decided to stay single and that I wasn't going to force you to marry or give up the child, they mostly shunned me. Only one friend, Chanda, has stood by my side. She said she wishes she had such courage years before. She was forced into a sudden arranged marriage, which is why she understands. We have lunch every few weeks. I only want friends like her: people who can move beyond the prejudices of outdated traditions."

"Maa, my heart breaks that I have caused you such pain," said Amahli. "It's not fair of them to reject you. It was my decision, not yours. It was not your fault."

"But in our culture, it is the parents' responsibility, not the daughter's, to ensure a proper marriage at any cost. Even for the British, an unwed mother is likely to be ostracized. I'm sure you've heard of girls who leave home to have a baby and never return, or return without the baby. Some go to America because the stigma is too strong to stay in England. Some families refuse to allow their child to marry a spouse who is illegitimate because it will spoil the family's lineage. You must be cautious. You must protect JJ."

"Oh, Maa. They shamed you because of me. It's my fault and I'm deeply sorry. Is there anything I can say to them to make it right?"

"No, there isn't. Your father and I faced such prejudice, but we faced it together, protecting you, bonding with people who saw the world as we do. You're alone and that's why I worry for you. That's why I want you and JJ to stay with us, to have our protection."

"JJ is a Jackson, but she's a Simmons as well, Maa. I will always cherish her father, but will not flaunt my unwed mother status. However, I won't keep JJ a secret stowed away behind the drapes either. I think, like you and Papa, I must face the challenges. I will stay with you until a new path opens to me. Together, the three of us are JJ's family."

Amahli tried to reassure her mother, but in reality, she knew many challenges would be hers alone.

JACK'S GIFT

PART II—DOROTHY

CHAPTER 6

Crisp November air tussled Joe Jackson's hair when he answered the door. He looked down on a delivery boy—barely twelve years old, from what he could gather—standing nervously in front of him. The boy thrust an envelope into his hands, then ran back to the sidewalk where he had left his fallen bicycle. Joe didn't even have time to tip the kid.

Such a delivery could be good or bad news. It was good news when Andy, already a major in the Army at only twenty-seven, telegraphed them to say he survived the first weeks after the Normandy invasion. Where, he couldn't say, but Joe knew from the papers that the Allies were putting Hitler's army on the defensive outside Paris. Good news again came in September when Jack telegrammed that he was safe, and loved being an airman.

However, this time Joe sensed something ominous. His inner voice told him not to open the letter alone. He took the envelope into the den where his wife Dorothy was sitting.

Two floor-to-ceiling walnut bookcases overflowed with their sons' trophies, framed photographs, and mementos from past family vacations at White Lake. A matching walnut desk was set against a wall beneath a John James Audubon print of two green-winged teal ducks, beautifully rendered in soft browns, black, and taupe, with the male's deep burnt-orange-and-teal feathers enhancing the room's décor. Two green glass and brass desk lamps lit the leather-trimmed pad with leaf green paper that protected the desk's polished surface.

The view was through a bay window facing the street. In it, two well-upholstered wingback chairs and a small circular Dansby oak pedestal table created a warm nook. The antique double globe lamp on the table had been Joe's mother's, and he wired it for electricity some years ago. Dorothy spent a month looking for the room's finishing touches to complement the lamp's cream, green, and burgundy colors. The room sheltered them, providing the warmth that was impossible to feel in the larger formal living room, with its French style stuffed-but-stiff furniture.

Joe sat in his chair across from Dorothy, who was quietly stitching an embroidery piece, her reading glasses tipped down on her nose, and listening to an afternoon radio presentation from The Bell Telephone Hour's Great Artist Series. She was a graceful woman, although not beautiful in the traditional sense. Some described her as handsome, with strength emanating from the way she held her head when she walked. She was a muscular farm girl by upbringing, and after careful eating and good beauty care for over thirty years, her body was still shapely at forty-nine. She dressed in a style that reflected her strength, whether at home or out; the clean lines and muted tones of her dresses and suits reinforced her inner power. Her stocking seams were always straight, her hair properly rolled, and her makeup lightly applied. Only at their

White Lake cottage did she abandon these clothes, giving way to bright cottons, floral prints, cropped slacks, and shorts.

***

Dorothy watched Joe enter the room without raising her eyes from her needlework. She admired his six-foot lean frame and solid features, still handsome at fifty, but the way he dressed was another matter. His legs were slightly bowed, so he hid them in loose hanging pants. He wore a tie and white shirt at work, but preferred shirts with open collars or plain white tee shirts often covered by a baggy button sweater or a light zippered jacket. He was nearly color blind, so Dorothy checked each day to see than his color combinations were acceptable. It was the best she could do.

Dorothy knew she was sometimes impatient and bossy, but always said "Please" and "Thank you." Joe did everything she asked, but at his own slow, careful pace. She could tell he did it deliberately, so it irked her much of the time.

Joe supervised auto production and, now in wartime, military vehicle production. They lived what many would call a solid middle-class life throughout the Great Depression. Joe was even able to purchase the small summer cottage with a big porch and dock on White Lake when the boys were young.

***

Joe knew Dorothy couldn't fathom the hardships others were going through during the Great Depression, believing himself to be a lucky man to have a well-paying, steady job. It wasn't an entitlement. Despite their financial status, they lived without extravagance. Dorothy maintained a lovely home, carefully managing the household budget but insisting that whatever they did acquire was the best they could afford. Joe often joked outside of her hearing, "Dorothy has the taste buds; I pour on the water to make them bloom."

He loved his wife despite not always understanding her—he let her be. Joe liked their settled life with its regular schedule and time for quiet evenings, weekend yardwork, and socializing with friends. What he missed most since sending their sons into the war was the time he and the boys spent working together on the car—changing oil and sparkplugs, doing tune-ups, and rotating tires while laughing and bantering about what to do with the parts left over after everything was reassembled. The great puzzle was why the engine always started and ran well.

Hitler's monstrous war changed everything for them, taking their boys away. Although they denied it to friends, the couple was at loose ends, coping with guilt and waiting for news to fill their empty hearts. The war hollowed out their lives despite the many activities Dorothy organized in an attempt to keep them from dwelling on sadness of the war and their sons fighting in it. They closed the lake cottage now that there was just the two of them. There was no joy in it.

Joe looked at his wife through the haze of the afternoon sun. His kept his fears to himself and waited for Dorothy to look up. She finished a row of stitches, then put down her embroidery and eyed the envelope with apprehension.

"I thought maybe that was Hazel and Bill at the door, but I see that it wasn't."

"No, Dorothy. It was a delivery boy with a telegram."

She turned and lowered the volume on the radio. Joe fingered the envelope, slowly breaking its seal to unlock the message. He adjusted his glasses, then silently read the words typed on white paper strips pasted onto the oat-colored telegraph paper.

The blood drained from Joe's face. His lips wouldn't form words as he gazed into space without blinking.

"What is it? What happened?" she cried. Too impatient for an answer, she snatched the paper to read it for herself, like a little girl who couldn't wait her turn.

Mr. and Mrs. Joseph W. Jackson Sr.:

The Secretary of War desires me to express his deep regret that your son, 2nd Lt. Joseph Jackson Jr, was declared Missing in Action on 08 November 1944. Letter follows = UL Adjutant General

Wails erupted from deep in her throat. She smashed the words, crushing the telegram in her clenched fists. Joe stood up, pulled her out of her chair, and embraced her. Beating her fists against his chest, she cried, her voice cracking. "No, no, no, no!"

Wordlessly, he held her tight, his breath caressing her neck and his arms bracing her from collapsing to the floor. His strength kept her upright. Their son, the sweet baby, the one they almost lost at birth, was gone. Disappeared.

Joe took her, one fragile step at a time, down the unlit hall to their bedroom. As he opened his arms she slid onto the bed, curling into a fetal position atop the satin spread, the one she finished sewing the week before. If she'd been coherent, she'd have protested, wanting the spread pulled back before she lay on the bed. This sturdy, in-charge woman had been diminished into an emotional, helpless little girl, exhausting herself into a fitful sleep.

Joe gently removed her shoes and covered her, fully dressed, with the blanket she carefully placed on the cedar chest at the end of the bed that morning. As he unfolded it, Joe remembered how proud she was about its purchase: "Joe, it's a Hudson Bay. Look at the perfectly balanced simplicity of four stripes woven into it." To Joe, it was just a blanket, a wool one, heavy enough to block out the Michigan winter's freezing night air.

Joe lay down protectively next to her, staring blankly at the ceiling, waiting for something, or for nothing…he didn't know which. His eyes were dry. A terror grabbed at him, turning both mind and body numb. They couldn't have lost their youngest son just four months after he flew to England.

It all must be a terrible mistake.

He drifted in and out of consciousness, fitfully wrestling with the news, but as darkness descended on the house, he knew he couldn't deny what had happened.

Dorothy was sleeping so he carefully turned, sat on the edge of the bed, and using all his strength, stood and walked down the dark hall, methodically making his way to the front door. Above the hall table with the telephone on it, he found the light switch. He picked up the receiver, put his index finger in the "0" on the dial, slowly spun the rotary, and then asked for Western Union in response to the operator's "Number please?" query. The telegram he sent that evening to Andy, stationed somewhere on the ground in France, read:

Jack declared missing in action November 8. Your mother needs you. Can you come home? Dad

There was nothing else he could do and he must go to work in the morning. War production quotas at the plant had to be met. Joe shuffled back down the hall to the bathroom, brushed his teeth and dressed in his pajamas, then lay down next to his wife once again. He slept the rest of the night. Ritual calmed him.

JACK'S GIFT

64

CHAPTER 7

Dorothy woke, her hair matted and her mouth foul. Rubbing her eyes open, she surveyed the dark room, trying to orient herself to the predawn reality. Light from the streetlamp painted a fanlike pattern on the ceiling above her, filtered through the window's open blinds. For a few moments she couldn't remember how or why she was sleeping in her clothes—only that her body ached and her mind churned, confused and conflicted. It was then that the news flooded back to her and doubts spilled out.

What happened? How did it happen? Did he escape alive, only to be captured by the Germans? Is he just missing, or is he really dead? Questions raced through her mind. She suspected that the government's letter wouldn't give her the answers she needed.

Joe slept on his back, gently snoring. Gazing at him, Dorothy saw more gray hair and wrinkles in his face. They both were aging. Her husband must go to work, despite the situation so she let him be at peace. It would take courage and commitment to plow through his unbearable sadness. She admired his perseverance, knowing that Joe was as devasted as she about Jack's disappearance. This tall, gangly, gentle man would tell her to be patient, that in good time they would learn if their son was alive or really lost. His easygoing disposition seduced her when they first met, but she learned over the years that he kept his emotions locked inside himself, paralyzing his ability to act. It would be up to her, a woman whose passion always propelled her forward, to battle the War Department's bureaucracy.

***

Showered, dressed, and alone, now that Joe was at work, Dorothy carefully lifted a cloth-covered box out of the bottom of the cedar chest at the foot of their bed. The floral pattern of white, pink, and blue summer flowers reminded her of her mother, who filled it with letters, birthday and holiday mementos. Now Dorothy did the same. The hunt for answers would begin with this box, the one in which she stored her sons' letters.

Like a sacred totem, she carried the box to the kitchen, placing it on her new modern bright-yellow Formica and chrome table. Sitting in one of its matching chairs, she retrieved the most recent letter from Jack, dated October 17, 1944, gently unfolding the pale blue onionskin airmail sheets as if they were a museum treasure. She read, hearing Jack's voice crooning in her head.

Dear folks,

How are things around Detroit this week? I'm now on a seven-day leave. Tommy…you remember Tommy? We met on the crossing to England. Anyway, he was going to join BJ and me on leave, but couldn't at the last minute, so BJ and I had the week to ourselves.

They couldn't find us any open flak homes, so we decided to spend it as tourists. BJ and I are staying in a city of about 40,000. It's a very pretty place and has some beautiful parks and gardens. It's noted for its health water and they have some Turkish baths. Also a pool and a stable with some pretty fine horses. BJ and I have been focused on the baths and riding. It's a bit challenging, as they use pancake saddles here, so we don't do much galloping. But it's swell!

We're not far from the Shakespeare Memorial Theatre, although we're not in Stratford-on-Avon. BJ convinced me to join him in seeing one of the plays. He loves the theater. If he's not reading a book, he's taking in a movie or play. It was an enjoyable and very interesting experience, even if I couldn't follow the actors' poetic speech very well.

Of course, by now you realize that at the rate the war is going, I won't possibly be home for Xmas. As for gifts for you folks, I'm in a whirl. I was going to buy you something the other day, but a lady friend told me I was foolish if I did because the prices are so high and only reduce after Xmas. Clothes are almost impossible to get because they require ration coupons.

Say, I wondered if you two would like a dartboard to put up in the rec room? It folds up into its own box right on the wall and has holders for the darts. English people really take the game quite seriously. Besides, it's about time I contributed something toward the rec room. I bought it and it's on its way to you now. Hope you get it before Xmas.

Well, gang, I'll sign off for now and go up and take a bath and shave, as it's almost lunchtime. Be good. Love, Your son, Jack

There was no inkling of the war or its damage in the letter. Jack had warned them that he couldn't discuss specifics about missions or locations, but the generalizations did get frustrating. Dorothy pondered who this "lady friend" in the letter might be. Probably some poor British girl looking for an American hero to sweep her off her feet, help her escape bombed-out London, and bring her to America after the war. The thought of Jack bringing home a foreign bride made her uneasy.

Dorothy yearned to keep thoughts of her son pure and untainted, but she knew war would change him. She imagined how she herself might fall for a handsome young man like Jack, flirting with him at a pub. Dorothy pushed these fantasies out of her mind. She had to focus on finding Jack instead of worrying about his love life.

Dorothy recognized two names in the letter: Tommy and BJ. She closed her eyes to see their faces and remember their last names.

"Let's see," she whispered. "Tommy's last name began with a 'P.' Piller… Piper… Pammer… Pitman? Yes. It's Pitman!"

BJ was simple—Martin. She peppered BJ with questions while visiting Jack at flight training school in Tennessee: Where did his family come from? Where was he raised? What did his father do? Did he go to college? What job did he have before the service? BJ answered all the questions, but she wasn't particularly pleased that her son had befriended someone from such a poor background. BJ, blond, slim, tall, and charming, was an affable young man, the same age as Andy, their oldest. He even looked a bit like Andy and seemed seriously protective of Jack.

Maybe these boys weren't flying with Jack that day, Dorothy thought. She knew airmen switched planes and schedules from time to time. She picked up her pen and began to craft letters, which she planned to send to the base at the same address where she sent Jack's. She set to drafting and rewriting until she was sure her message was right and the script clear and readable, remembering that Jack often described her handwriting as chicken scratches.

Long shadows announced the approaching evening by the time Dorothy put her pen down. It was time to start dinner—Joe would be home soon. Removing her reading glasses, she looked out through the kitchen side window. There he was, right on time: their 1941 two-door sedan with its dark-blue paint was in the gravel driveway next to the house, ready to collect a storm of dancing snowflakes. Joe bought the car with his employee discount just before civilian car production halted. It was another trophy of her husband's success.

After growing up on a farm, tramping through fields of wheat and corn and slogging down rutted dirt roads splattered in cow dung, nice things consequently became important to Dorothy. Neither of her parents finished high school and had struggled financially to keep the farm afloat. She and her two younger brothers lived with them in a clapboard house with a tin roof that hadn't seen paint in years. A single wire provided electricity to the house. There was no telephone, nor indoor sinks with running water or flush toilets.

Her future seemed a dead end, but she managed to graduate from high school because Grandma insisted, surrendering her small savings so she could stay in school her last year instead of working on the farm full time. However, there was no money for teacher's college, one of the few escapes for girls like her—rural and small-town girls who were expected to marry by eighteen to become exhausted farm wives with broods of children. She wanted a different life. She believed she deserved a different life.

It was Joe who rescued her. At the 1912 state fair, Joe smashed into her during a square dance round and Dorothy sent him to the floor when she turned in the wrong direction at the same time. Dorothy's rich mahogany hair, brilliant brown eyes, and strong smile caught Joe's eye. When she discovered that his father was not just a farmer but also owned a farm equipment store in the next county, and that Joe had graduated high school and was working at the store, she knew she had found a man with potential. They were married a year later. She was nineteen and he was twenty-five.

Dorothy was right proud when they built their home in 1935, letting go of renting for the rest of their lives. The house was one of the first new home designs in the Detroit area—a rambler. First seen in the 1920s, ramblers were considered modern, with open rooms and a large, low-pitched roof presenting a strong horizontal expanse, so different from the two-story, foursquare brick-and-white trimmed houses they rented. It was located in what some people were calling a suburb, a development of new houses constructed by a builder who offered buyers some customization options, yet kept the price in line with what they could afford.

Dorothy worked diligently to keep every room clean, tidy, and nicely decorated. The house had three bedrooms, a full bath, formal living and dining rooms, a den with a bay window, and a modern kitchen with a breakfast area. Joe said they couldn't afford all the offered options, so they chose to have the basement paneled in a high gloss knotty pine, complete with a wet bar, instead of a more practical garage. Dorothy had always wanted a recreation room for casual entertaining, like she saw in the latest home décor magazines. Now she had one.

Although the yard looked stark without much vegetation, trees and bushes would grow soon enough. The distance from the city's center announced that they had joined the middle class. The home's location separated Dorothy from the people who migrated to Detroit from southern states and Appalachia to fill thousands of wartime manufacturing jobs in the area. There would be no more farmers in their family.

When Andy asked her one day why she didn't like to drive into the city or near the plant, she said, "Those people don't have anything. Back on the farm, drifters and homeless families would steal anything they could get their hands on. I don't feel safe around people like them."

"Well, Mom, I'm not sure I agree with you. Times are changing, but I'm glad you feel safe at home."

Dorothy sensed his disappointment. Her boys, along with Joe, who worked with all types of men every day at the plant, never said a negative word about them. She thought them naïve to believe that no matter a person's color, or where he came from, he deserved respect. Dorothy believed no one had her respect until they earned it.

***

Two days after Joe sent word to Andy, pleading for his return, a telegram was delivered.

Dear Mom and Dad:
*   "Missing in action" does not mean dead. I cannot*
be released unless Jack is declared dead. War Dept will
do all they can to find him. Have faith.
Love, Your son, Andy

"We'll just have to be patient," said Joe.

Dorothy bit her lip and scowled. "I can't wait until we get a letter from the War Department. I drafted letters to Tommy and BJ yesterday. I can delay sending them, if you want, until we get the formal letter, but I don't want to."

"Dorothy, please wait. If we don't hear as they promised, then we'll send the letters."

Two weeks later, they did receive an official letter.

*   ...Since your son, 2nd Lieutenant Joseph W.*
Jackson Jr, was reported Missing in Action 08
November 1944, the War Department entertains the
hope that he survived and that information will be
revealed dispelling the uncertainty surrounding his
absence. No finding on his status will be made until he
is either recovered or, according to law, will be presumed
dead 12 months after the expiration of his absence on
08 November 1944...

This letter said nothing that reassured Dorothy that the War Department knew what it was doing, other than keeping secrets it had no right to keep. In fact, the letter only increased her anxiety and frustration. Their son had become a statistic to the War Department, an object with a status to be tracked. She told Joe she wasn't going to wait a year. She had to figure out what happened. The next day she mailed the letters inserted into Christmas cards to BJ and Tommy.

***

When Dorothy kissed Jack goodbye in Florida, just before he flew to England after navigation and artillery training, she gave her son his assignment. "Jack, write us after every mission you fly. We need to know you're safe."

He gave her a big smile, pushed his brimmed hat back on his head, and then hugged her. "Of course, Ma. Now don't worry."

Once in England, however, while Jack endeavored to write as his mother requested, he discovered that his Air Service life couldn't be expressed in letters. He kept his letters simple and light, unlike the weekly detailed and sometimes serious letters he wrote from training school in Tennessee and Florida…when life was still normal and war was an exercise, not a reality. But now, normal life vanished. The unending pace and trauma of multiple twelve-hour missions a week absorbed so much of his time that he managed to write only one or two letters a month. Luckily, the spine-chilling dreams of near-death experiences that plagued some of his comrades hadn't overtaken him. Yet.

***

The lack of letters from Jack frightened his mother. By early September she lost patience, so she wrote him expressing worried concern. The newspapers were full of horrific stories of what Germans did to Allied soldiers, now that the Nazis were being pushed out of France into their homeland with their backs against the Russians, who were encroaching from the Eastern Front. She received a speedy telegram in reply.

All well and safe. Please don't worry. Love Jack

Two weeks later, after a ten-hour production day at the plant, Joe walked into the house with a letter that Dorothy would recognize without opening. He brushed the snowflakes off his jacket as he stomped his feet on the kitchen door mat, careful not to splash onto the floor. She saw the letter in his hand, recognizing immediately that the handwriting on the envelope was her own, and grabbed the letter after wiping her hands on her apron. It was stamped in red ink…

New York, Received December 10, 1944.
Missing in Action. Return to Sender.

She sent the letter the first week in November, the week their son was declared missing. Opening it, she read her own words.

…We still haven't heard from you since we received your letter in the first week of October. Are you writing to us? Perhaps your letters are being held up again. Are my letters coming through ok? How long does it take for them to reach you?

Uncle Meyer just called and asked to be remembered to you.

Your Dad and I played gin rummy recently. We each won one game (31 cents)—'tain't much. I haven't heard from Grandma this week, so I must call her in a little while.

We were out to dinner at Peg and Al's Saturday night, and Tuesday we went to the Webers', where she held a surprise anniversary dinner. The Bassetts were over last night for bridge. They read some of your and Andy's letters. They always seem so interested in what you are both doing. We are going to the Delaney's for dinner tonight, so you see we haven't been doing badly this week, have we?

I am almost done sewing the new bedspread for our bedroom. I quilted it myself and the blue color is perfect.

I've just called up Ann of the Sunshine Beauty Parlor in Royal Oak. I'm having a permanent and manicure Friday. My hair's so long that I'm tired carrying it around.

Tootie feels as swell as a bear in honey. She just hasn't any bad faults at all…but the one of barking when people come in the house…

"How could I have filled this letter with such drivel about our everyday little lives when our boys are facing death every day? How useless." Dorothy's eyes teared as she stared at her husband, who stood at the counter while she sat in a chair at the kitchen table.

"We write that news because Jack and Andy need to remember home, that you and I are waiting for them, and that there is such a thing as a normal, everyday life to come back to."

Dorothy groaned and handed the letter back to him. "I knew there was something wrong. I sensed it in my bones when I wrote this." She pointed at the first paragraph.

Joe took the letter from her. "Even if you had a premonition, you know that you couldn't have stopped what happened. Jack did what he had to do because it was his job. We know he loved flying. We don't know he's dead, only missing in action, so let's be patient."

But Dorothy knew that whatever he said, there would be no convincing her. She believed her sixth sense more than cold facts. Joe said no more.

"We won't have to wait. I sent letters to BJ and Tommy. Remember? I asked them what happened." Dorothy barked the words. She walked her letter down the hall, took her memento box from the cedar chest once again, and added it to the collection.

***

Joe hid in the den with his pipe, knowing that Dorothy couldn't be stopped. If writing letters calmed her, then let her do it. It calmed him to have a smoke. Whatever happened to Jack happened—all the letters in the world wouldn't bring him back any sooner, if at all. He would wait. War was war and it had to be won, no matter what cost. If Jack's life were sacrificed in the war effort, he'd be heartsick, but he'd also be proud of his son's service. And if Jack were alive and came home? Well, he would be happy and proud.

He could hear Dorothy slam a pan on the stove and rustle silverware for the table. He took a flaming match to his pipe, taking long draws to ensure it was properly lit.

CHAPTER 8

Even now, as a seasoned airman, Tommy looked like a scruffy Nebraska farm kid with his bushy, incurably crimson hair, face full of freckles, and compact body of sinewy muscles. But melancholy and moodiness overwhelmed him this first Christmas away from home. He lay on his bunk yearning to sink into the mattress on his Army-issued barracks single bed. Letters from his missing buddies' parents and presents from his girl Janice were scattered about. The loss of his flying comrades depressed him, and the passion bubbling in his groin was driving him crazy.

Janice accepted his proposal to marry, but before they could set a date, he decided that it was his patriotic duty to join up to fight the Nazis.

"We'll get married when I get back," he told her, but since Arf & Arf went down, he now knew the truth was *if I get back.*

The gray, clammy English chill trapped him. He couldn't do what he always did when he was confused—escape to breathe and clear his head in the crisp Nebraska winter air, wandering plowed fields covered in snow under radiant robin's egg–blue skies, and the sun's heat melting the glistening icicles hanging from the barn's eaves.

Tommy was the youngest of his squadron's crew and one of the best aircraft engineers at the base. He'd flown with Jack and BJ since July when they arrived at Glatton together. Despite having no aviation experience and only a high school education, the Army transformed him into an aircraft engineer, which surprised him no end. When he signed up, he lied to the Army recruiter about his age, saying he was eighteen, so he begged and his dad reluctantly signed the release form. But he told the truth about being his dad's tractor, truck, car, and general engine mechanic on the farm. The Army immediately hustled him off to aircraft mechanical training.

He loved tinkering with any kind of engine or equipment. Now it was planes. As an aircraft engineer, he walked the plane to declare it airworthy before each flight. If he found a problem, or if a problem occurred during flight, it was his job to diagnose its seriousness, repair it if he could, and advise the plane's captain on its risk to mission completion for their survival. Whether it was a jammed gun, broken radio cable, or leaky oil line, Tommy could fix it. His fellow crewman had a big laugh when he naïvely explained to them why he couldn't climb out on the wing in midair and fix an engine oil leak.

Tommy stretched and picked up Mrs. Jackson's letter from the foot of his bunk. Reading her pleas to know what truly happened to Arf & Arf only intensified the guilt he felt for not being on the plane with Jack that day. But he hadn't been in Jack's plane—and there was nothing he could do to change that now. He would live with guilt in his gut.

But what was abhorrent was that he couldn't talk about the details. He could only speak in generalities, trying to not give Jack's mother false hopes of the plane's crew.

> *Dear Mrs. Jackson,*
>
> *Thanks for the Christmas card. It was swell. I really appreciate it. I'm in the finest of health and hope this letter finds both of you the same.*
>
> *Now to your questions. I want so much to tell you what happened exactly, but I just can't. You see, we're not allowed to mention any details of casualties whatsoever in our mail. I hope you understand.*
>
> *All I can say, Mrs. Jackson, is "I'm also praying for all of them."*
>
> *Your son's friend, Tommy*

Dorothy wrote to thank him as soon as she received his letter. Then she wrote again, begging for the names and addresses of the other men assigned to that mission because the War Department had not responded to her requests. Missives from Dorothy appealing to him for information were not the only ones Tommy received. He found himself the correspondence hub for the mothers and wives of the Arf & Arf crew members. He wrote them all, resolving to help these mothers, fathers, and husbands—people without answers. Tommy responded to Dorothy's pleas in early February 1945.

> *Dear Mrs. Jackson:*
>
> *I received your swell letter and was more than happy to hear from you. I also received a letter from Mae Wisner at the same time—I answered hers a few minutes ago. I think you know Mrs. Wisner and stay*

in touch with her. I've enclosed her address along with that of Louisa Leonis in this letter.

I also received a letter from my girl Janice, back in Nebraska. She said that one of my buddies who was on that mission is now home, and stayed at her family's house overnight. He told her what happened and instructed her to tell Mae. I also suggested Mae get in touch with him through my girl.

Jack gave me the enclosed good luck charm. He put it together on our flight to England out of Newfoundland back in August. The guys signed it when we flew missions together and carried it on different missions. It was my turn to have it during our November missions… Maybe if it had been with Jack, his plane would've made it back that day.

You should have it. I wish I could give you more hope, but I honestly don't know myself.

Try not to worry too much and please write again, as your letters are always more than welcome.
Your son's buddy, Tommy

***

Dorothy devoured Tommy's letter as soon as it arrived, then examined the strange-looking charm he sent. At first glance it meant nothing. It was a four-foot string of paper money taped end to end, then fanfolded so it fit easily into a man's back pocket. It consisted of currency notes: a yuan, a franc, a lira, a pound, a peso, a kroner, and a US dollar bill. Very colorful, but of no value.

Dorothy knew that Jack hadn't been to all of those places. She guessed that the Army's censors dismissed it as meaningless, so they let it come through the mail.

She examined the bills more closely. There were signatures on them as Tommy stated, but they were nearly illegible and the notes had been signed by numerous people. She needed better light if she was going to decipher the signatures.

In the den, Dorothy turned on her sewing lamp, a magnifying glass encased in a circular neon lightbulb. There was an annotation on the dollar bill: Crossed Ocean 07–15–44, Short Shooter Jackson—was at one end. The names Al Francin, Warren Raymond, Leroy Samson, and some others, with abbreviations next to their names, were scattered about the bill on the front and back. At first, she didn't understand why her son had the nickname Short Shooter Jackson because his position was navigator. Then she remembered that Jack, like the other men, received gunnery training in Florida just before being shipped overseas. She smiled, thinking that he must have been a great shot.

The pound was more interesting. In a feminine script in a light-blue ink, instead of navy or black, were names around the edges. These signatures were not scattered about, like on the other notes. The names were not easy to decipher, but after a bit of matching, it was clear to Dorothy that most likely the Arf & Arf crew declared missing in action on November 8, 1944, consisted of Booker, Brown, Francin, Jackson, Leonis, Milligan, Raymond, Samson, and Wisner.

Joe sat across from his wife as he smoked his after-dinner pipe, reading the evening paper as a smile crept over his wife's face.

"Look at this! I think Tommy was trying to tell me who was in the plane with Jack that day." She pointed at the pound note. "Could that be the crew list of Arf & Arf?"

Joe, his pipe gripped between his teeth, put on his reading glasses and took the note string from his wife, inspecting it carefully. He put his pipe in the ashtray on the table between them.

"Looks like Tommy has provided the linchpin to solve the crew mystery. You know that the boys didn't always fly together in the same crew, but let's see if we can find their positions in the plane that day." Together they scoured the notes, finding names and sometimes bomber assignment abbreviations. As Joe deciphered a name and position, Dorothy carefully listed it in a spiral notebook of lined paper. Joe translated the cryptic abbreviations into understandable flying positions. In the end, there were nine positions matching to nine names—pilot, copilot, bombardier, radio operator, left waist gunner, ball turret gunner (nose), tail gunner, aircraft engineer, and navigator.

"Tommy was pretty clever to send the note string," said Dorothy. "I didn't think a farm boy could be so clever."

"The lads we sent to fight this war are young, but they aren't stupid. Their training and flying time gave them talent and made them crafty."

"That's true, I suppose," Dorothy replied, then with a twinkle in her eye she said, "I will thank him cleverly in my next letter. We won't alert the censors or he'll get in trouble."

Dorothy held the list between them as they reviewed it one more time.

"At this point, this is your list of families to contact here in the States. Plus you have information in

Tommy's and BJ's letters from Glatton. Do you have any addresses?"

"I've got addresses for Louisa Leonis and Mae Wisner, and Tommy's girl, Janice Baines. It's a good start."

Within two days, Dorothy drafted and sent them letters in her continual search to solve the puzzle of Jack's plane. But the results were disappointing. Everyone she contacted received the same vague Missing in Action letter from the War Department. No one seemed to be aware of anything more than she and Joe knew.

That was until she received a letter in March 1945, five months after Jack's disappearance, written by Sterling Booker, the copilot's father. It was forwarded to her by Jane Wisner, the tail gunner's mother.

Dorothy's sixth sense whistled in her ear after she pulled the letter from the mailbox, telling her that this message contained the clue she was waiting for. She turned the postmarked envelope over and over and held it up to the sunlight, but didn't open it. What if it told her that Jack had perished? She couldn't face that alone, so she waited for Joe to come home, keeping herself busy for the afternoon with changing bed sheets, running the sweeper, emptying ashtrays, dusting tabletops, and mopping the kitchen floor.

Each time the hand in the grandfather clock in the front hall edged forward to the half hour mark, striking a solemn tone, small beads of worried sweat appeared on her brow. She stood, wiping her forehead before returning to her cleaning, then looked up after putting the sweeper away to see the minute hand was just four ticks from six. Dorothy quickly unbuttoned her cotton cleaning jacket, hanging it in the utility closet. She then carefully pushed loosened strands of hair away from her face, tucking them into her bun, and positioned herself by the kitchen table, letter in hand and standing tall as if she were a soldier waiting to be relieved of duty.

***

Before Joe could put the car keys on the hook by the kitchen door, she rushed to him, helped him remove his jacket, then pulled him by the hand into the den without a word. Sitting in their chairs in the bay window, she said, "Joe, please, you must open this letter. I can't—my hands are shaking too much. I won't be able to hold the pages steady. You read it… I'm afraid of what it might say."

She rubbed her hands on her knees, clutching a delicate handkerchief with its hand-embroidered four-leaf clovers and daisies. It was the one that Jack gave her before he left. Joe gently took the letter from her hand and leaned to one side to extract the small Swiss Army knife he was never without. It was also a gift from Jack before he left.

Joe carefully slit the envelope along its side, not along the top, to preserve the envelope for the letter once it was read. Glancing at the ever impatient Dorothy, he extracted and unfolded the off-white vellum with the sender's imprint at the top of the first page. The letter was typed. Joe cleared his throat and in a low calm voice that matched the darkening evening sky, read the copy of the letter sent from the father of the copilot to Mrs. Wisner that she forwarded to Dorothy. She pulled her chair closer to his, now sitting on the edge of the chair, her knees brushing up against his with her eyes closed.

> *Dear Mrs. Wisner:*
>
> *Your letter of the 16th received yesterday. My wife is visiting our oldest daughter, so I will attempt to answer your letter.*
>
> *First allow me on behalf of all our family to extend to you and family our deepest sympathy. I assure you that Mrs. Booker and I sympathize with you in this sad and dark hour; we pray that through God's divine power and loving grace, he has seen fit to save and protect our dear boys, and in due time will return them safely to us. We can't and will not give up hope. Yet Mrs. Wisner, the picture looks pretty dark.*
>
> *We are grief-stricken, for as your son said, our Sterling was indeed a fine boy, and I am sure your son was the equal of any. We feel that this ill-fated bomber had aboard a group of young men—the finest among the greatest that America could offer.*

Joe paused, looking over at his wife. "Are you ok? Should I continue?" She opened her eyes, rubbing her hands up and down her thighs to release her body's tension, and nodded.

> *Mrs. Wisner, in today's mail came a letter from a Miss Patricia Perkins, a young lady who is a friend of Bill Bonnet, whose plane, Dragon Girl, was flying in formation with Arf & Arf when an accident happened. My son Sterling was Bill's friend.*
>
> *She wrote: "Bill was flying right beside Sterling when it happened. In his opinion, Sterling did not have*

a chance in the world. Everyone else who saw it said the same thing. The plane completely broke in half, right behind the wing. The boys in the back half might have had a slim chance, but the boys in the front half did not have a chance in a million."

"The navigator position is in the ball turret in the nose of the plane!" Dorothy screamed, "He's dead! Oh, my God, he's gone!"

Joe placed the stunning evidence carefully on the end table next to his chair. The worst was confirmed. Hope vanished…Jack was dead. Weeping, they stood and once again walked in an embrace to their bedroom. They slept closely together that night, Joe wrapping himself around Dorothy, who curled into a fetal position with her back in Joe's encircled body.

The next morning, Joe called the plant and didn't go into work. Dorothy was grateful. Neither of them were hungry, but they managed to choke down a bit of the toast Dorothy prepared and drink some of the rich black coffee for which she was famous. As she removed the dishes from the kitchen table, Joe asked, "Do you want me to read you the rest of the letter?"

"There's more? Yes, we should know everything we can." She set aside her dish towel and sat at her husband's side at the table. Again, her hands rubbed against her knees. Joe reopened the letter and continued reading Mr. Booker's words.

…Now as to the letter we all received from the War Dept., I wrote the War Dept. on Jan. 8th asking if they could verify Miss Perkin's story… On Feb. 3rd I received a letter from a Major Brandeis, acknowledging

my letter and stating that only one boy was seen in the water of the channel and that a raft was dropped to him. His identity could not be established.

Mrs. Wisner, we know that the plane broke in half, but the War Dept. has given us no other detail… I shall write the War Dept. another letter soon. I am just waiting for some more definite information. I will keep you informed.

You know, Mrs. Wisner, this is the hardest blow my wife and I have ever experienced. I am almost crazy—I worshiped my son. I won't say anymore. I know you all know just how I feel.
Sincerely yours, Sterling H. Booker Sr.

"Crazy!" said Dorothy, looking at her husband. "Just like Sterling Booker, I feel crazy. I don't understand why the War Department didn't tell us this from the beginning. They must have known what happened after they interviewed the crew from the two planes that returned. It sounds like all the boys and their friends over there knew."

Her sorrow quickly morphed into rage. "Joe, BJ and Tommy lied to us! They knew everything the day it happened. How could they not trust us with the truth?"

Joe kept his voice low and steady. He couldn't and wouldn't rebuke her fury. Rather, he said, "Dorothy, listen to me. It's like the boys said. The War Department bureaucracy classified the incident as secret. No one was supposed to know, fearing the Germans might see a weakness. It's not an excuse, but we can't undo what has been done, and we can't blame BJ and Tommy." Joe put his hands on her shoulders, gently massaging them.

Dorothy took a deep breath. "I want to forward this letter to Edna Francin, the pilot's mother. She's been a dear, keeping in touch with me these last months."

She rose from the kitchen table, walking directly to the desk in the den, where she pulled out the old portable typewriter from the closet. They bought it before the war so Andy could type his college papers. Within an hour she had typed a copy of the letter, then added a handwritten note at the bottom:

Keep this letter. It's a copy of the one we received. We have such sorrow to bear now. All of us.

From the den window, Joe watched Dorothy turn north on the sidewalk, heading for the post office seven blocks away, knowing she'd be moving fast to clear her mind. He sat quietly in the den, smoking his pipe, allowing himself to descend into the numbing silence of their son's death.

***

When Dorothy returned, Joe was still in the den. She recovered the original letter from the desk to store it carefully in her memento box with the others, directly on top of the December news report with Jack's profile picture in uniform. She sobbed quietly as she reread the article that documented the Air Medal he was awarded.

...for exceptionally meritorious achievement was awarded to Lt. Joseph Jackson Jr. while navigating a Flying Fortress in sustained bomber combat operations over Germany and Nazi-occupied continental Europe.

The courage, coolness, and skill displayed by Lt. Jackson during these occasions reflect great credit upon himself and the Armed Forces of the United States. At this time, he is Missing in Action.

Yes. Our youngest son is a war hero, but it would be better if he were alive and with us once again, hero or not.

In the back of her mind, denial began to fester. Could it be possible that the Bookers' tale of the plane's fiery demise was just the fantasy of a British girl who didn't know what she was talking about, or had drunk too much beer to remember the truth?

Jack remained in the missing-in-action void. Dorothy struggled through the rest of the spring and into the summer of 1945, trying to keep hope alive, trying with her husband to live their ordinary lives, unable to sleep soundly. With Andy still away, the house was eerily quiet. There were days when the two barely talked to each other, much less spoke with friends.

*****

A month and a half after May 8, 1945, V-E Day, Dorothy and Joe received a letter from Bob Short, who also flew in the same squadron as Jack. Dorothy had written to his mother.

Dear Mrs. Jackson,

I just arrived home yesterday and the letter you wrote was here. There isn't much I can add to what you already know, but here goes. I was in Dragon Girl. The weather was rather hazy, and we were getting lower.

The next thing I know there is a shout over the interphone that there was a collision. Bad Time's prop wash had forced the plane up and then down toward Jack's plane. It's left wing, and then the propeller, hit Arf & Arf. That plane's fuselage broke right in half at the wing, and both pieces went straight down.

We were just five miles off the Dutch coast. Our whole crew was too stunned to do anything but follow orders. Bad Time lost an engine and was ordered back to the base. We made several runs over the spot, dropping life rafts. Someone reported one man in the water, but we had to withdraw after two runs as we were being fired upon from the shore.

As to who the man in the water was, no one knows. He was never heard from. No one was picked up, as I checked every now and then with Intelligence until I left the group on January 5 of this year.

There isn't much else I can say. My own opinion, as hard as it may be, is that there was hardly any chance of getting out. If someone did, he should have been heard from by now. I hope I have written you what you wanted to know.

I remain as always, with my deepest regrets,
Bob E. Short

P.S. My mother thanks you for your letter.

Bob's firsthand account confirmed Sterling Booker's secondhand story. Dorothy reluctantly coerced herself back to the reality that Jack would never return.

CHAPTER 9

On Sunday morning August 8, 1945, nine months to the day their son was purported to have died, Dorothy poked Joe. "Wake up, Joe. Joe, wake up!" she cried.

He rolled over. "What is it now, Dorothy?"

"Remember what I told you last December after receiving the letter from the War Department?"

Joe saw a happiness on her face and a hopefulness in her voice that had been missing for months. He knew that she was going to tell him whatever it was, so he might as well sit up and listen. With his brain foggy, he reached for his glasses on the night table.

"Ok, Dorothy. I don't remember, so explain what has you so energized." Joe pulled his long body up into a sitting position and adjusted the glasses on his nose.

"I woke up from a dream at four, a dream that erased my sadness and electrified me with new hope. I couldn't wake you that early, so I got out of bed as quietly as I could and ran to the den to record the dream so I wouldn't forget any details. Two hours later, with the sun on the horizon, I came back to bed, but couldn't get back to sleep.

"That's when I woke you, unable to wait any longer to tell you about this strange, powerful dream. I remember the time exactly because I looked at the clock. I think the dream is a message that Jack hasn't left us." Dorothy took a deep breath and pushed her spiral notepad with its lined pages into Joe's face. "I wrote it all down when I woke up."

"A message from where?"

Dorothy ignored his question and began to tell her dream, putting herself into a meditative-like state as she spoke.

"I was outside. I couldn't identify where—maybe a park or a playground—but I found a piece of broken metal that could have been a dog tag. I just knew it was connected with Jack. Then suddenly the scene shifted and I was in a hospital corridor peering into a ward with ten beds in two rows. Jack was sitting on the second bed on the left, dressed in his uniform, like he was ready to leave. I went to him and hugged and kissed him. He looked swell, just like when he left the training camp in Tennessee.

"I said, 'Jack, at last I've found you! Come home with me now.'

"He told me that he really didn't want me to find him because he couldn't come home; that the tag must have been lost in the laundry. Jack said, 'I'm not the kid I was when I left. I'm a man over here in England.'

"I said, 'Jack, I don't care. You'll be your own self after you're at home with us for a while.'

"His reply was, 'No, Mom. I'm not coming home.' Then handed me a letter saying it would explain what changed him. I left him and went into another room to read the letter. I wasn't crying because I thought it was what he wanted me to do. Then, I was copying his letter instead of reading it—"

Joe interrupted. "Do you remember what the letter said? Was it the letter he wrote like all the boys did before they left the States, in case they didn't make it back home?"

"No, I can't remember what it was about, just that I was copying it." She continued. "I was working on the last paragraph when a woman came into the room and said that Jack wanted to see me in his accommodations, so I left the letters and followed her. It wasn't the ward—it was like an apartment or something. Jack came toward me, but his toes didn't touch the parquet. Then he floated to a cupboard in the corner of the room and started putting his clothes in a sack. Then he was gone—vanished without saying a word.

"The next thing I remember was that I was in the ward again, leaning over his bed. Jack was in it but he was a baby. I picked him up and carried him out to the corridor. I looked back into the ward to see nurses putting someone else in his bed."

Dorothy was animated, bursting with intensity. "Can't you see? I think it's a message from Jack. He's still alive somewhere! I believe it, don't you?"

Joe swallowed and shut his eyes for a moment to gather his thoughts. He closed the notebook and took off his glasses, placing them on the night table on his side of the bed. He bent over, pulling his wife of thirty years to him in his embrace.

"Dorothy, my love. I know and you know it was a dream. But I also know that you continue to hope that Jack is still alive. If you must, then keep the dream in your heart."

She hugged him back, snuggling in his arms. "Oh, Joe. I feel it in my bones. We have hope."

***

Despite Dorothy's dream, Jack's status was officially changed to Dead by the War Department on November 8, 1945, one year after he'd been declared Missing in Action. Andy, now returned from Europe himself, on behalf of his parents asked for and, because of his military standing, received the detailed official accounting of the events that led to his brother's death. The letter confirmed that his brother and the rest of the Arf & Arf crew died in an air collision accident with another B-17 bomber.

In early 1946, Jack's parents received another and final confirmation of what happened. This time it came from BJ in a letter telling them what he couldn't tell them during the war: that he saw Arf & Arf split in two by the third plane in the formation. All nine men disappeared and were never recovered. Although some of the details differed, all the accounts of Jack's death came to the same conclusion: The demise of the plane called Arf & Arf on November 8, 1944, was a tragic accident.

Joe hoped that these additional confirmations would help Dorothy let go of her dream that he would come home. But it wasn't settled for her. A letter from Edna Francin, the mother of Arf & Arf's pilot, reignited her fantasy that Jack was somehow still alive.

Dear Dorothy,

Today I was on the bus going to Crawfordsville and a boy in the Air Service sat in front of me. Of course I had to talk to him. He was with the 8th Air Service Squadron on a B-17 ball turret bomber, just like the one our boys flew.

I told him I had never given up. He said this: "If it were me that was missing, I wouldn't want my mother to give up." He explained that his two brothers were pilots, and one was shot down two years ago in February.

"My mother has never given up, even though the government has declared him dead."

Apparently in some parts of the channel, the water is warm—he'd put his hands in the water, along with some of the boys he was with. Also, there are nearly always Danish fishermen out there, and he seemed to think they would rescue the boys. He said the Germans wouldn't fire on the boys going down.

He told me that after such a circumstance—when the boys go through a shock like that—many want to forget everything in the past and start a new life. He thinks his brother will show up some day. He's seen some come out of planes or show up when you just couldn't think it was possible.

He said the B-17 has three exits that could be used in an emergency. I told him our boys' plane was in the lead with two others on each side. He said that was quite an honor.

Dorothy, I received so much comfort from talking to him. I just had to write and tell you. Good night. Sincerely, Edna

In March 1948, Dorothy and Joe received Jack's Purple Heart, Air Medal, and a boxed American flag accompanied by a letter from the War Department informing them that the date of the death of Joseph W. Jackson Jr. was official. Joe knew that Dorothy, like her friend Edna, let her fantasies and yearning for her son fester, continuing to harbor the belief that her youngest son would return to her someday.

PART III—AMAHLI

CHAPTER 10

A knock on the front door intruded upon Amahli's play with JJ on the front room carpet. Although deeply immersed in her studies at university, she devoted Saturdays to her daughter, giving her parents time for a bit of shopping, luncheon, and entertainment.

Amahli lifted JJ and parked the baby on her hip. Then, with quick light steps, she went to the front door while cooing to the baby, who giggled and fiercely grabbed at her fingers. Expecting repairmen to come by after lunch, she swung the door open.

"Well, gentlemen, glad to see you have finally—"

The shock of who she saw standing before her caused her to stop mid-sentence, erupting into unladylike screams of delight. Instead of crusty menders, there was a tall, nattily dressed man with a head of flaxen blond hair slicked back from his forehead. The baby squealed in unison with her mother as Amahli threw her free arm around him.

"BJ! It's really you! I thought you'd be back in the States by now. What are you doing in London? Are you visiting?" She thrust the child into his arms as BJ steadied himself, letting the flowers he brought fall behind him onto the stone entryway. "JJ, meet your dad's best friend, Uncle BJ." The baby gave the man a wide-eyed ogling, then snatched his tie with her chubby fingers.

BJ poked back at the little girl, making funny faces, then gazed at Amahli. "She's charming. And you are even lovelier than when we parted. You look terribly well and quite fine in those slacks—as always, defying convention. Even in the throes of motherhood, you make your own fashion statement."

BJ clutched the baby as he swooped down to retrieve the colorful bouquet. He presented it to Amahli with a deep bow, as if greeting the queen. Still laughing, she accepted the flowers, curtsied, and then jumped up to give BJ a huge kiss on the cheek.

"I guess you've lost some of the famous British reserve," he said as he followed her into the house.

"Can you tell that Jack is her father?" asked Amahli as she led him down the hall.

"Amazing—she's the reincarnation of him. Poor little girl has his ears. Just like Jack's, they stick out. She'll be hiding them under that thick black hair when she's a teenager for sure."

BJ tickled JJ's ears. The little girl squealed again with delight, reaching for his fingers. Amahli's eyes filled as she shuttled BJ into the kitchen to prepare tea.

"You're family, BJ, so I can't bear to leave you alone in the front room for a minute right now." She settled BJ and JJ into her father's favorite spot at the well-worn oak table. While the tea steeped, she plated her favorite sweet shortbread biscuits.

The two chatted casually about her family's health, the weather, and other unimportant things as they settled into each other. With everything on the table and the tea poured, Amahli asked, "What has happened to you since we last saw each other? When was it, April?"

BJ handed JJ back to her mother. He exhaled a relaxed breath, slowly stirring a bit of milk into his tea. "Yes, it was April when you left. Tommy and I were released the last week in July, but there was nothing for me to go home to in the States. Mom wrote that she knew I didn't want a miner's life, and neither did she want it for me. She told me she loved me and to live the rest of my life doing what I wanted—and living the way I wanted. So here I am in London."

"I imagine you miss her. I can't fathom your situation."

"More than anything I miss her when I'm in my flat, alone. I can see her standing on the wooden porch of our weather-beaten house on the side of the mountain, her flowered apron covering her simple dress with her hands out, welcoming me home after school. She was always there for me." BJ slowly sipped the tea. "I miss her voice, but we write often."

"What about your father? Has he changed at all?"

"Not in the least. He hates what he can't understand."

"Oh, BJ. I am sorry."

"Don't be. I really didn't have any friends back in the States either. Since I know London some, I decided to come here. A RAF bloke at Glatton gave me a couple of names to call when I got here. Within a week I had a construction job and found a room until I could get properly settled. I can swing a hammer as well as any of them and they're desperate for workers.

"One day I found myself repairing a theater in the West End and fell in with some guys about my age who work there. These new friends appreciate my excellent construction skills, as well as my view on life, if you know what I mean." He paused to take a biscuit, then continued.

"I've always loved the stage. Even got a Midwestern guy like Jack interested in Shakespeare, remember? Now I'm starting to work backstage in my free time."

"Oh, how wonderful! But please, BJ, don't take risks. Remember the laws in Britain."

"I know, but I can't go home. You can get lynched for being Black or gay where I come from, much less be put in prison. I'll take care of myself and my new friends will help me learn the ways. At least here, there's some level of acceptance. Right now, London is where I'm supposed to be. Londoners like us Yanks and I'm being useful. And when I'm with my friends, I don't have to hide who I am."

"Then your second home is here, where you will never have to hide who you are, and your friends are welcome to join us. My parents will always receive you, whether I'm here or not. They're quite unique themselves, you know. And I love having you so close." She handed JJ to back to him so she could clear the table. JJ immediately lunged at her Uncle BJ.

***

The curved arches of the front room greeted BJ and Amahli after they left the kitchen. The room's floor-to-ceiling drapes, which replaced the wartime's dark maroon blackout ones, were a pale green silk. When pulled back, they revealed cream sheers that let the afternoon sunlight fill the room. BJ immediately admired several of her parents' powerful, intense abstract drawings by 1930's artists like Evengy-

Voitendo, Max Bill, Luigi Veronesi…and even a Modigliani.

Amahli put JJ on the floor on a blanket, where she played with her fingers and toes for a bit, then fell soundly asleep. BJ and Amahli sat in twin stuffed Art Deco chairs her parents purchased in the 1930s, before the war stopped the acquisition of such handsome items. Settled by the fire, its heat radiating warmth into the room, she said, "You never told me what it was like flying with Jack. Tell me everything about flying in those B-17s, about Jack's flying, and then about the last mission."

BJ looked at this strikingly handsome tall woman, wishing once again he were not homosexual. But there was no changing that. He took a cigarette from a case in his inner jacket pocket, offering one to Amahli. She declined but indicated for him to go ahead.

After lighting it and taking a long draw, he said, "Are you sure? Do you really want me to bring up memories that could upset you?"

"BJ, I am fine. Our child has replaced my grief with joy. I know you two were inseparable since meeting in Tennessee at flight school and gunnery training in Miami before flying with Tommy. But I want to know more. That's what I want right now."

JACK'S GIFT

CHAPTER 11

Jack had been flying bombing missions over Germany for four months and returned from all twenty-four flights in one piece. Every time his B-17 Flying Fortress cut through the sky with the sun glinting off silvery metal, Jack felt complete and self-assured—a member of a skilled crew. Even flying for hours in below-zero temperatures at 26,000 feet, Jack felt an intense inner satisfaction. He often told me that his was the best job a guy could have, flying in the nose, guiding it through the sky, sitting next to the ball turret gunner with pilots above him. I watched Jack morph from a meandering, catch-as-catch-can, rebellious life-of-the-party kid when I met him in Tennessee into a serious man who took great pride in his work.

Jack came into flight operations ready to plunge into action despite the awful weather on the morning of November 8. For this twenty-fifth mission, he was assigned to Arf & Arf, which he flew in many times. He loved that plane, even though she suffered from an embarrassingly bad two-tone paint job. It was constructed by taking the tail section of a silver B-17 and marrying it to the front section of an olive-drab one. The mechanics fabricated, fit, welded, and bolted the parts together to create her in twenty days.

We roared when we learned why they named the bomber Arf & Arf. Some said the name was stolen from Britain's famous Half & Half Biscuit—one half iced white and the other half chocolate. This was the story Jack and I related in our letters home. But the mechanics who put her together really named her after a notorious pub drink: the half-bitter and half-beer Arf & Arf.

The bomber squadron normally flew in a thirty-six-plane box formation—a strike force to be reckoned with. Each B-17 plane, powered by four unfailing engines and large fuel storage, could stay in the air for up to fourteen hours. Because of this, the squadron could fly deep into enemy territory, wreaking havoc on the land below. The successful bombing made a difference, providing cover to American and British ground troops.

The Glatton squadrons were big and tough, so tough that they didn't need fighter escorts. Each was a phalanx of deadly firepower: twelve trios of bombers staggered to the right and left, above and below each other. Over 100 gunners attacked enemy fighters or ground fire, while thirty-six bombardiers concentrated the bomb releases on mission targets—airports, fuel facilities, bridges, roads, or cities, if need be.

Bomb drops were followed by flak spraying up from the antiaircraft ground artillery, or from enemy fighters that managed to get airborne. Some men were rattled, but for Jack these air fights were exhilarating, daring, and dangerous. The ground fire and enemy strafings galvanized all of us to think and act as one. What was tough for us were the monotonous, wearying hours spent flying to and from the targets.

Jack's seat in the plane's ball turret next to the gunner gave him a 280-degree view of the sky. On his seventh mission, with me in the gunnery position next to him, we witnessed six bombers explode, crashing to the ground after a Nazi fighter attack. It was then that Jack's casual attitude gave way to a consistently weightier, more directed, and committed focus.

Jack and I were also together on Arf & Arf the first time she was severely attacked, leaving dozens of bullet holes in the plane's hull, which exposed us to frigid air that blew against our sweaty skin, instantly chilling our bones. No one died that day, but it was too much for the plane's radio operator. An invisible terror took over the kid's psyche, ripping through his body once back on the ground at Glatton. He never flew again; however, he did recover sufficiently to serve as a ground-based radio man.

Jack was built for bomber flying. I saw it in his eyes: the mastery he felt for a job that needed to be done. At twenty-two, Jack found himself and liked what he found.

In the predawn morning of November 8, 1944, frigid wind, rain, and sleet beat against everyone and everything. We were in the trio of planes, Arf & Arf, Bad Time, and Dragon Girl, first off, climbing into a sky filled with low steel-gray clouds and foggy haze. We were taking point for the squadron, flying to the English coast, across the channel to the Dutch coast, then deep into enemy territory. The rest of the bombers wrestled to take off and assemble into formation, fighting what was now slashing weather.

The mission was scratched and the base commander issued a recall that was passed forward from plane to plane. However, our trio of lead planes were beyond the horizon and never received the message to return to base. We flew to the target, totally exposed and vulnerable over enemy territory.

By the time the planes' captains realized we were alone, we were less than thirty miles from the target. Like an orchestra building to a crescendo, all three planes dropped their bombs at the target in unison, then banked hard left to return to Glatton. The escape was good, evading heavy but inaccurate shelling from Nazi ground forces. After that it was a slogging five-hour flight at full throttle to reach the Dutch coast, where we could reestablish communications.

The drone of our planes' engines powering the monstrous propellers blanketed us, making talk impossible without intercoms which, for safety and security, could not be used. Nor were voice communications between planes allowed. All was radio silence. Jack passed the time Morse light coding with me in Dragon Girl, flying to the right and above Arf & Arf. The lights couldn't be seen on the ground when cruising at such high altitudes. We often did this kind of chatting in silence to keep ourselves alert. That day, we discussed our plan to connect with Tommy after the ops debrief, then go for the postflight ritual pub decompression. Jack would leave earlier than the rest of us to rendezvous you. Jack wanted to be with me and Tommy, as well as you, every minute he could eke out of the onerous bombing schedule.

Our three planes were exposed, ghostly flying shadows as they descended and broke through the overcast sky, skating 500 feet above the sea off the Dutch coast. The planes' captains, all well-seasoned men, held their positions within the trio. Buffeting wind and piercing rain smeared our views out the planes' noses. Something sliced through Arf & Arf's fuselage, splitting it in two just behind the wing and throwing it out of the sky and into the churning sea below.

***

BJ put out another cigarette in the nearby ashtray, stood, stretched, then looked directly at Amahli. "I should have been with Jack that day, but my back went out during the previous mission. That morning, I was released at 0600 from the hospital, but my gunnery seat next to Jack was reassigned. I pleaded with the ops center and convinced them to assign me to another plane. I ran to Dragon Girl, its engines already revving. If I couldn't be in the same plane with Jack, at least I'd be close by to keep an eye on him."

BJ sat back. JJ had awakened, cranky, screaming, and twisting on the floor. "BJ, get something from the bar. I'll be back right after I change this girl's nappy and get her a bottle. She's hungry as well as wet." BJ gratefully poured a three-finger Scotch adding a splash of soda. He was surprised at the agitation he felt in his gut from telling the story.

Amahli returned with JJ devouring her bottle. BJ sat across from Amahli, overwhelmed emotionally but relieved that he was sharing his story with her: someone who accepted his love for Jack…

***

I was a self-made six-foot-two philosopher, a lanky blue-eyed blond with no formal education—an escapee from a dirt-poor Appalachia mining family of nine children. Five-foot-six Jack was the youngest of two sons of Michigan middle-class doting parents, a muscular brown-eyed man who refused his parents' offer of a college education, opting for adventure and casual jobs when he needed money. It was easy for me to be Jack's big brother, the designated pitch hitter for Andy, his older brother. Andy, the college graduate, was an Army officer fighting somewhere in France.

I enjoyed meeting up with Jack at the pub after missions. After he was killed, I often retreated to my quarters with a book instead of drinking. But with Jack at my side, I enjoyed the pub. Jack's confidence, mellow voice, and authoritative manner helped me feel safe, protected. Jack never raised his voice, but everyone knew he meant what he said when he spoke. He never threatened or made fun of me so I trusted him and he trusted me.

Jack wore his hat cocked to one side of his head and had piercing eyes, but was never full of himself. He didn't chase women. His aura alone drew women, and men, to him.

I loved Jack's consistent positive thinking, warm humor, and big smile. I believed Jack smiled so much because he had a mouthful of what American GIs call pearly whites. His parents had money for regular dental care throughout the Great Depression. I thought that was a huge advantage, because I never saw a dentist until I joined the Army Air Service. They fixed my teeth as best they could, but my teeth never looked like Jack's so I am always reticent to smile in public.

Jack had what I never had as a child: a secure life free from need, wrapped in a blanket of parental security. I knew that Jack would have a happy life ahead of him after the war. I wasn't so sure about myself.

I knew I was different since I was ten when classmates started to bully me. My shyness exacerbated their terrorizing. By sixth grade, I was taller than most of them, so I could run faster. And I knew where to hide, where they never went—the town library. There I read books and magazines and the librarian, Miss McDermott, urged me to pursue my interest in theater and scholarship. Mr. and Mrs. Fibbons, who owned the diner, gave me a quiet corner in the back where I read or listened to music, baseball, or the news on the radio. They didn't make me buy anything, since they knew I never had any money and these kind people did not want to shame me.

My uncles and dad told me I was lazy and odd because I didn't want to work in the mines. However, after high school I was forced into them. There were no other jobs and college cost money, so mining was my only option.

When the US declared war in December 1941, I made my escape, immediately enlisting before the draft called my number. The war pulled me out of oblivion. In the Army Air Service, the loneliness and differentness of all those years melted away with Jack. Jack's confidence and affection convinced me that I would not only survive the war but find a place in the world afterward. I absorbed his positive attitude despite an array of near-death experiences. We lived through an attack that left over fifty bullet holes in the fuselage, and another where two crew were wounded, but we were unharmed. Another time our plane had to limp home after flak disabled two of the four engines. Neither of us cracked under the pressure.

On that November 8 mission, I signed off after light coding with Jack, and turned back to my job. I surveyed the sky from my gunnery seat in Dragon Girl's ball turret, flying above Arf & Arf and Bad Time, which were parallel to each other. Without warning, a blazing flash just below my plane lit up the sky. I jerked and swung my seat around and down just after Bad Time's propellers slashed through Arf & Arf at the wing. Within seconds, the fuselage, now in two pieces, spiraled down, piercing the ink-black sea, leaving nothing in the churning waves. There were no parachutes in the air or in the water.

Breaking radio silence, I yelled over the intercom: "Plane down! Arf & Arf is down!"

Dragon Girl's pilot, the most senior captain, immediately commanded Bad Time to regain her heading and head for Glatton. Amazingly, she only lost one engine in the collision. Dragon Girl dove through the air to the crash site, scanning the black water, looking for signs of life. I felt sick and helpless, watching the man I loved disappear below. Over the intercom another crewman yelled, "I think I see someone in the water. There's a Mae West!"

The copilot quickly radioed the communications center at Dover Tunnels to send the Air Sea Rescue Service. I released my harness, then sprang to help the bombardiers throw inflated rubber life rafts as close as they could to what appeared to be a man floating in the water. Can it be Jack? If he were alive, there was a good chance he could crawl into a raft and stay afloat until the rescue squad could reach him. But after a third 360-degree run over the crash site, no one had climbed into any of the life rafts and German batteries on the Dutch shore started popping at our circling plane, forcing Dragon Girl to leave or end up in the water as well.

After landing back at base, I, along with the remaining airmen, deplaned from the surviving bombers and were told to assemble immediately in the base's operations center before talking to anyone or returning to barracks. Jack had jokingly called the base's Quonset huts Hot Dogs because their tin roofs wrapped the buildings' circular frames, just like a bun wrapped around a hotdog.

Still in our flight suits, leather helmets, and sweat-stained jackets, we straggled solemnly into the ops center, taking our places with backs to the operations wall. As I am sure you remember, its massive blackboard was full of chalked matrices, tracking the four squadrons' pilot assignments, available planes, flight status, and other data. In front of us was a dog-eared long mahogany table surrounded by heavy straight-backed chairs. The ops team normally sat there, receiving position data coming from Dover Tunnel communications. If ops was short on personnel, communications specialists like you were called in to post data on the board. The glaring overhead fluorescent tube lights magnified the dust floating in the air and the dirt accumulated around furniture legs and in the room's corners.

The base commander stood in front of the table facing us. "I know this has been a tough day. We lost a plane and a crew of fine men, your buddies. However, remember: Do not to talk or write about anything you saw or heard to anyone—not each other, other crews, friends, or family on base—in bars or in homes here or in the States. Like all missions, this one is classified as secret. Any violation is a criminal offense. Although no one was recovered at the scene, the Arf & Arf crew has been given a Missing in Action status. That is all you can say. That's all I have to say. This status will be in place for one year until proven otherwise. Do you understand?"

We saluted and snapped back, "Yessir!"

Tommy, who was the flight engineer on Bad Time that day, eyed me as we started to file out. I stood frozen until I forced myself to turn and put one foot in front of the other very slowly, falling behind the others as we left the ops center. I was seeing double, and my whole body felt like one sickening, overwhelming panic attack. My hands shook so much that I couldn't keep them in my pockets. It felt just like what happened to the radio operator.

Tommy saw me start to collapse. He ran and quickly put his arm around my waist, bracing his smaller body against mine as best he could. We walked, slowly dragging each other down the muddy gravel road to the base hospital as rain soaked our clothes. Our pained moans echoed in the night air. Tears streamed down my face. Tommy held me tighter and kept me walking.

There was nothing either of us could say—no explanations. Neither of us could have stopped what happened. Tommy managed to get me in front of a doctor. Walking back into the rain, dry-eyed now, Tommy went to get drunk at the pub. I didn't leave the hospital for a week. When I did recover and went back to flying, I never felt the same about it again, during or after the war.

CHAPTER 12

In London, BJ became a weekly visitor to the Simmons' home. Thomas and Amita welcomed him into their family circle, realizing how much Amahli's and BJ's sharing drew them close to each other. They loved BJ for who he was, enjoying his company and relishing his role as uncle to their granddaughter.

It would be years, and many infusions of cash and materials from the US, to restore London. BJ's construction skills continued to be needed as Londoners wanted to return to the normal—theater, cinema, and cultural events—now that the war was over. The distraction was critical to recover individuals' and the country's mental health.

As JJ grew up, she regularly attended matinée productions with her mother, Papa and Nani, and Uncle BJ. With her uncle's connections, they always had tickets to the new plays and the best seats. But most of all, they enjoyed BJ's backstage tours, enabling them to admire his expert scenery construction, meet the stars, and catch backstage gossip.

***

Before dinner during one of BJ's weekly visits, Amahli announced that Tommy had written. Sitting at the table after pudding and coffee were served, BJ was holding JJ while Papa and Nani sat across from Amahli.

Dear Amahli,

I hope this letter finds you, JJ, your parents, and BJ well. Thanks for writing to me and sending pictures.

It's good to be home here in Nebraska. I feel like the war and all we went through together will always be with me, but it also seems like a lifetime away as I sit here on my dad's porch, looking out over the farm outbuildings and the fields. It's definitely where I belong. We've planted winter wheat now that the corn and soybean crops are harvested. Dad's got cows, so we have a dairy operation. It's a lot of work, but we hired some good hands to help us out.

Janice and I got married in August. All I can say is that being married is really swell. We missed each other so much.

Dad's getting ready to retire, he says. I don't believe he'll ever really retire, but I'm helping out with managing the farm as well as maintaining all the equipment. When it's slow in the winter, I do mechanical work up the road at a gas station. It helps me save a bit more because, as you might guess, we're expecting a baby next year! We're blessed.

How's JJ? I bet she brings you massive joy and helps you remember good memories of her father. He was such a good man—a true friend to me, and someone I will never forget. Nor will I ever forget you and BJ.

Well, it's time to go, so please tell everyone hello for me. And please write when you can.

Maybe someday you'll want to get in touch with Jack's parents. Here's their address if you need it. I corresponded with them and some of the other parents over the past months. I continue to keep your confidence. Your friend, Tommy

A worried look came over her mother's face. "Such a nice letter. I'm glad that he's happy. But what do you think about his suggestion of contacting JJ's grandparents in the States?"

"Maa, I don't know. I've always said no, never going to consider it, but now I'm not sure. Maybe someday they should know that they have a granddaughter, but I'm not ready to face them with the facts about her father and me, nor do I believe are they. I never met them, and I don't want JJ to be rejected because their son died without marrying me first." Happiness escaped out of her like air leaking from a balloon.

"Well, you'll know in your heart when the time is right. Everyone has endured so much in the last few years. Wounds need to heal," said BJ. Her father agreed and BJ continued. "When I met Jack's dad in Tennessee after we completed flight training, he greeted me with a warm handshake and a cigar. There were no questions. He just invited me to join them for a celebratory dinner, saying he prayed that we'd both be safe and return home as soon as possible.

"His mother, on the other hand, was cautious, almost suspicious for some reason. She peppered me with questions. I told her bits about my background and that my parents emigrated from Italy in the late 1800s. She said nothing. When I told her about how I mostly grew up in the library and hung out with my aunt, a teacher, she was about to ask more questions, but Jack cut her off. He said quite firmly to her, and I quote, 'Mom, BJ has more book learning and expertise than most college kids and lots more sense than either Andy or me. He's my best friend.' That settled her and she put away her questions."

BJ sat back in his chair. "I have to be honest. She's a strong lady with many well-formed opinions. But then, Amahli, so are you. It'd be interesting to see the two of you together. My guess is that in the end, she will accept you and love JJ because she loved her son. JJ is his legacy. But it may take some time."

Amahli cringed. "Well, I'm certainly not ready to face someone like that yet."

He reassured her. "Remember, you'll have support when the time comes. Jack's dad and his brother Andy will be your allies. Andy is a welcoming and open guy, just like his dad. They'll take you as you are. I met Andy in Florida before we were deployed. He's tall, blond, blue-eyed, and beautiful—like me, except his teeth are perfect, just like Jack's were. If you ever decide to unite JJ with that side of the family, start with him."

CHAPTER 13

Thomas's work in the Foreign Office focused on building alliances with the United States and Western European nations to ensure that never again would Europe be devasted by war. With Soviet Communism taking root in Eastern and Central Europe, a strong military defense of Western Europe became imperative. The culmination of his and his colleagues' efforts came in 1949 with the founding of the North Atlantic Treaty Organization (NATO). Its member countries vowed to defend threats against any one of them to prevent a resurgence of aggressive nationalism.

Inspired by her father's work and her own wartime experience, Amahli immersed herself in the study of the foreign relations and business alliances that were becoming critical to Britain's recovery. This was an unusual career choice—a daunting one—for a postwar woman. Her first career challenge came when she attempted to reenter the university and register for classes. She was told flatly by a snotty registrar that open seats were reserved for returning men. Refusing to be rejected, she went back two days later with her certificate of service signed by the Glatton base commander, proving her returning veteran qualifications and winning reentry without her father's intervention. She took her seat at the opening of fall classes in 1945 and picked up where she left off two years earlier.

After she graduated, even with a degree it wasn't easy for a woman to find nonclerical work. Amahli set her sights on working in the postwar Foreign Office that was now rapidly expanding, in desperate need of analysts and officers. She applied for entry-level analyst positions in four sections. Three directors wouldn't interview her. The fourth agreed to an interview, but after a few perfunctory questions, Mr. Smith said he would be happy to hire her to translate and transcribe documents for his analysts. She thanked him but said no, explaining that with her WWII work experience, a degree in foreign relations, and having experienced numerous European cultures while her father served overseas for the Foreign Office for twenty years, she believed she qualified for more substantive and sustainable work.

At the mention of her father, Mr. Smith asked, "Who is he?" to which she replied, "Thomas Simmons, who is now working on the NATO effort."

She hated having to drop his name, but she was desperate. Mr. Smith didn't acknowledge her statement, or even look at her as his secretary arrived to escort her out of the building.

"Buggers," Amahli said under her breath. "He didn't even listen to me."

That evening at home with her parents, she explained how poorly the interview went. "Papa, it seems that now the war is over, women aren't wanted or needed for any kind of work that requires thinking."

Papa smiled that wily smile he sometimes let come to his face. "Don't give up. Mr. Smith's reputation as backward and less than innovative is well known. Let's see what happens."

And so Amahli waited, taking JJ for long walks to calm herself.

***

Two anxious weeks later, the phone rang. "Miss Simmons, I've reviewed your qualifications again and found them acceptable for a junior analyst position in another section, one headed by Sir Anthony Williams. Although if you are interested, you must be willing to start work immediately."

Amahli put her hand over the receiver, jumped up and down as quietly as possible, then pulled herself to her full height. Using her most authoritative voice, she said, "Why, Mr. Smith, that is most welcome news. However, I have several conditions that must be met before I accept the position."

"Well, Miss Simmons, I'm not sure. What are they?"

"My conditions are that I will not be asked to transcribe other analysts' work and that I will have access to the same secretarial resources they do."

She could hear Mr. Smith's labored breathing. He sighed audibly, then said, "Yes, Miss Simmons. Sir Williams may agree to your conditions, as you call them, but you'll have to confirm them with him."

"I will accept the position if he agrees to the conditions. Thank you very much."

***

For her first day at work, Amahli arrived dressed conservatively in a forest-green skirt suit and starched white collar shirt finished with a black Windsor knot

121

necktie. It was unusual for a woman to wear it, but Amahli decided to mirror her colleagues' business suit look. Black heels, pearl earrings, and matching necklace completed her ensemble. Her new bobbed hairstyle transformed her from an alluring exotic to a strictly business, low-key professional. After being processed by the personnel section, she was given her office supplies, which she placed in the box she brought from home, along with several other items. Amahli was then escorted to Sir Williams's office.

"So, you're Miss Amahli Simmons," he said, reaching out to shake her hand. She immediately recognized the deep, clear, and forthright voice.

"Sir Williams, first let me say I am pleased to be here. Thank you for the opportunity." Amahli paused slightly before she continued. "I believe we met some time ago when I visited the Foreign Office with my father during the war."

"Yes, we did, and I remember you. Welcome back. I understand that you gave Mr. Smith a difficult time when he offered you the job."

"I'm afraid that I had to make it clear to Mr. Smith about the kind of work I was searching for."

"Yes, you did, and I'm pleased to accept your working conditions." He chuckled as a man walked into his office. "Charlie Sachs, I want you to meet our new junior analyst, Miss Amahli Simmons."

"Welcome. I'm glad you could start so soon. We're bursting at the seams with work that needs to get done. Come with me to your desk so you can get settled before the Monday morning briefing."

"Mr. Sachs, thank you. I'm ready to go to work."

Amahli followed him and found herself in the middle of the large central room filled with analyst desks, and those of several secretaries. Nine analysts, all dressed in gray, brown, or navy suits and ties, surrounded her. She hoped they were not going to attack immediately. She was a new fish thrown into a pond, left to sink or swim. It was obvious to her that everything she said or did would be observed and scrutinized by her new colleagues.

The young men gawked at this tall, well-dressed woman with raven hair and olive skin as she set up her desk, placing a flowering plant, a brass desk lamp, and two framed small photos on it: one of JJ and one of her parents.

The silent staring was brought to a resounding end with Amahli's unabashed statement: "Good morning, gentlemen. I'm the new analyst, Amahli Simmons. I'm joining you in pursuing peace in international alliances. I hope to get to know you all well very soon." She sat down. The words sent the men to rustling papers at their desks, trying not to look at her.

"Is your father Thomas Simmons?" one man asked and snickered in a rather loud dismissive tone, eyeing the picture of her parents and implying that she was in the job because of her father's connection. The room went silent again, but before she could respond, Sir Williams entered the room and heard Henry Mayer's comments.

Talking directly to her he said, "Miss Simmons, welcome to the analysts' world." To her new colleagues, he said, "Gentlemen, please follow me to the briefing room, where you can introduce yourselves and brief Miss Simmons on our work. Then we'll take some time to organize her into our projects with her first assignments."

With that he turned, walking briskly to the conference room. His minions trailed behind him, looking dead ahead and silent. Amahli, struggling to keep a straight face, followed at the end of the line.

In the conference room, Sir Williams was a king holding court; the high-back leather chair at the end of the polished cherry table dwarfed the other chairs. Amahli observed him closely and liked what she saw. He was dressed in university tweed rather than Oxford Street serge. He was most likely in his late forties or early fifties. A fairly distinguished gentleman, his body not thin nor thick, he stood six feet tall with tawny-brown, close-cropped hair. Fine wrinkles framed his eyes when he smiled, and his ruddy complexion hinted at a Scottish heritage. He was clean-shaven, wearing tortoiseshell-framed glasses that highlighted his green eyes. His chin didn't recede, as was often the case in the nobility, so he must have been knighted for some other reason. His serious look was intimidating, but she anticipated that he was also full of good humor.

"Henry, let's start with you. You seemed out to impress Miss Simmons when I came to gather you all up for the meeting. What are your current projects and how do they contribute to our overall industrialization strategy?"

Henry blushed and stumbled through his projects' descriptions without sassy remarks. After Henry, Sir Williams proceeded around the table with introductions and project summaries. Amahli took detailed notes, as each man spoke, documenting his name and projects. The last person to speak was Amahli.

Sir Williams said, "Please tell us a bit about your war experience, language skills, and schooling so your colleagues can get to know you."

She did, and the men never teased her again about how she won the position.

***

In the first months on the job, Amahli observed this swirling sea of dull-suited men. She became invisible on purpose, continuing to wear muted conservative suits and ties, wanting the men to forget that she was special in any way. She fancied herself a spy among them. Not to steal, but to learn, to put the puzzle pieces together so she could find a niche of her own success.

Her strategy worked: her colleagues and Sir Williams's peers soon talked openly around her, as if she was not there. Amahli was so pleased that they took her for granted, thinking her head empty—for now, at least. They began to discuss matters of importance on an array of topics, as well as local gossip. She listened and learned, soaking up strategic, tactical, and key player information.

As she did in the war, she took on all the work thrown at her no matter how meaningless, except typing others' papers and proposals. Like many of the analysts, she conducted research and did translations as requested by Sir Williams and his colleagues, the other senior directors. The more she learned, the more she could annotate the work with connective tissue and discussion points she had gleaned from listening, and from her own research. By the end of her first year, her work was well noticed, and the directors came to rely on her.

Amahli patiently waited for the right opportunity before stepping forward. The need for competent people around the globe to support expanded operations was obvious. Embassies and consulates were reopening in war-torn European countries, as well as new offices throughout the United States in major cities. A wide range of political, commercial, security, and economic alliances needed to be nurtured and championed. The Foreign Office was taking the lead in trade and investments that would benefit the United Kingdom.

Amahli intended find the right place to make her mark. She kept learning and building her own network of relationships, as her father coached her, while enjoying living with her parents and their nurturing love and care for JJ. The happy, growing, cheerful little girl adventured out into the world as fast as they would let her. Amahli could not imagine how women without her family's resources and support could succeed. She wrote to her friend.

Dear Patricia,

I think about you often now that I'm settled back in London and have a new job. My daughter JJ is growing and always amazing me. She is my love and my joy. I hope you and Bill are doing well out in Cornwall. Between your nursing and his keen work with engines, I'm sure you'll both do well in the country. Smart choices come easy to you.

I want to thank you for all the advice and support you gave me back in January '45. Everything you said was absolutely true. My career is underway because I fought for it, like you told me. The pain of losing Jack has faded into memories of our good times together, just as you promised.

Your sense of persistence and insights to survive have been well applied, and I am blessed with a strong family and much support. I know that other women have fewer resources and less support. I am here because you helped me realize what it means to carve one's own path, no matter how many potholes may slow me down. Thank you. You can reach me anytime about anything here at my parents.

Much love to you and your family, Amahli

CHAPTER 14

The Boeing 377 Stratocruiser, heading to the States, lifted into the afternoon sky from London's Heathrow airport in early April 1952. Taking young JJ with her and away from everything familiar was a risk, but Amahli couldn't leave her behind. It wasn't just the separation anxiety. More importantly, leaving the child with her parents would destroy any attempt to connect JJ with her US grandparents.

Sitting in the coveted window seat next to her mother, JJ unexpectedly asked, "Mummy, who was my daddy?"

"Why, your father was an American who died in the war. Don't you remember me telling you about him, and how very much we loved each other?" Amahli opened her ring locket and once again showed her the miniature portrait.

"Yes, I see, but where is he?" JJ's eyes bored into her mother's face. "What does it mean to be died?"

"Sweetheart, the word is dead: What does it mean to be dead?"

"Ok, what does it mean to be dead?" JJ persisted with corrected grammar.

"People, just like animals, are born into the world. When they die, they leave the world and no longer exist."

"But where do they go when they leave?"

"Some say that when someone dies, they go to heaven, where we'll meet them some day. Others say that after you die, you disappear to into the cosmos, the universe of stars. But truthfully, no one really knows. We just know that we'll never see them here on earth again."

"So, he died and I'll never see him until I die?" JJ frowned. "But I thought someday, maybe when I was grown-up, I'd get to see Daddy."

"No, you won't see him, nor will I, here on earth. We are like all creatures—we are born, we live our lives, and eventually we die, JJ. Some people, like your daddy, die unexpectedly. Other people live to be very old before they die."

This conversation was becoming way too philosophical for a six-year-old, in Amahli's opinion.

"You won't surprise me and die, will you, Mummy?"

"No, JJ. I'm going to live for a very long time, and so are you. So, how old are you now?" Amahli asked in a feeble attempt to change the subject.

"Goodness, Mummy—I know that. I'll be seven soon." JJ furrowed her brow. "I thought we were going to see Daddy, but he's not here. So why are we flying to the United States?"

"We're traveling to the United States because of my work, but we may also get to meet your daddy's parents. Just like Nani and Papa are my parents and your grandparents, you have another set of grandparents, Daddy's parents."

Amahli held her breath, waiting for the next question. Being a mother required more than logic, but she never expected a child's questions could be so challenging.

"Well, if Daddy's dead, are his mother and father dead too?"

"No, JJ. Daddy's mother and father are still alive, as far as I know."

"It would be so fun to have another Nani and Papa. When are we going to visit them?"

"I'm not sure, but we'll sort it out when we get there," Amahli replied, hiding the worry of how she was going to make such a meeting happen.

JJ opened her coloring book and her long wavy hair, unruly as always, fell around the book. She was so much like Jack—easily accepting of herself and her circumstances. At least for the moment.

One step at a time, Amahli thought as she pulled JJ's hair back into a ponytail and studied her daughter's ears. They were still like Jack's, standing out a bit too much. My God, how I loved to nibble at those ears.

Today JJ's questions were innocent enough, but Amahli knew they would persist. No matter how much devotion and affection she, her parents, and Uncle BJ gave her little girl, she was beginning to develop an emotional hole that would need filling.

Connecting with Jack's family might help herself, as well as help JJ. However, the thought of Jack's parents believing that their granddaughter was the bastard child of a mixed-race trollop was almost too much to bear. Amahli needed them to embrace their grandchild. Then they might accept her.

As a child, Amahli experienced rejection as mixed race girl, and was sometimes bullied. She grew up stronger for it, but it took both of her parents to see her through. JJ only had one parent to help her. How was she going to protect her? Amahli had no idea. She only knew that her first step was to get to Detroit.

Amahli smoothed JJ's hair again, but the child ignored her mother's touch. She had abandoned her coloring book and was pressing her face solidly into the window, watching the earth far below them.

"Look, Mummy, we're flying! Isn't it just wonderful? Do you think we'll go as high as heaven?"

"No, my dear," Amahli said. "Look at the map in the back pocket of the seat in front of you. We won't be going to heaven."

She opened the map, pointing out that they were most likely over Ireland and on their way to New York. "Our plane must land at Ireland's Shannon Airport and at Gander, Newfoundland, to get fuel. From New York we'll transfer to another plane to fly to Detroit."

JJ used her red crayon to mark the route on the map. Later she would sleep, color in her coloring books, and play with the two dolls she had carefully placed in the seat pocket.

After dinner, JJ dozed off. Before putting her own head to a pillow, Amahli reviewed her briefing book, memorizing the biographies of everyone she was to meet and work with. Charlie would help her with the presentations and the required socializing before and during the conference. Being the Foreign Office's first and only woman on a project of this importance was both a challenge for her and a new experience for the people she would be working with.

However, Amahli recognized that the conference work would be easier than what it took to convince her mother that bringing JJ to the States was a good idea.

Maa protested for a week before she succumbed to Amahli's determined refusal to leave her daughter in London. She reminded her mother that she and Papa took her all over the world. And Maa reminded Amahli that she was a single parent doing what the two of them did together. Only after explaining that the consulate promised to help her find a trustworthy and kind nanny and tutor for JJ while she worked did her mother agree.

Just before Amahli finally succumbed to sleep, she opened the locket on her ring. Looking at his photo, Amahli whispered to the ring, as she often did in times of stress. "Jack, I'm doing this for JJ, and your family. I just hope it works out somehow."

JACK'S GIFT

CHAPTER 15

Two months before Amahli and JJ flew to the United States, Sir Williams offered Amahli a promotion: a full analyst position to support NATO. Its headquarters were in Rocquencourt, France, a suburb wedged between Versailles and Paris. Now that Lord Ismay was its first Secretary General, there were ample opportunities for work requiring research and coordination with the US and the other Western democracies to make the emerging transatlantic security agreement a reality.

Papa and Maa encouraged her to accept the position. She could travel back and forth to France while JJ stayed protected under Maa's watchful eye. The job would be challenging, but not overly stressful. Her well-honed translation skills, knowledge of European culture, project management skills, and Foreign Office experience prepared her well for such an assignment.

On a Thursday afternoon a week after the offer, a brilliant day that polished much of winter's dullness, Amahli was called into Sir Williams's office. He told her the position could lead to a much-expanded role in another two to three years. As her advocate, he fought the not-so-subtle resistance among his peers who believed that the only women with sufficient skills were the young Queen Elizabeth and Eleanor Roosevelt, both of whom got their positions through their families—one by heredity and one by marriage.

Amahli knew that if she wasn't going to accept the position, she must instead offer an alternative, and she must create the impression that the idea was his, not hers alone. *When did I become so Machiavellian?* But she learned from the best. For years, she watched her parents interact. Her father knew when to be firm, how to implant ideas for his wife to adopt, and when to let go. Her mother knew when to resist and when to accept her husband's ideas, shaping them to make them her own.

Amahli straightened her collar and tie and smoothed her skirt over her hips. Her long legs melted away the distance to Sir Williams's office, where she entered with a proposal in hand. She sat squarely in front of his intricately carved mahogany desk that miraculously survived the war. He nodded for her to begin.

"I know this isn't the most logical decision I've ever made, Sir Williams, but I believe it's the right decision for both of us. I'm declining your offer of the NATO analyst position."

He sat back in his chair, calmly smoking a still-difficult-to-come-by American cigarette. The room fell silent, so silent that she could hear her breath bounce against the office walls.

"Are you sure? There are others waiting in line if you pass it by."

"I appreciate your offer and your concern, but I've been researching something you talked about several months ago: the condition of our exports."

Again there was silence.

Sir Williams leaned forward, putting an elbow on his desk. "What about our exports? I'm not sure this is your area of expertise."

"It wasn't, sir. It is now and I've discovered some opportunities you won't want to miss." Amahli voiced cracked slightly as she spoke.

He frowned. "Let's see if you educated yourself. Tell me what you're thinking. I've ten minutes before my next meeting." He looked at his watch.

Amahli nodded, then handed him the proposal. He took the paper and read the title, then slid it onto the desk.

"The ten-minute version is simple. The biggest push for British consulates in the US since the war has been to champion trade and investment between the two countries. We desperately need US financing to power our manufacturing recovery. We've nationalized our steel industry—much to the conservatives' objections—but it's profitable, unlike the others. Our economic recovery here in Britain has been slow, housing is in short supply, and bread is still rationed, along with many necessities. American loans and Marshall Plan grants keep us afloat. Like you, I believe there's opportunity in this time of austerity."

She paused to confirm that he was listening. "As you also know, during the war, car production in the US gave way to commercial and military vehicle production, and many motor vehicle plants were converted for aircraft and aero engine production. Now the British government controls the steel supply and priority has been given to supporting foreign-revenue-raising export businesses. In 1947, steel was available only to British businesses who exported at least 75 percent of their production. By the end of the 1940s, 75 percent of British car production and 60 percent of its commercial vehicles was exported—"

"Amahli, I know all this. What's your point, if I may ask?"

"My point is that America is going to get its auto production volume to exceed prewar levels soon, and that will take ours down…unless we invite American automakers and parts manufacturers into partnerships with us. The faster we act to start discussions and negotiate agreements, the better our chances of success." She held her breath.

"And why is this so important to do right now?"

"Time is of the essence, sir. From what I've calculated, in two years US financial support will ebb. We need partnerships in place and operational before that happens."

"And why can't we leave this partnership-building to the current consulate staff in Chicago?"

"Because, sir, they need help to make it happen."

Sir Williams continued to sit forward.

Amahli explained. "Based on my five years with the Foreign Office, some diplomats have come to believe that because of our special relationship with the States, US financial support of our economy will continue forever. Neither of us believe that will be the case, correct?"

He nodded, seeming to know he was being drawn into her web, but letting it happen.

"What I propose is a way to kick-start partnership building and make it operational before the end of this year. We can host a conference in June to define specific partnership opportunities, share ideas, and build relationships with the American automakers and parts manufacturers. Based on my experience working with Americans at Glatton, not only will the Americans buy into it, but they'll also adopt it as their own because it'll have the look and feel that is important to action-oriented American sensibilities. Immediately after the conference, our negotiators can begin to finalize the alliances, which should be concluded before the end of December."

***

"Let me guess." Sir Williams raised his eyebrows. "You propose that you are the one to organize the conference?" He smashed his cigarette butt out in the large cut-glass ashtray, a present from his wife.

"Yes, sir, I do. With some help, of course. I've learned from working with Americans that a direct approach, focusing on building collaborative commitments before the conference, will work. Americans do not like to be told what to do. Nor should we British appear to be begging. I think the Americans will see the need for this kind of collaboration. It will quicken their ability to enter global markets by having production operations on this side of the Atlantic. A conference hosted by us in the United States, on their playing field, will bring the teams together."

He was pleased with what he heard. What spark, what energy he saw rising out of her, and the proposal was brilliant, with its strategic and practical advantages. She proved herself reliable, smart, and a strong team player during the past five years. This plan proved she was no longer just participating in executing other's ideas: she was creating her own solutions.

He was sold; however, he wasn't going to pave her way. She had to convince his peers—the other senior directors—that her idea was the correct action. Their people stationed in the States and their sections' funding assistance were needed to make the conference successful.

Sir Williams stood, walked around his desk, then sat next to her in the companion chair. "Here's what I can offer you: As you said, you can't do this alone. That would be too risky. I'll have Charlie call a senior directors' meeting three days from today, at which time you'll present the proposal and demonstrate to all of us what you're capable of. If you can't convince them, you can't convince the Americans. Am I correct, Miss Simmons?"

Amahli nodded.

"Can you be ready to make the presentation to the senior directors in three days?"

"Yes. Thank you, sir. It's all in my proposal. Is there an overhead projector we could use? I saw one used at Glatton."

He saw her excitement, and noticed that she dove into the details before he could rethink his decision.

"Well, yes, we have one. I'll have Charlie show you the equipment." Sir Williams and Amahli stood and shook hands. "Good luck to you, young woman. I think you'll need it."

CHAPTER 16

Amahli, Charlie Sachs, and Sir Williams entered the same briefing room where Amahli met with her colleagues on her first day on the job five years before. Charlie went to the back, ready to dim the lights. The directors strolled in at the last minute, chatting, shaking hands, and then taking their usual seats. The men sat smoking their after-lunch cigars and cigarettes. To clear the haze, Charlie cracked several windows in the back of the room, letting lazy curls of smoke escape.

Sir Williams opened the meeting. "Gentlemen, thank you for taking time to meet with us today. You know Amahli, who's done research and writing for all of you over the last five years. She has an idea that I would like you to consider. Miss Simmons, please share your proposal with the directors." He walked away from the table to stand by the wall, observing the unfolding scene.

Show time! echoed in Amahli's head. "Thank you, Sir Williams." She stood and turned to the table. "Sirs, in front of you is a copy for your later reference. I'm going to present to you this afternoon the key points and highlights of the plan, with the expectation that you'll agree to support us in proceeding with the project. Time is of the essence. We'll need your cooperation and financial assistance to make this partnership a success."

Amahli paused and inhaled, her chest rising. With her knocking knees hidden below the tabletop, she looked around, unable to gauge whether they would listen.

Who is the most significant player? Amahli applied what she had learned from watching these men interact in other meetings. If she could get support from the most influential director, the others might fall in line fairly easily.

"Mr. Sachs, would you lower the lights, please?" Amahli turned on the projector. The room went quiet and she began her presentation. The men were attentive for the first ten minutes, but then started chatting among each other. Sir Williams looked at Amahli with a slight smirk on his face and his eyebrows arched.

She nodded recognition of the situation, then abruptly stopped speaking, transforming her panic into calmness.

"Mr. Sachs, please turn up the lights."

Charlie obeyed and the men stopped talking amidst the haze. Amahli spoke softly, but very clearly and with significant authority. She wanted them to lean into her words.

"Gentlemen. There are significant opportunities for quickening our alliances with American industry to ensure British economic manufacturing success. Forgive me for being so blunt, but we have less than two years before the Americans forget about us and go about their own merry way if we don't take leadership now and act.

"If you have little interest in exploring partnerships with US manufacturers, then I'll say nothing further and close the meeting. It's your decision. Sir Williams's section will pursue what his office can do on its own."

She raised herself to her full height, looking straight at the men, saying nothing more.

Chairs shuffled, heads turned, and hands clenched on elbows on the table. They looked at each other, sending the message, Say something! Somebody say something!

Sir Wentworth, the eldest member of the senior directors, sat at the end of the table, opposite Amahli. After what seemed like an eternity to her—but was actually less than a minute—he spoke.

"Miss Simmons, no offense was meant. I believe my colleagues didn't contemplate hearing such an arresting proposal today. And I think they expected Mr. Sachs to present." He let that message settle on the men around him. Faces reddened. "We all know the quality of Miss Simmons' work, so why shouldn't we at least listen to what she has to say? I'm intrigued by her perspective."

The men around the table nodded and came to attention like young lads reprimanded for talking without permission during a university lecture. From the side, Sir Williams nodded a thank-you to Sir Wentworth.

"Thank you, everyone. I understand you'll have concerns. Mr. Sachs and I are here to answer all of your questions at the end of the presentation. Mr. Sachs, please dim the lights." She then continued, holding their attention until the end.

With the lights bright once again, Amahli closed. "Gentlemen, thank you for listening to our proposal.

We will answer your questions and address your concerns now."

Charlie came forward, standing next to her at the podium. There were a dozen questions over the next twenty minutes and the two answered them. Sensing the audience was ready, Charlie took the meeting to the next step, as he and Amahli discussed in the previous day's practice session.

"Miss Simmons, I think we have answered their questions. Let's move forward to the decision-making." He stepped aside, standing next to their mentor. Amahli glanced at Sir Williams, then turned to the men sitting at the table.

"As I stated, we need financial support and human resources to get the conference planning started. We would like to hear from each of you." Amahli targeted her new ally with a soft voice and smile. "Sir Wentworth, do you have any questions before we begin?"

"No. I think they're all answered for me."

"Then do you agree that the section you lead should provide the necessary resources to move forward with this project?"

"Yes, Miss Simmons, I do. I support you and Mr. Sachs to lead the conference to its successful completion with all due haste. Let me know what I can do to assist."

"Thank you, sir. We're incredibly grateful."

Amahli's knees stopped shaking as she turned her attention to the director at the right of Sir Wentworth, asking the same question. He made one inquiry, which was answered, and then he agreed to move forward as well. As she worked her way around the room, using the same words to address each director, a consensus was built. In the end, it was a chorus of "Yes, do move forward" led by Miss Simmons, their conductor.

Amahli and Charlie thanked everyone, vigorously shaking each man's hand as they departed. Her visible excitement was infectious.

After the others left, Sir Williams said, "Now that my colleagues agree to support the conference, you will fly to Detroit to organize and execute it in June, in coordination with the Chicago consulate. You will share the responsibility for its success with Sam Toller our administrator in Chicago who has connections within the US auto industry. He'll work with you to ensure the right industry people are invited and the right protocols are followed, and assist with attendee logistics. You will design the agenda and obtain participation commitments from the Big Three automakers. A travel budget must be prepared for me to approve by the end of next week."

Charlie laughed. "Amahli, it looks like we're going to be mates for a while."

"Yes, we've got a lot of work to do." Amahli, glowing from the inside out, followed several respectful steps behind the men as they started the walk back to their offices.

Charlie gruffly whispered to Sir Williams, shaking his head in amazement, "I can't believe she was ready to stop the meeting like that."

"Do not underestimate Amahli, Charlie. Believe me, she will succeed. Help her where you can. She's as good as any man around here, as I'm sure you have discovered."

JACK'S GIFT

CHAPTER 17

Amahli, her daughter, and Charlie were exhausted from the many hours in planes. Even though the flight from London to New York was perfectly uneventful and smooth—much to their delight—the flight to Detroit was delayed for three hours and encountered unexpected turbulence from storms whipping across the Midwest, adding a strong dose of anxiety to their fatigue. Only JJ seemed undaunted by the chaos, telling anyone who would listen that the bumpy flight was as much fun as riding a county fair Waltzer.

Sam Toller arrived earlier in the day from Chicago and met their plane. "Welcome to Motor City," he shouted over the noise on the tarmac. He led them to the baggage area to claim their suitcases, then ushered the trio into the private car he hired to take them to their hotel.

"I'm glad you pushed back on us to have the conference in Detroit instead of Chicago, near the consulate. It was a sound maneuver to come to the automakers' home court. Very diplomatic of you," said Sam.

Amahli smiled. "Thank you. We do know what we're doing…usually."

"Of course! I didn't mean to imply you don't," Sam said.

"No offense taken," Charlie said, looking out the window. "Amahli and I are really impressed with Detroit as much as we were with New York. After years of England's rubble and slow rebuild, it's all candy to our eyes."

As the car wove through the traffic, Sam explained the accommodations. "I've rented a large suite at the Cadillac Hotel, a historic place centrally located with easy access for everyone attending the conference. General Motors, which everyone calls GM, is the largest corporation, and its headquarters are just a couple of blocks away. The others are scattered about the area. And the airport is not far from downtown, as you will see. The overseas arrivals will appreciate that."

He removed and opened a black notebook from his pocket, ticking off items with his pencil.

"The Cadillac Hotel should be a good place for the conference as well, but I'll leave that for you to decide. It and two other conference hotels have availability for the period you requested. Once we settle on the place and dates, I'll reserve them on the ambassador's calendar. He'll be flying in from Washington, DC, for the opening. Hopefully he'll stay for the conference and be able to close it as well."

Charlie asked, "A hotel suite for the three of us? I appreciate your effort to keep us together, but surely you realize that Amahli and I are colleagues, not spouses. I'm married, with children back home. Amahli and her daughter will need their own rooms."

Sam blushed a deep red. "Yes, of course, I know. Forgive me for not being clear. Seems I have a bit of foot-in-mouth disease, as Americans are apt to say. It's really two smaller suites, each with their own hall entrances, sitting room, bedroom, and bath. They're connected with a larger shared living area that has a small kitchen, and dining and meeting rooms. You'll have your privacy and a central place to work. I'm arranging a nanny for JJ." He turned to Amahli. "You'll be interviewing several candidates tomorrow. When men come over with their families on extended stays, we usually arrange for family apartments, but since your stay is less than three months, it made more sense for you and your daughter to be close to where you'll be working with Charlie."

"Thank you, Sam. That's kind of you," replied Amahli.

Sir Williams initially resisted when she announced that JJ would be traveling with her, thinking it better that she should remain in London because Amahli was single. But Amahli did her homework, telling Sir Williams that there was nothing prohibiting her from bringing the child. The policy language was written in such a way that it assumed the traveling diplomat was a man who brought his wife along to care for the children and their schooling. Amahli countered by saying she would pay for a nanny and tutor.

Sir Williams admitted that the language and rules were outdated. Although there was nothing in it explicitly stating that babysitting and tutoring could be expensed, he said that the Foreign Office would cover the cost since it was for only three months.

Switching to the conference plans, Sam said, "When we notified the auto manufacturers that we were organizing this conference, they were excited at the prospect of partnerships that will put them into international markets. As you requested, they're waiting for your preconference meetings to offer their ideas." He puffed up a bit and his face was back to its normal color.

"Good. Sounds like you've picked up a bit of the American preference for action, as well as some of their slang. Is there something in the water over here?" she asked.

"Well, it's different here for sure," Sam batted back. "I came to Chicago with the postwar consulate expansion program. I enjoy living here—it's really quite brilliant. Americans have no reservations about their wishes, and they're determined to get them. It's all about the future, not past traditions. The demand for goods and services is extraordinary. Americans don't wait for what they want, they just invent it! It's very refreshing to know where you stand. If I had my way, I'd stay in the States for the rest of my life."

"I completely understand your attraction to Americans." Amahli remembered how direct Jack was. "Will you be staying with us here in Detroit?"

"No, I'll be in Chicago as your consulate liaison, but you'll have a direct line to my office. Anything official, like invitations, must be sent from the consulate. We will also handle attendee logistical inquiries so you can focus on the conference organization and content. Once word gets out, both parts suppliers and smaller auto manufacturers will queue up to attend, as well as the Big Three. I think you can count on more than 100 men participating."

"Well, we certainly have our work cut out for us, don't we?" Amahli said. "Let's start tomorrow after a decent night's sleep and breakfast."

***

Within a week they had a firm date for the conference, selected the Cadillac Hotel as the venue, and drafted a list of British and US attendees. They also made meal and reception plans and confirmed the preconference meeting appointments with GM, Ford, and Chrysler. After those talks, Amahli and Charlie would integrate the collected ideas, assuring everyone that they had been listened to. Then they'd design a conference structure to bring the program to life.

"Brilliant," Sir Williams said when the two updated him on a call to London at the end of the first week.

***

Near the end of the third week, Amahli and Charlie were completing the last of the three preconference meetings. He led the first appointment and she, the second. GM was the biggest, so she expected that Charlie, her senior, would take the lead. But he had a different idea.

"Amahli, I want you to run this last meeting. You're a sharp and good-looking woman—even when you try to hide it in those conservative suits. Let's put those qualities to work for us. When I compare our performances at the first two meetings, you had better interaction with the men and they were certainly engaged. They offered more ideas and quickly made additional commitments. Do you mind?"

"Oh, Charlie, I thought you liked me for my brains. What will your wife say?" Amahli teased. "Of course I'll do my best, but don't get your hopes up. I only brought my gray and navy suits for work." They both laughed, then retrieved JJ from the nanny's care and went to dinner.

***

Amahli was ready. Smartly dressed in a gray suit, white silk blouse, and pearls, with her hair, now long again, pulled back into a seriously stylish upsweep highlighting her elegant neck, she stood to her full height at one end of the boardroom table opposite the GM International Markets Senior Vice President Mr. Joe Withers. At the end of the formal remarks and open discussion, she summarized.

"Gentlemen, your ideas for both content and structure are brilliant. Together we can make this event a success for everyone involved.

"Soon you'll receive the formal invitation to the Vehicle Manufacturing Partnership Opportunities Conference directly from our consulate in Chicago. We do hope you'll attend, with your most knowledgeable staff. Our leading British steel, automotive manufacturing, and import-export experts will be there, ready to engage. After the occasion, it's our intent to formalize the partnership agreements and put them in place before the end of the year."

Charlie joined her at the head of the table for the final question and answer session, then thanked their audience once again and retook their seats, waiting for the senior vice president to speak.

Amahli watched Joe Withers scan the room with a satisfied smile before he spoke. "Miss Simmons and Mr. Sachs, thank you for coming to us. We're looking forward to the conference. I've asked one of my department managers to work with you. Until we see you again at the event, thank you for taking the initiative to pull all of this together."

Everyone stood, gathered up their papers, and readied to leave the room. Amahli and Charlie shook hands with each executive as they filed out, but one lingered behind. Amahli watched the slim, impeccably dressed blond-haired man approach. He was about five foot eleven with piercing blue eyes and looked amazingly like Uncle BJ, but there was something else. *What is familiar about him? Is it his head or face?* She couldn't put her finger on it.

"Miss Simmons, Mr. Sachs." The man reached out to shake hands. "I'm Colin Jackson, but everyone calls me Andy, please do the same. I've been assigned to assist you, as my boss said, so I'd like to start by taking you to dinner this evening to get acquainted. Then we'll be ready to start on the conference planning. I know most of the players who'll be attending, so at dinner I'll paint some portraits." He paused, then smiled. "And I'd like to introduce you to our famous local cuisine."

Amahli shook his hand; his touch made her dizzy, forcing her to abruptly sit at the conference table and inhale deeply. Both men stared at her.

"Are you all right?" Andy asked. "You look like you are going to faint. Is it something I said?"

"No, I'm fine." Her voice was strained, but she quickly regained her presence and stood. "We're just pleased for your assistance, and we certainly can use the help. Charlie and I would be delighted to join you for dinner."

***

Andy gazed at this handsome, well-made woman. If only he could have asked just her to dinner, but that would have been bad form, and he wasn't about to do anything that might jeopardize his company's needed relationship with the Brits. There was something riveting about her that drew him. It was more than her confidence, combined with her slightly exotic look and charm. Her gaze penetrated into him and told him she was more than she seemed, but he couldn't pinpoint it.

"That's swell. I'll meet you and Mr. Sachs at the hotel at seven. The restaurant's a short distance from the hotel, if you don't mind a walk."

"That sounds fine, but please call me Amahli, and this is Charlie. Fresh air after three busy weeks would be delightful." They shook hands again.

***

Amahli watched Andy leave the room, her eyes following him down the hall visible through the conference room's glass wall.

As they walked back to the hotel, she was drowning in her thoughts. Entering the hotel, Charlie asked, "This may be none of my business, but what was that all about back there? I have never in the five years we've worked together known you to be so completely upended. Are you sure you're ok?"

Amahli stopped, taking Charlie's arm. "I did almost faint. Meeting him was a shock. I know who he is, but he doesn't know who I am."

"Well, who are you, Miss Simmons, and who is he?" Charlie chuckled.

Amahli stood, looking down, letting herself be mesmerized by the mosaic floor tiles of the building's reception area for a moment.

"I really shouldn't tell you, Charlie. It's about Jack's family—the American side of JJ's family. I didn't want anyone at work to know."

Charlie grinned. "Really, Amahli? Is that what you think? We all knew Jack's father was an American, even though you never displayed a photo or talked about him. Your ring gave you away—Sir Williams and I recognized the American Air Service ring. When you asked to take JJ with you, we surmised that you might have orchestrated this trip to find Jack's family. Am I right?"

Amahli looked at him, wide-eyed. Her heart pulsed as if were exploding out of her body among shots of guilt and shame that plunged into her gut. She pulled Charlie to a sofa in the hotel's reception area, where she sat before her legs gave out.

"You mean you two knew all along? I'm profoundly embarrassed. Is that why Sir Williams agreed to my bringing JJ with me?"

"I do believe that's the reason. But don't worry. He believes in you and the conference first and foremost. Remember, the decision to send you came first." He pulled her up by the arm and steered her toward the elevator. "Now, who is Andy Jackson?"

"He's Jack's older and only sibling."

"Oh, goodness. This is a pickle of sorts. How about I don't join you tonight for dinner? I'll dine with JJ. We'll make an evening of it."

"I'll get the nanny to stay. I—I need you at dinner tonight," she stammered as panic set in.

"No, you don't. Don't go all victim on me. Be the strong woman you always prove yourself to be." Charlie punched his finger at her chest. "You don't understand, do you? Even though he asked both of us, his eyes were on you. I recognize the symptoms because I remember when I first met my wife right after the war."

"I didn't see the invitation that way."

"You want to connect with Jack's parents, right? Well, here's your opportunity," Charlie said. "Maybe it's not exactly how you planned it, but Andy is definitely a lead worth pursuing, as salesmen like to say."

"I don't know what I planned. BJ met Andy in the States before they flew over to Glatton and said he was a good man. Tommy, another war buddy who lives in Nebraska, gave me Jack's parents' address here in Detroit some years ago. I didn't know if they're still living there, or even alive. I thought that perhaps after the conference, I'd reach out to Andy, and then to the family."

"Well, there's no time like the present," said Charlie as the elevator doors slid open and they stepped out into the hall together. "Go enjoy dinner. And don't forget to ditch the gray suit. Tell JJ she's got a date with her Uncle Charlie." He walked toward his suite's hall entrance and Amahli toward hers.

"All right. Thank you, Charlie. At least, I think so." Amahli pushed a smile onto her face, but her brow remained furrowed. It took her three times to get the door's lock to work.

CHAPTER 18

"What are pan-fried perch?" Amahli asked from behind the oversized laminated menu. The restaurant felt like a British pub. Its dining room, paneled in distressed wood, was filled with worn armchairs and sturdy tables, Detroit sports memorabilia pinned to the walls, and people who seemed to know one another. Only the dartboard and beer-splashed, sticky floors were missing. This place had aged red carpeting and a billiard table in the back room.

"It's the local cuisine I told you about earlier. Perhaps I should have picked a more elegant restaurant." Andy gazed at her over his menu. She had exchanged her gray suit for a featherlight blue silk shirtwaist dress with a plunging neckline and high collar. She was stunning: a person of substance with a flair for fashion.

"Michigan inland lakes are major breeding grounds for this small-sized variety. They flourish in our many spring-fed lakes. You can't get them overseas, or even in Chicago. The chef fillets the fish to remove their spines and large rib bones, then gently sautés the morsels in salt, pepper, butter, and lemon until golden brown with curled edges. They're so tender that they melt in your mouth when you wrap your lips around them."

"Why, that sounds almost French," Amahli said. "I wasn't sure if Americans knew what 'sautéed' meant."

"Oh, come now. We're not all lumberjacks wearing coonskin caps. True, pan-fried is not a fancy way of saying it. The French, as I have learned, would add shallots and call it perche sautée au beurre citronné et échalotes."

Amahli opened her eyes wide. "Très bien, monsieur. Tu parles bien le français."

Andy laughed. "Not really. I know enough to read a menu and find a bus. I started eating perch when I was a kid, fishing for them with my dad. He taught me how to clean and then cook them over an open fire in a cast-iron skillet. We fished as much as we could. Dad managed to buy a small cottage north of Detroit on White Lake, where I spent many, many days fishing with him and my brother Jack. Catching perch was a favorite, mostly because it was easy and they were plentiful." Andy relaxed into his chair. "Wait until you see them served. They'll make you a freshwater perch lover forever."

"Ok, nothing like a surprise for dinner. I will order them," said Amahli, placing her arms casually on the chair's arms. Andy had many of BJ's looks—the height, blond hair, slim figure, and clear blue eyes. Perhaps that was why Jack had been so close to BJ. He'd seen his brother in BJ. Andy definitely didn't look like Jack, except for his ears.

"How about a cocktail before we eat?" he asked.

"A gin martini would be most welcome. I presume the bartender is properly trained in the mixing of gin? Make it extra dry with olives, please."

After the martinis were served, Andy held his glass up to hers. "Well, Miss Simmons, here's to our working together."

"Yes, to our working together, Mr. Jackson." She took a swallow, stopping herself from slugging it down in one gulp.

***

"The perch were quite a pleasant surprise." Amahli sat back in her chair as the waiter cleared her plate. "So light and tender, just like you promised. Thank you."

"And you're a pleasing wonder. You're smart, poised, and obviously able to handle men. Does your work suit you for a career, or are you looking at a future with a husband and children?" Andy dabbed his lips with his napkin and flipped it to his lap. His direct words matched his direct stare.

Amahli shifted uneasily, put both hands on the table, and leaned forward, matching his stare. "I'll take that first part of what you said as a compliment. But as to the second part, I'm not a woman looking to being taken care of, if that's what you imply. And why would being married prevent me from having a career? If I were a man, you wouldn't ask me that question. What is it with men? You come back from the war after we women have worked in every kind of job men have done, only to be told we should step aside and be happy taking care of a man and children."

Andy shifted. His napkin fell to the floor and he let it lay there.

"Both of my parents have careers. My father works in the Foreign Office, and my mother is a medical doctor. I have one as well." Amahli's words cut like the jagged edge of an overused axe. "Does that bother you?"

"Absolutely not. I apologize for making any assumptions." Andy stumbled through the words. The air was silent between them. "Look, I say foolish things sometimes. Can we start again?"

Again, silence.

"I'm sorry. I didn't mean to be hurtful. It's just that I'm very sensitive when it comes to my career and place in the world," she said. "Yes, let's start again."

"No matter what you say, I do believe you are unique and I like that. Can you tell me more about your parents?"

"My father is British and my mother is Hindu. That makes me mixed race. I've lived a half-and-half existence all my life, not fitting into anyone's camp particularly well. And it looks like with this conference, the situation will be the same. Everyone I've met in any kind of position above waiter or secretary is very, very white and male."

"Yes, it's true. I witnessed segregation during the war. Racism is the elephant in the room that no one talks about."

"Well, your country is not alone on this issue. I guess we cover it up with the British class system."

"Amahli, it's an issue we're all going to tackle if the West is going to succeed globally, long term. The largest potential markets for our US vehicles in the future are not the English, or even Europeans. They're Chinese, South Asian, South American, and eventually African, from what I discovered through my research. The US has work to do if it's going to succeed internationally." He paused. "Amahli, have you ever seen the movie Gone with the Wind?"

"Yes, but what does that have to do with anything?"

"Do you remember what Rhett Butler said to Scarlet when he was leaving her?"

"Why of course. Who could forget that?" Amahli grinned. "He said, 'Frankly my dear, I don't give a damn.'"

"Good. Because that's how I feel about you, and anyone else. I don't care where you came from or what your heritage is—I take people as they are," he said. "Career and marriage or not."

She searched his face but remained silent.

His eyes met hers. "Let's order dessert and coffee, then I'll walk you back to the hotel. Or would you prefer tea?"

"Yes, tea would be nice." They sat in an uneasy silent tension until dessert was served. She took a spoonful of the vanilla ice cream from atop her apple pie, then put it down.

"Andy, I did come across angry. I apologize because I know it made you uncomfortable, but as a mixed-race woman trying to make her way in what is, quite obviously, a white man's industry, I have to know with whom I'm working."

"And I apologize for asking so many questions and making so many assumptions about you."

"Apology accepted, Andy. So, enough about me. Tell me about you." They both relaxed and continued to eat dessert.

Looking up from his apple pie, Andy said, "I was in France in the war—a captain, and later a major in the artillery. It was a gruesome time, fighting on the ground and seeing so many innocent civilians struggling to stay alive. I landed at Normandy five days after D-Day. Too many men died, or were wounded so badly that their lives were never the same. Then we lost my brother Jack in November of '44. He was stationed in England, a navigator on a B-17. I find it difficult to talk about the war with people who haven't experienced it.

"What about you? Did you live with your parents in London during the war?"

Amahli stopped eating and put her hands in her lap to hide her locket ring, hoping Andy hadn't noticed it. She couldn't lie, but she was not ready to make the family connection. As she spoke, she carefully removed the ring from her hand and placed it in her dress pocket.

"Actually, I worked during the war. My parents wanted me safely out of London. Instead of staying at university, I helped with translations and communications outside the city. My father's not nobility, but because of WWI, he became well connected with many in the Foreign Office and was able to join after the war. He's a well-respected diplomatic administrator. I guess Americans would say he is the man everyone asks to get things done when others can't. We lived in Europe, the Middle East, and northern Africa while I was growing up. I learned French and several other languages. After the war, I returned to university and graduated. Unlike most women who settled for teaching, clerical work, or nursing, I was determined to work where few women fear to tread: diplomacy and international relations. I persisted until I got my first job as a junior analyst in the Foreign Office. I'm sorry to say that I didn't get the job because of my qualifications alone. The man interviewing me ignored me until I dropped my father's name."

"Men do the same thing, shamelessly, and qualified or not, all the time. You shouldn't be afraid to connect using any reference that might give you a leg up on the competition. It just makes you stand out from the others." Andy obviously admired her. "As you've probably learned, initiative drives us here in the US more than heritage. My family were formerly struggling farmers and country storeowners from rural Michigan. Dad worked his way up to a really nice middle-class life here in Detroit in auto manufacturing. Started as a plant laborer, putting in countless hours and effort to become a supervisor during the war. He was rewarded with a plant manager's job, which suits him well. I'm the first in our family to graduate from college, so I never had to work in a factory to get a foot in the door."

Amahli put her hand on his forearm, encouraging him.

"When I returned to the States, I got a job here at GM, not at Ford where my dad works. I was in the finance department, but found it boring, just dealing with the numbers. Last year I got lucky and started working in the international markets department, where I'm putting my knowledge of Europe to good use. The job is a combination of economic and market analysis to forecast primary international market locations, timing, and growth. I put context to all the numbers, and I paint pictures in my own way. It's not exactly artistic work, but definitely not boring. It's swell, in fact."

Their eyes were locked on each other. Amahli was served tea and Andy, coffee.

"So, how do you like the States?" he asked.

"Well, I do like America. It's new and polished silver, always gleaming, where people seem to ignore their circumstances and always look to the future. In Britain, silver is always elegantly old and tarnished, with people fully aware of their circumstances, accepting their place. I'm a bit overwhelmed with the size of everything here, from the buildings to restaurant food servings and the expanses of space. New York is like London, but with more energy, more vigor. Why, even Detroit, a manufacturing hub, is brighter and bigger than anything we ever had, even before the war destroyed so much. The sidewalks here are wide. The buildings, skyscrapers, and the hustle and bustle are kinetic."

"Would you like to be working here permanently?" he asked. His voice had the soft timbre of a friend, rather than the sharpness of a formal professional.

"I'll be returning to London after the conference. We're working closely with the consulate in Chicago. I do hope I get to see Chicago before I leave. I hear it is actually a windy city."

"That it is," he said. "Look, I apologize again for coming across so rude tonight. It's just that I'm so pleased to meet you and Charlie. You're both savvy, modern, and engaging. So many diplomats I've met over the years come across as stuffy and old school. They talk down to people like me, plain people who are willing to work hard for success. You and Charlie are refreshing, diplomatically speaking. Let's work together to make this conference special. I'll help you in any way I can." His face reddened a little.

"Again, apology accepted, Andy. I did so enjoy dinner, especially those wonderful little perch arranged in a ring round the plate. Very clever. Too bad Charlie missed them."

Andy paid the check, and then the two strolled back to the hotel, side by side, not arm in arm. Amahli felt electricity jump from him to her. She made the space between a bit wider.

JACK'S GIFT

CHAPTER 19

Amahli tapped the lectern microphone, found it was on, and welcomed the overflowing room of attendees to the conference. She scanned the room, finding only four women among the 150 men. She quickly put that thought aside and focused on the agenda, knowing it clearly reflected their suggestions from earlier meetings. She turned the lectern over to Charlie and Sam, who introduced the British ambassador. She disappeared quietly to the back of the room where she listened to his opening address, which stressed the importance of partnerships to both nations.

As the conference progressed, Amahli, like her father, made things happen. She ensured that all speakers and breakout sessions started and stopped on time, that both the American and British participants were personally introduced and correctly connected to each other and to the consulate staff, and that everyone was tended to during the evening receptions and dinners.

On the third and last day, at its closing ceremonies, the ambassador's booming voice once again radiated over the audience.

"Gentlemen, it has been a pleasure to host this partnership-building event. The Chicago consulate will be following up with you in the coming weeks with draft partnership agreements. The Foreign Office in London will follow up with our British executives." He cleared his throat.

"Now, before we end, I want you, with me, to thank the creative forces behind this conference: Miss Amahli Simmons, Mr. Charlie Sachs, and Mr. Sam Toller. Without this team's dedication, persistence, and organizational skills, it would not have been possible. Amahli and gentlemen, please come forward."

She stood with Charlie and Sam in the back of the room, blushing and frozen as everyone rose and turned, applauding. With a push from Sam and Charlie, the three walked forward to the stage, graciously smiling. At the lectern, the ambassador whispered in her ear, beckoning her to speak as the applause slowly quieted. He stepped back, allowing Amahli to stand at the lectern.

"Thank you, Ambassador. We've made this happen together. In addition to Mr. Toller and Mr. Sachs, please thank Andy Jackson of GM, who became a most valuable team member. Andy, please join us on the stage."

As he obeyed, applause erupted again. After the crowd became silent, Amahli said, "Most of all, I want to thank all of you who gave our team the ideas and insights for the conference content and structure. And thank you, everyone, for being so incredibly open. I love my country, but I've also come to love the United States and its people, who work so energetically to help us make the world whole again."

She bowed slightly and in closing said, "I hope, sometime in the future, to again work with you here in the United States."

***

The conference room was given back to the hotel, and Sam had the ambassador safely on a plane back to the Washington, DC, embassy. Charlie and Amahli were weary. With their last bit of energy, they sat at the hotel bar finalizing their to-do list for post-conference follow-ups. Sam walked in, returning from the airport, and read the list approvingly, adding only one item. Andy joined them after a short stop at the office after the conference. He ordered a round of celebratory martinis.

The four sat shoulder to shoulder, toasting to each other's accomplishments. "I feel like we climbed a mountain," Amahli said. "I've never felt such exhilarating accomplishment before!"

The men toasted her. Sam said, "Now all we have to do is figure out how to get down this mountain without falling off a cliff." They all laughed and toasted again.

At nine, Charlie went to his room to get much-needed sleep so he could get up to call his family in the morning, British time. He was flying home Sunday night. Andy left because he had to stay sober enough to drive home. Only Sam and Amahli continued at the bar, quiet now, sipping their last martinis, swishing their pimento stuffed green olives around in their glasses.

"It's been swell working with you, Amahli. I mean, it's been brilliant to be with you." He slipped his fingers into her hand. "I wish you could stay to take a position in Chicago for a while."

"Sam, this endeavor with you and the others has been exceptionally good, but I'll be heading to London as soon as I clean up a few things next week. I've got to get JJ ready for school in the fall, and we both miss my parents."

"Yes, if you must go back, you must, but why don't you come to Chicago for a few days before you leave? Everyone at the consulate wants to meet you, and you'd have a chance to see the best city outside of New York. Lake Michigan; the Art Institute with its magnificent Impressionist collection; the Palmer House, our most elegant hotel; and Wrigley Field are aching to meet you." He gave her hand a squeeze. Amahli didn't withdraw.

"What's Wrigley Field?" she asked with a slightly slurred voice.

"Just like Americans can't understand the British until they know cricket, you can't understand Americans until you understand baseball. Wrigley Field is the home of the Chicago Cubs, my favorite baseball team. They're not often a winning team, but the field is so intimate because you sit close to the players. It's like they're playing in your garden. I can't for the life of me stop watching them play so I have season tickets for all their home games. I'll take you to a game when you come to Chicago." He dropped her hand and put his arm around her shoulder.

"Are you asking me to come to Chicago to take me on a date?" Amahli, almost choking on her olive, sat upright, pushing his arm from her shoulder, but in a most friendly manner.

"You could put it that way, or you could just say I want to give you and JJ a taste of the true American experience." Sam looked at her with a sheepish grin.

How un-British. Amahli's head spun. The martinis and a dinner of only shrimp appetizers, nuts, and cheese were beginning to take a toll.

What is happening? Why am I feeling so happy? Is it the alcohol talking? Her body pulsed in a way not experienced in years. Not since Jack.

"It does sound interesting and JJ would be thrilled, of course." Amahli searched for her formal voice, which was unavailable. "Let me talk with Charlie. Perhaps I could get approval for me and JJ to take the train to Chicago, then fly out of Chicago to London."

When she pushed away from the bar and stood, her legs were jelly. She grabbed Sam's arm to steady herself. Sam took it, paid the tab, then walked with Amahli safely at his arm. They stepped into an empty elevator. He leaned toward her as the door closed, taking her face in his hands, gently kissing her on the mouth. She returned the kiss, then caught herself.

"Sam, goodness. How delightfully unprofessional of you."

He stepped back, didn't apologize, and watched as Amahli knew her cheeks were turning red: Bing cherry red.

The elevator door opened. Sam put his hat on his head, cocked it to the side, winked, and then waved to her as he backed out. "I'm on a morning plane back to Chicago, so call me when you've decided what to do."

What an old Frank Sinatra move, Amahli mused, almost swooning. She giggled, falling against the back wall of the elevator, and then got off two floors later, swaying down the hall to her room, humming Doris Day's hit, *A Guy is a Guy.*

JJ was snuggly tucked into bed and sound asleep. Disrobing in the bathroom, Amahli looked at her naked self in the mirror. Sam was trying to seduce her…and she didn't mind. She smiled at the woman in the mirror and touched her breasts. It electrified her all the way down her body. Were these new emotions replacements for past feelings? Or were these past feelings reawakened? It was all a complicated jumble. The woman in the mirror had no answers for her but smiled back. She touched herself again and again until she erupted, falling to the floor in a self-induced ecstasy not felt since 1944.

She had no idea what time it was when she awoke, finding herself with legs spread open on the floor, her back resting against the bathtub. She shook herself, put on a gown, swallowed an aspirin, drank a large glass of water, and went to bed.

***

Sober, and thinking clearly again, Amahli did not call Sam on Saturday. She was not going to Chicago. Sam awakened the wildness she had with Jack so many years before. It was unholy—violating his memory, violating her plan. Instead, she fulfilled JJ's wish to visit Monkey Island that Saturday after breakfast. The taxi deposited them at the Detroit Zoo—only four miles north of their hotel. She and JJ walked the zoo, downed hot dogs and Coca Cola, then left to shop at Detroit's famous Hudson's Department Store. There she bought JJ a new outfit for school and surprised herself with a new silk dress. The color wasn't a favorite, but her skin glowed in it and she read a recent Vogue article claiming that men loved orange. Honey orange was her choice, so deeply creamy—a good compromise. The afternoon ended with a tour by JJ, leading her mother proudly to a playground in a large park near the hotel. JJ played there often, accompanied by her nanny. For dinner, they joined Charlie for a long farewell.

***

As the sun crawled up the eastern sky, ringing broke the morning's silence, waking Amahli. She grabbed her head, shaking herself awake, then reached for the telephone on the nightstand. She pulled the cord around the corner into the bathroom, barely able to close the door behind her. JJ rustled under the blanket but didn't wake up.

"Hello? Who is this?"

"So, you want to work in the US, do you?" Sir Williams bellowed.

"Good morning to you too, sir. It's before six on Sunday morning here. Is there an emergency or something?"

"Do you remember what you said at the conference closing, Amahli? I just received a cable from the ambassador, asking for you to be stationed in the Chicago consulate for the rest of the year."

"What? Asking for me? Why?"

Did she tell the ambassador anything about staying in Chicago? Racking her brain, Amahli remembered her closing words at the conference.

"Sir, the only thing I said was 'I hope, in the future, to work with you again in the United States.' I was just being polite. I needed the Americans to know that we like them. Anyway, why would the ambassador request me?"

"As I said, the ambassador said you are needed in Chicago until the end of the year. That was his order," Sir Williams barked.

"Oh, sir, I don't know how this could happen. I never spoke with him about such a thing, during or after the conference. I didn't say 'now' when I spoke at the closing ceremony. I said 'sometime in the future.' I would've discussed it with you first if there was any inkling of an offer."

"Amahli, I appreciate that you were careful with your words, but that really doesn't matter. You are wanted, for whatever reason. I guess you outperformed to their expectations. It's your fault, young lady. You have one week to get yourself to Chicago. They want you to coordinate the partnership negotiations process because, the ambassador said and I quote, 'Everyone likes the way she gets things done.' Your job will be to keep the lines of communication open and the negotiation teams organized and on track. There'll be deadlines to keep and issues to resolve. There's an army of people working in the Chicago office, in Washington, DC, and here in my office."

"But why can't Charlie or Sam handle it all?"

"Because Charlie is my deputy and will work on this end. Sam won't be of much help in Chicago—he's got other assignments, it seems. He can help you the first weeks to get settled, but that's all. That's why you're needed…from what I surmise." Sir Williams inhaled and went silent.

"I need a few days to think about it, sir." Amahli could not wrap her head around the idea of getting her mother to agree.

"Like I said, the ambassador wants you in Chicago by the beginning of next week. Please figure out how to get there and what to do with your daughter," Sir Williams snapped. Amahli knew her success would shine brightly on him. "Enjoy Chicago—I hear it's cold as hell in the winter. Cheers." With that, he ended the call.

Amahli sat on the edge of the bed, dumbfounded. Pulling on a sweater and slacks, she splashed cold water on her face, ran her fingers through her hair, and checked to see if JJ was still asleep. She was. Softly closing the bedroom door behind her, she walked across the suite's shared living area with fists clenched, ready to knock on Charlie's door. He opened it, surprising them both.

"What are you doing up so early on this lovely morning?" he questioned with coffee in hand. Unable to hold back, she told him what just transpired.

"Well, I'm happy you're staying here, and not me." His knowing look made Amahli wonder if it was Charlie who recommended she stay in the States. "I'm looking forward to seeing my wife and boys." Charlie gave her a hug. "Chin up, girl. Looks like you've got plans to make and work to do. I'll help you. I don't leave for the airport until three. Wake JJ with the good news while I order breakfast."

This was the perfect opportunity to prove her ability to act quickly and adapt to a fluid situation. She laughed when she received a copy of the cable Sir Williams sent in response to the ambassador:

Miss Simmons graciously accepts the opportunity to coordinate the partnership agreement negotiations in the Chicago consulate until the end of the year.

***

There were plane reservations to change, train tickets to buy, and calls to Sam in Chicago to set in motion new living arrangements for herself and JJ.

Amahli called her parents. Maa was distraught but acquiesced after only an hour of lively discussion and promises. Amahli considered it a win. By two in the afternoon, everything was set. Within a week, Amahli and JJ would be in Chicago.

Amahli and Charlie laughed as JJ danced around the room, celebrating the continuation of her great American adventure. At least they'd still be working together, even though it was long distance. Amahli hustled JJ into their rooms for a nap.

"By the way," Charlie said as he gathered his cases, preparing to leave. "Did you ever do anything about meeting Jack's parents? What did Andy say when you told him?"

Amahli tried to make herself disappear into the overstuffed couch. "Oh, goodness, Charlie. I didn't tell him. I didn't lie, but I did not tell him."

"So much for our brave new diplomat." Charlie chuckled. "You can't leave town until you talk with him, you know, especially since you are going to be here in the States for six months. I thought your scheme was to introduce your daughter to Jack's side of the family."

"I know, I know. I just don't know how to do it" She pulled her knees to her chin and hid her head between them. Charlie sat down next to her.

"Just imagine how JJ's grandparents might react if they learn—eight years after their son's death—that they have a grandchild. "I can't imagine what they would feel. I'm afraid they'll reject her because of me, or maybe attempt to steal her away."

"First of all, they can't take JJ away from you. You're her biological mother, able to fully care for her, and you both are British citizens with British passports. That gives you all the protection you need."

"You're right. It's very logical when you lay it out that way, but I feel like a big baby about the whole thing. I'm a coward."

Like the big brother he'd become, Charlie stood and pulled Amahli off the couch onto her feet. He put an arm around her. "It's not going to be easy, for sure, but don't mope about it. Start by telling Andy the truth. He likes you very much, so he'll be an ally you can rely on to help you find a way. The good news is that being here for six more months will give you some time to plan and see it through, one way or the other."

"Yes. You're right, I suppose. I just wish I felt more confident about it working out properly."

JACK'S GIFT

CHAPTER 20

Andy welcomed Amahli's call. He was intoxicated by her presence, her smell, and her manner, but kept his emotions in check and to himself, treating her as the professional colleague she was. Now that she was headed back to London, it was too late to say anything anyway. Her time in the States was over, but he still wanted to see her, so he accepted her invitation.

From watching her, Andy learned how a woman could be tough and persistent but also kind and generous. He wasn't sure if he could live with someone as headstrong as her, but maybe it would be possible, making marriage more of a partnership rather than the traditional relationship, like that of his mom and dad. Since knowing Amahli, Andy did know that if he ever had a daughter, he would raise her to set her sights on a career with financial independence as well as a happy married life, doing whatever she wanted to do.

As he walked to the hotel, the air was fresh against his face, dry and sun filled, not hot and humid like so many summer days. Amahli was an energy, creating a sensation that somehow told him that he was connected to her. It haunted him. He couldn't shake the feeling as he rang her suite, then made himself comfortable in the lobby, waiting for her to come down. He'd abandoned his suit and tie for slacks and a navy-blue crewneck sweater over a white shirt. He wanted her to see him in a new light.

Amahli walked from the elevator through the lobby, her stride long, her arms swinging at her side, her face without expression. How odd, thought Andy as he watched her approach. What happened to the jubilant, conquering warrior from the conference, with her gleaming smile and bright eyes?

"I'm so glad you called." He stood to greet her. "How about we walk and find a nice place for an early dinner? I did so want to see you before you headed to London."

"I'm not really hungry, but I do need to talk with you." She looked at him in a matter-of-fact way, then turned to follow his lead, walking to the hotel's front door.

"What makes you so serious today? I thought you'd be excited to be heading home." He opened the door while she studied the ground.

"Andy, when we first met, I didn't tell you everything about me, and I'm afraid you won't be happy when you hear what I have to say."

"I doubt that anything you could reveal would make me unhappy. Except maybe saying you never want to hear from me again."

"No, that's not it at all. Come, take me to that diner around the corner. I can use some coffee."

"Coffee? Not tea?"

"Yes, coffee. Something strong, with a full-bodied aroma."

He obliged, steering her toward the diner, her heels drumming on the pavement as they walked. They found an empty booth with a picture-window view out onto the West Side of the city. The glow of summer lit their surroundings, making the booth warm and welcoming.

"How about some pie with that coffee?" the waitress asked when she took their orders. He looked at Amahli to see if she was interested. She shook her head.

"No, no thanks," he said to the waitress, then returned to Amahli. "Tell me what's troubling you."

"I knew who you were when we first met, but I didn't tell you." Her words were flat.

"Well, that's a bit of a surprise. Who am I?"

"Andy, you're not just the man from GM who was going to help us with the conference. You shocked me. I had no idea that you would just appear in my life."

"You still haven't told me. Who am I?"

"You're Jack's brother."

"Did my name give me away?"

"Well, that and your ears…"

"What about my ears?" Andy frowned.

"It's a little thing, but you and Jack both have ears that are just little too big for your heads."

"Well, you can blame that on my dad. All Jackson men have these ears." He sipped his coffee. "Hey, how do you know my brother had ears like mine? Who are you?"

Amahli sat straight. "I'm the woman who fell in love with your brother in England. We were together for four months. I'm the woman who had his child. Andy, you're the uncle of a little girl who will be seven in August."

Andy sat speechless for a moment. "Tell me everything."

"You want to hear it all—about me and Jack? About our affair? About JJ?"

"Yes, the whole story from the beginning. I want to know the truth."

CHAPTER 21

It was a brilliant July afternoon on my day off. I met my two girlfriends, Alison and Patricia, for lunch at the Addison Arms, Glatton Village's ancient pub, a place built sometime in the 18th century. We planned a hiking excursion for the afternoon.

While we waited for our sandwiches, I watched some Yanks standing about in the pub and was not impressed. They looked and acted like all the others I encountered at Glatton since my arrival in the summer of 1943. American servicemen were friendly and exceptionally hard working, but they were also a cliquish lot who talked much too loudly, displayed rakish manners, and generally ended up taking over wherever they appeared.

The pub became a popular gathering spot for US crewmen after the Americans transformed the fields surrounding Glatton Village into a bomber airfield. American flight crews in their B-17 bombers flew constant raids against the Nazis in Europe out of Glatton. I appreciated their critical role in saving Britain and Europe from the Nazis, but I refused to get close to any of them. My mother had warned me.

As we ate our lunch, Alison stated the obvious. "Looks like our dartboard's been commandeered by Yanks."

Her voice boomed across the pub, loud enough for three men to hear despite the chattering and laughing among themselves while drinking and playing darts. They stopped talking and looked toward us.

"You're embarrassing. Hush," I whispered to Alison.

"Oh, come now, Amahli," Patricia said, swinging her newly bobbed hair across her face. She was really quite fresh. "They look harmless enough. It might be fun. Invite them over, Alison. There's nothing wrong with a friendly chat."

My friends waved while I sat chewing a bite from my sandwich, keeping my eyes downcast onto my plate. The men looked at each other and, without a word between them, put down the darts, grabbed their pints, and walked over to our table.

"Ladies, good afternoon. What brings you into this den of flying Yanks?" asked the one I later learned was named Jack. I thought him too much, too full of himself. He was short and dark haired—not handsome in a chiseled John Wayne or Cary Grant kind of way, but his face had character. I liked that. I broke loose from his stare, turning away and going back to my sandwich.

Alison gave them a welcoming smile. "We're having lunch before a walk across the fields. We've been cooped up working six days straight, so when we can, we get out into the open air, rain or shine." She then introduced herself, Patricia, and me, pointing to each as if instructing students, like she did as a teacher before the war.

BJ introduced himself, Tommy, and Jack. They'd been together since they arrived at Glatton.

Patricia teased, "I thought you'd be flying on a day like this. It's easier to see the Nazis, isn't it?"

Jack was quick to respond. "We just finished our second run this week, so we've earned a couple of days off to recover before heading out again. Does that answer your question, milady?" He laughed. "How about we chat while you eat your lunch and we drink our beers?"

Before the girls could answer, the men pulled chairs from the next table, their legs scraping across the uneven floor. Jack put his chair next to me. He was soft but intense, trying to make small talk. Then he would blurt out things like, "You're beautiful, so different. I want to wrap my arms around you right now."

"That's very brazen of you," I slammed back at him. "You have bad manners as far as I'm concerned."

Jack smiled. "I'm telling you the truth. You're different from the girls back in the States. You're interesting."

"Interesting, maybe, but no pushover. Let me finish my lunch."

Jack blushed, trying to recover. He said nothing more, but didn't move away. Finally, he bent his head close to my ear. "I'm sorry. I didn't mean to make you uncomfortable."

I looked at him closely. "You didn't. You embarrassed yourself."

He persisted. "I can't help it. You smell of lavender and your hair shines like the sun."

I started laughing. "You are too much. Here, eat some of my chips. Maybe that will keep your mouth busy for a time." Jack obeyed. Then, looking straight in his eyes I said, "I'm not going to fall for a man who is shorter than me, nor a man with such a messy mane of hair with a sassy mouth."

He laughed from deep in his gut. It was then that I saw how extraordinarily compelling his smile was and how penetrating his mink-brown eyes were. I also realized that his ears were slightly too large for his head, protruding a bit. Here was a man who was attractive not because of good looks, but in spite of his looks. He must have the confidence and the strength to go his own way, doing what he wants. Maybe there was a sublime soul in this man somewhere.

"Do you like the out-of-doors? My friends and I planned to hike this afternoon, but I think they're going to stay here in the pub, playing darts and drinking with your mates. How about hiking with me? I desperately need exercise."

"Great idea! Let me help you with your jacket." Jack stood to reach for it on the back of my chair, but I twisted first, pulling my jacket as I stood up. Jack's eyes popped out of his head. "My God, girl, you're a giant. You must be four inches taller than me!"

I laughed. "Well, I'm just two inches shy of six feet. There's nothing I can do about it. Can you deal with a woman who can see over your head?"

He laughed from his gut again. "It's a piece of cake. Being with you is like being with BJ over there. He's six foot and blond, as you can see. We make for interesting conversation wherever we go."

Jack threw his head back, bowed with a sweep of his arm, and pointed for me to lead the way out of the pub.

As Jack and I passed the dartboard, Alison whispered to the group, "He's a goner. I say he doesn't have a chance."

BJ countered, "No, she's the goner. She doesn't have a chance." Overhearing the comments, Jack and I, walking closely, touching elbows, looked at each other and laughed as our friends ordered another round of drinks.

As we walked, we talked, telling each other our stories. Jack told me he was determined to make his own way. He didn't want to jump into college, like…you. He couldn't cope with the idea of being stuffed into an office. He even refused to take a job at the plant where your dad worked.

He wanted to drive west from Michigan across the country using the old family car your parents gave him for graduation. All he had was $50, but he knew he'd find work when that $50 ran out. However, your mother wasn't going to allow him to take such a trip until you came to his rescue, telling your mother, "I wish I took that long camping trip around Michigan's upper peninsula before I went to college. Having a break between high school and college would've made my first year easier." Jack got all the way to New Mexico on Route 66 before he turned around after Pearl Harbor was bombed.

Jack told me that he enlisted to become a flight navigator as soon as the requirements were stripped down to essentials. The Army Air Service was so desperate for men that the engineering degree requirement was eliminated. All he needed was a high school degree if he passed an aptitude test. Jack found he had a good aptitude for math, tinkering with instruments, and mapping, so he jumped at the chance. He loved solving puzzles and learned to tease out a flight path given many variables, like the wind, weather, and time of year.

He said that again, your mother wasn't going to allow it. She was furious, considering flying the most dangerous job anyone could have. But Jack had his own ideas. He would risk her fury, even rejection, to do what he thought was right. Your dad came to his rescue. By the time they visited him in Tennessee at training graduation, she supported his flying, finally seeing that he was no longer a child.

Exactly the opposite of Jack, I wanted a career. I was determined to finish my degree in foreign relations and international business, join the diplomatic corps, and travel the world. My mother and father were both professionals, but somewhat unconventional because of their mixed marriage, my father being British and my mother Hindu.

After two hours of walking and endless conversation, we circled back into the village. We were standing in front of my boarding house. Jack took my hands in his.

"This sounds crazy. We're so different in so many ways and we've just met, but I have to tell you that you belong in my life."

No one had ever been so forward with me. All I could say was, "I don't know how I feel about you, but you're sort of good looking and I certainly like your attitude. I could tolerate seeing you the next time you're on the ground."

We went out twice the following week. On our third date, I looked at him and said, "Yes, it's crazy. I feel the same way about you as you feel about me." We kissed for the first time, letting desire not just bubble up, but explode.

Nothing seemed to affect Jack's love for me, or mine for him. He didn't realize that I was older than him until one evening when we were talking about school, the difference become obvious. I asked, "Does it bother you that I am older? Don't most American men want women younger than themselves, as British men prefer?"

"I really don't care what other men want. I relish the fact that you're smart, determined, beautiful, taller, and older. It'll keep all the other blokes away."

Maybe it was the urgency of the war all around us, the loneliness of it, or the fear that tomorrow wouldn't come, but we didn't waste time with a traditional courtship. Even though everyone sensed the Allies were winning the war, life was still fragile. It was not fear we felt, but a deep magnetic attraction that stole our emotional control, while helping us feel safe at the same time.

Instead of time at the pub with the Arf & Arf crew before meeting up with me, as he usually did, on the evening of November 7 Jack asked me to a private dinner with him. I found that earlier in the day he arranged a dinner at the pub, reserving a table in the quiet, warm corner by the fire. Through his own connections, he managed to procure a bottle of white bordeaux which the pub owner, Roger, cooled for him.

This was the first time that Jack formally asked me to dinner, so I sensed it was going to be special—the tone of his voice gave it away. I wore my best dress, a flowing blue silk shirtwaist dress. It wasn't new, but it was the last one I found in London before the war descended.

He met me at my boarding house wearing his dress uniform. Very unusual. We walked to the pub, where Roger sat us at our table; a fire burned in the hearth, smothering both of us in glowing golden light. Roger brought the wine, uncorked it at tableside with a dash of flair, and poured two glasses…not a normal pub service. We toasted to each other's good health and were served roast chicken, boiled potatoes, and peas. It certainly was not an elegant meal, but it was wartime, and it was the best to be had in the area.

After the plates were cleared and the last of the wine poured, Jack held my hands across the table. "Tomorrow is my 25th mission. That means I have only ten more before I'm released from flight duty. Do you know what that means?"

I held my glass to the side of my face with my elbow on the table, leaning in, smiling, looking romantically into my lover's eyes. Jack coughed, then cleared his throat to find his most formal voice.

"It means that sometime after the New Year, after that last mission, we could marry and make our affair official. Would you like to marry me?" He held his breath, waiting for my answer.

"Why not now?" I could tell I surprised him. "For the past month, every time we're together, all we talk about is our future. Would you stay in Britain for me? Would I go to America for you? What would we tell our families? How would we convince them that we were right for each other?"

Jack laughed, proclaiming, "Well, milady, if that's what you want, then that's what you'll have. Right after tomorrow's mission." He pulled a small package, wrapped in an embroidered handkerchief, out of his pocket and gave it to me. I placed the package on the table in front of me, then slowly unfolded the silky material to reveal a ring, a man's ring. I picked it up, turning it over, examining it.

"I couldn't afford, much less find, a proper engagement ring for you in this village, so I'm giving you my Air Service ring." I gave him the ring and held out my left hand. He slipped it on my ring finger and said, "Will you, my beautiful Amahli, be mine forever and marry me?"

"Yes, and yes!" I said, throwing my arms around him in such a wide sweeping motion that my wine glass tipped over, creating chaos. Neither of us jumped out of the way as it spilled on the table, but we laughed heartily.

I said, "What could be more perfect than living together, with all the joy that it brings? No more secrets." Thinking about my parents, I added, "And the challenges that it will bring."

Jack said, "I want nothing else. We'll get married next week. We'll file the paperwork and find a justice of the peace after the mission. I'll re-up for another set of missions, or get transferred to a ground job here at Glatton. Then after the war we can make other decisions and get our families used to the idea of us."

"How did you know my ring size? It's a perfect fit."

"Alison borrowed one of your rings a couple of weeks ago."

"Ah, that's why she wanted that ring. She told me she had a date she wanted to dress up for." I looked more closely at it, noticing that it was an official sterling locket ring with the US Army Air Service emblem embossed on the top of the locket. Inside was a photo, our faces smiling out to the viewer.

I was awestruck by all the effort he put into making the ring perfect. He took a negative of a photo that BJ took earlier in September to a photographer in the village, who cropped out everyone but us and reprinted it in just the right size. Jack took care in everything in a manner that made it all seem effortless.

We stood. I took his face in my hands, kissed him again. Leaning against his chest, our hearts together, the world around us disappeared for those few moments.

Applause erupted, filling the pub with happy noise. We turned together and faced the pub's customers, including BJ, Tommy, Alison, and Patricia at the bar. We blushed, grinning from ear to ear, making deep formal bows to more applause. Then we grabbed our coats and went to the bar to pay the bill on the way out, but we were refused. Roger wouldn't take Jack's money. We thanked him and then ran into the night, hand in hand.

We entered my boarding house room, creeping through the back door and up the back stairwell, thinking that no one would see us. The landlady heard us, but Mrs. Kershaw, I learned later, was well aware of our rendezvous since the beginning, choosing to ignore us because, despite being a proper lady, she blamed the war on destroying proper courtship.

That last night we ignored precautions. All our passion ignited in a desperate need for each other, clawing and enrapturing at the same time. He was gentle. I was ravenous, I am embarrassed to say. He was tender, giving me pleasure, electrifying my body as if I never felt his touch before. We wrestled, screamed and collapsed, laughed, cried, and then did that all over again. For the first time, he stayed the night, neither of us wanting to part. But at 0600 in the dark, Jack rose, kissed me one last time, and left for the base.

JACK'S GIFT

CHAPTER 22

Andy and Amahli were quiet for a time. "I hope I didn't embarrass you with all those details."

"I'm not embarrassed at all. My brother, true to form, got what he wanted," reflected Andy. "However, what you told me just proves what I always knew. Although I followed the wishes of my stoic parents, Jack did what he wanted, not what they wanted. He didn't inherit our parents' cautiousness, nor quiet formal manners. I think I did, always wanting to please them. I wish I were more like Jack."

Amahli liked his honesty. "Jack never tried to be someone he wasn't. You should do the same. It's perfectly all right to be totally different from him and still be a wonderful person." They sat a few minutes watching the sun set.

"Tell me more about yourself."

Amahli smiled. "My story is simple. Like I mentioned when we first met, I'm the daughter of a British university man—but not nobility—Thomas Simmons, who's done well in the British Foreign Office as an organization administrator. My mother, Amita, a raj's daughter born in India, was one of the few female medical doctors trained in England in the 1920s. They met in her first year in medical school in London, a classic case of love at first sight. They defied

British colonial conventions and Hindu arranged marriage traditions and produced me."

"So why did you work at Glatton? Why didn't you evacuate farther to the north, like so many others?"

"I didn't evacuate because I was not a young damsel in distress that needed protecting. My father stayed in London for work and my mother stayed with him. As a doctor, she was also needed in the city, so he couldn't ask her to leave. We lived, and still live, in the same home.

"My parents conspired to make me leave, but were highly unsuccessful at first. I committed to stay unless there was work elsewhere that I could do toward the war effort. So much to my parents' chagrin, I stayed, supporting medical teams on the streets wherever I could be of help. In 1943 my father organized an interview for me for a position at Glatton. He thought I would be safe working as a communications specialist, transmitting and receiving messages between Glatton, the Allied command center in Dover, and contacts in Europe. I'm fluent in French, Dutch, and a bit of German, so it was a good fit."

"How did you get all those language skills?" Andy leaned toward her over the table, taking her hands. She didn't withdraw them.

"Papa was posted in Europe and Asia in the '30s. My parents sent me to immersion school wherever we were living. This impressed Jack, as you can imagine. I remember him saying, 'I only speak American—certainly not proper English.' Then he added, 'I guess that puts me at a disadvantage.' I laughed. He was never at a disadvantage with me."

"That sounds like my brother, all right."

"Andy, he told me some of your family's history, but it was sketchy. What can you tell me?"

"Before the war, none of us had traveled outside of Michigan. Mom is a farm-raised stay-at-home mother and Dad is the son of a farm supply storeowner; neither progressed beyond high school. Dad was lucky to have worked through the Great Depression right in Detroit. We were better off than most people then, but they had their struggles. They wanted their boys to do better and go to college."

"Was your dad disappointed that he was still working in a plant after so many years?"

"No, not all. Dad's fine with what he's been able to accomplish. There were no opportunities or money back then when he was starting out. I became the poster child for their dreams; went to college and became an accountant. As you know, Jack had no idea what he wanted to do and, being the youngest, he got away with it. I think the war was his lucky star. It opened the world to him."

"I agree. Besides loving flying and navigation, I think most of all Jack loved working so very closely with a team of men in life-and-death situations. He said that his future would figure itself out."

"You've certainly cut your own path, just like Jack did," said Andy. "I've met very few women with a professional business background. You really pushed. Would you have taken the same path if Jack lived and you married?"

"Yes. I will continue my career, single or married. I know now it will be a continual challenge, since the war is over. It's disheartening sometimes." She looked down, away from Andy's gaze.

"The biggest obstacle to my own future was my mother, believe it or not. She thought a career was acceptable, but what was more acceptable would be a marriage to a high-ranking diplomat or Hindu businessman, having children—as soon as possible, so she could be a grandmother—and living near her. She was introducing me around, as she puts it, before I left for Glatton." Amahli paused. "But I had defenses. Papa would never tolerate an arranged marriage, only a marriage he could bless after I made my own choice."

Andy and Amahli continued to sit in the diner, watching the evening approach. The deep orange sunset gave way to an ink-blue sky. A slip of a moon rose. Venus was visible. Later that night, away from the city lights, the glitter of the Milky Way would split the sky.

Andy looked out through the window as he spoke. "So, was it pure coincidence, or were you searching for me and my parents when you came to Detroit?"

"I came here knowing your family lived in Detroit. Tommy gave me your parents' address. Meeting you and your family was my priority, but as time passed, the more reticent I became. So here I am, wanting you to accept my daughter into your family."

He leaned forward, framing his coffee cup with his forearms. Slowly he raised his fists to hold his chin.

"Anyway, my daughter, your niece, will be seven on August 8th. She's a clever girl who started asking about her father and his family." Amahli paused. "You're not upset, are you?"

He whispered, "A little girl. What a wonderful gift! I would love to have a little girl." He corrected himself, "I mean, Jack would have loved to have a little girl. I'm so pleased. I'm thrilled to know he had a chance to find such a deep, enduring love. I'm just surprised you didn't try to find us sooner."

"I'm a coward who is afraid that you and your parents will reject her because of me. My little girl won't be content until she knows the whole of her ancestry. The older she becomes, the more important knowing her roots will be to her…and the more resentment she may have toward me for not connecting her to the family.

"You see, we have no pictures, no letters, no family stories. She knows only that her father loved me. She needs to know what he was like as a baby, what he looked like as a kid, and that her Grandma and Grandpa Jackson and her Uncle Andy love her. Jack's wartime friend, BJ, is Uncle BJ to her. He's able to tell her some things about her father and certainly loves her, but she wants to know more. Like all children, she thinks having additional family will be exciting and fun because she'll have a multitude of people to play with."

Amahli hung her head, looking into her hands, that were now on her lap. "I'm so sorry and embarrassed to tell you all this after working with you for three months, not telling you the truth."

Andy's eyes brightened. He sat straight up and in a clear, full voice said, "There's nothing to forgive. I have a niece. I'm an uncle! What's her name?"

People around them in the diner turned their heads. Amahli and Andy winced. Her voice went soft. "I gave her the Hindu name Jaya. But her middle name is Jack, so everyone calls her JJ. That way she'll never forget who her father was, nor will we."

"That's great!" Andy seemed genuinely happy. "Now I have a grand excuse to visit London regularly."

"We'd love to have you." Taking a deep breath, Amahli got to the crux of the matter.

"Like I said, I've been a coward. I don't know how to connect with your parents. I'm afraid they'll reject her because of me. Jack and BJ said your mother could be opinionated, was suspicious of outsiders, and was always very protective. I'm afraid they'll reject her because I'm brown, or because Jack and I weren't married, or both. Maybe they'll think I'm out to con the family. They know nothing about me."

"That's a bundle of assumptions that aren't necessarily true," Andy said, waiting for her to calm. His blue eyes lit up and his lips stretched into a grin. "First, it's true you kept all this a secret from us for years, but more importantly, you haven't given us a chance. You just assume my parents will reject you and JJ." She nodded.

"Let's compare those two facts against what I know. Number one, Mom desperately wants grandchildren. She's been pestering me to marry since the day I got home and won't stop until I do. Dad will embrace you and JJ immediately, no questions asked. That's just the kind of guy he is. I love JJ already because of how I feel about you, her mother, and I haven't even met the young girl."

He blushed and she paled. They looked at each other in silence. Amahli waved the comment aside as she flipped her napkin onto the table. "What about your mother?"

"That may take some time and strategy. Too bad you have to go back to London so quickly."

"I don't, Andy. That's the good news. I'm assigned to the Chicago consulate until the end of the year. I'll be living in Chicago."

"Well, then, this is all a very correctable situation. That's great news."

"I don't care if your mother accepts me or not. I can handle the rejection as the adult, not the child, in this situation. I care desperately that they honor their lost son and embrace their grandchild. They should know that Jack gave them a granddaughter to love. They can ignore me, but they just can't reject JJ."

"They can't refuse you either. Do you hear me? They can't have JJ without you, Amahli. Believe me, I feel very strongly about this. Dad will too—he and I will tackle Mom together."

Amahli envisioned a military campaign with Andy in command, leading the charge. He continued. "Let me think on it. In the meantime, how about you introduce me to my niece?"

"Absolutely! She'll fall in love with you."

They left the diner and walked back to the hotel. "Amahli, I'm sorry I blurted out what I said earlier. Now that I know about you and Jack, I apologize and won't mention it again."

Amahli slipped her arm into his and gave it a squeeze. "We don't know where life will lead us, remember? Like Jack, we need to let life happen. It can't be all be planned out. Now, let's take a first step at a new beginning and go meet your niece, shall we? Then next weekend, perhaps you can help me move."

PART IV—DOROTHY AND AMAHLI

CHAPTER 23

With Andy safely home from the war and flourishing in his new civilian career, Joe Jackson was enjoying the postwar years. He was blessed with the routine and normalcy of his plant manager job with its solid salary, benefits, regular hours, and restored vacation time. He commuted to and from the plant with the car windows down, letting the wind swirl around him as he drove. Even in humid July or in the cold of December, he loved it. Only rain forced him to cocoon himself in the car.

He arrived home Wednesday evening right on time, looking forward to tomorrow morning when he and Dorothy would drive up to the White Lake cottage for a long lazy weekend. As was often the case, Andy planned to join them Friday night. Over the weekend, the men would fish, spending quiet and unhurried time on the water in a rowboat, throwing lines out into the placid lake water that you could see into for fifteen feet. Last season Joe found a broken one and a half horsepower outboard motor at a boat dock across the lake. Father and son got it working again. It was loud, but they put up with the racket as it transported them to and from their favorite fishing spots more quickly and with fewer aching shoulders at day's end.

Dorothy would visit with her girlfriends, playing bridge or canasta on someone's cottage porch. In the evening, Dorothy and Joe invited their lake neighbors over for a Saturday night grill with bourbon and beers. Life was good again. It was peaceful.

Joe parked the car in their newly built garage and walked to the mailbox. How strange, he said to himself. Wedged among the bills and advertisements was a letter from Andy. He recognized the handwriting immediately. Why would Andy write and not call from work or his apartment? Dutifully he took the letter in to his wife. She greeted him with a kiss and stopped her dinner preparation, wiping her hands on her apron. She took the envelope, then opened it.

Dear Mom and Dad,

I'm away from the office and in Chicago for a few days. I have a minute to drop you a short note. I can't come to the lake this weekend, as I am helping friends move into a new apartment. Seems they were unexpectedly transferred from Detroit to Chicago. I just wanted you to know (before I forget and get tied up in work again) that at a conference in June, I met someone who knew Jack when he was at Glatton. See you in a couple of weeks. How about we meet at the lake?
Love you both, your son, Andy

*****

Chicago was good. In fact, living in an apartment just two blocks from Lincoln Park, its zoo, and Lake Michigan was more than good: it was near perfect. Fresh breezes blew; the lake was gorgeous, with its shoreline for sunbathing and swimming; and the park was an excellent playground for JJ. When fall arrived, the trees would be on fire with color, creating breathtaking views. The consulate staff helped Amahli find an after-school sitter, and it was easy to register JJ for school. She knew that JJ would adapt, love the adventure of it all, and find friends among the children.

But tonight, Amahli's clock dial glowed 4:00 a.m. In the twin bed next to hers, JJ was sound asleep. Why couldn't she sleep through the night like her child? Instead she bolted awake, breathless, sweating, and shaking from a dream so real that she had to inspect her hands for the mud. She slipped out of bed, grabbing a notebook and pen from her night table and made her way to the kitchen. Seated at the table, she recorded the dream, rushing to capture its details before they retreated into her unconscious…

***

I stood in a whitewashed clapboard house across from a muddy churning river. A dirt road and embankment separated the house from the river. A thunderous, horrific storm suddenly blew through the house, breaking windows, ripping up carpets, soaking the floors, and overturning furniture. Then, just as suddenly as it appeared, it retreated, leaving behind a disastrous scene.

I searched for an escape out of the chaos left behind by the storm. I saw a man, but couldn't see who it was and I couldn't call out, as if I were in an old silent movie. He beckoned to me to come to where he stood, just outside the front door. I went to him, but I still didn't recognize him. He offered his hand. I took it and we walked silently down the gravelly dirt road, the river on our left side.

The storm threatened to return as low leaden clouds hovered over what was again a raging river. I stopped and gazed at it apprehensively, attracted to it and yet afraid. The man dropped my hand and started to walk forward without me. I turned, attempting to catch up with him, but it was difficult, even though the road was flat and empty. His rapid pace lengthened the gap between us until I found myself alone on the road. The man had disappeared over the horizon.

I continued walking, but the road was no longer flat. It was now leading up a hill. The gravel and dirt transitioned into a wet, clingy clay mixture as the incline became steeper. Like a rat on a wheel, the faster I walked, the more exhausting the road's steepening incline became. As the storm engulfed me, I dug into the ground with my hands and feet as if climbing a ladder, flinging mud as I struggled. With my arms and legs radiating pain, progress slowed to a crawl. I couldn't see over the hill's horizon…The dream abruptly ended.

***

Amahli sighed, realizing that her life was too complicated, and of her own doing. *Why would I try to follow someone who purposely left me? Will I ever see the horizon? Are the answers there?*

What a soupy mess.

Her relationships with Sam and Andy were frustrating, even though she convinced herself they had nothing to do with each other. But when she mentioned to Sam that Andy was coming to Chicago to help her get settled, he reacted defensively, as if Andy might steal her away from him. As if she somehow belonged to Sam. Why can't he understand that Andy is about family, not about romance or sex?

She didn't give into Sam's tantrum, so the result was several awkward moments that were saved only through JJ's playful ways and questions about Chicago. Amahli would not and could not make commitments to anyone, and at the moment, she wanted neither of them and both of them. Ugh! she screamed silently. When the two men left on that first Sunday evening, Amahli collapsed on her new couch, thankful to be alone with her daughter.

The dream beat against all other thoughts. She'd been left in the muddy mire, alone, to struggle. Who was the man she couldn't identify? Sam? Andy? Jack? In past dreams, Jack always stayed close at her side, embracing her. Was the dream about moving on without him, or was he telling her she'd be lost if she gave him up? She couldn't figure it out.

Amahli stared out the window. Streetlights glittered, raindrops splashed against the glass. One thing she was sure about. She didn't want to live in the past anymore, but she couldn't fathom what her future life would be, and that frightened her. She didn't see a path in front of her… Except it had to start with Jack's parents. JJ needed that connection. The rest could be sorted later.

***

As Sir Williams often grumbled, "Don't come to me with problems; bring me solutions." He said it again and again. The words, now embedded in her muscle memory, were at the top of her mind as Amahli wrote her first bimonthly report. She documented negotiation progress, identified emerging issues, and suggested potential solutions to resolve them. The assistant, Miss Kress, typed the report, and Amahli was making the final edits. She looked up to find Sam in front of her desk, watching her. How long had he been there?

"Just to remind you, I'm being nice, not pushy," he said. "How about we have dinner before either of us heads home? It's been a long week. We deserve a treat."

Amahli put down her blue pencil. This was the fourth time this month that Sam asked her to dinner. He always paid, refusing to let her share the bill, as colleagues would. And he was spending Sundays with JJ and her, taking them to a Cubs game, the Adler Planetarium, the Museum of Science and Industry, and the like. JJ looked forward to the outings and Amahli particularly liked their visit to the Art Institute because Sam knew his art history. Their conversations were filled with perspectives on paintings and sculpture. His knowledge of theater was sound, almost as scholarly as BJ's. He was romantic, even a bit possessive in attending to her, but she liked being with this surprisingly open and assertive Englishman masquerading as an American.

"Why not? I'd like dinner. Just let me take these changes over to Miss Kress."

***

While they walked to Amahli's home after dinner at a restaurant near her apartment, Sam took her hand.

"Listen to me for a moment. You've turned my world upside down, Amahli. I love my bachelor life here in America. It felt good after so many years at war.

But for you…I'd give it all up. I believe that I'm falling in love with you."

Amahli stopped walking and looked up at the star-filled sky, avoiding a direct look at him. "Sam, you make me forget the past and focus on the future. Why else would I keep accepting your dinner invitations and let you spend the weekends with us?"

He pulled her to him, gently moving her head to his shoulder, his arms around her. She stepped back a bit awkwardly. "But I don't know what I want. I do like being here, despite missing life in London sometimes. I don't know if I'm ready to be one half of a couple again. I don't know if I want that kind of commitment."

"Amahli, I'm not trying to rush you. I'm just telling you how I feel. I can't hide it. The time I spend with you is the best, and I want it to be the best for you."

Amahli didn't know if he believed everything he was saying or was just making it up, but he certainly wasn't stopping himself. She knew he wanted her. He took her chin with his hand, bringing her face to his. The heat of his body and breath caressing her lips again awakened her inner hunger. She responded, pressing herself to him and letting herself be aroused, kissing him deeply.

"Sam, whether I feel love or just have an appetite for you, I don't know. However, these feelings also cause me dismay, because the last time I felt this way, I was crushed by it."

Sam stood back from the embrace, then caressed her face and said, "I'll be here until you see the path that lays before you…until you tell me otherwise."

They stood in silence in the middle of the sidewalk, gazing at each other. Suddenly, an elderly man walked toward them with such ferocity that they had to jump aside to let him pass. They laughed, watching this overstuffed fierce little man rush by them, breaking their spell. Amahli was relieved.

Sam looked back at her. "We'll have each other soon. I am your path to happiness. I'm willing to wait for you, like I said."

"I have no idea how long that might be." Amahli smiled and kissed him on the cheek.

"Well, now that we've settled that, let's get you home. JJ will be wondering where we are."

***

Despite his determination to remain platonic friends, increasing desire pulsed through Andy every time he heard her voice. He found himself calling her several times a week. She was rich in laughter and caring. They chatted about work, JJ's adventures, and the wonders of Chicago. Andy updated her on his plans for meeting his parents. Amahli made him laugh as she read her parents' and BJ's letters from London to him over the phone.

Amahli's kind nature was fresh, abundant, and visible. It was the perfect counterbalance to her hard-driving, persistent pursuit of a career in what was still a man's world. She sent electric sparks through his body, but he wouldn't tell her that—he'd never tell her that and he wouldn't pressure her, but no other woman ever made him feel so alive. He wanted her in his life someday, somehow.

On his last call, he said, "Amahli, I've done some research and I have good news. Did you know that JJ is entitled to US citizenship, as well as her British citizenship?"

"I had no idea. Won't the facts that Jack is dead and I was never married to him prevent dual citizenship?"

"Our government recognizes her rights because of a 1946 amendment to a 1940 US citizenship statute. If a father served in the US armed services during World War II, between December 1941 and December 1946, and the father resided in the US for ten years or more, five of which were after age twelve, then his child, legitimate or not, born outside of the US is a citizen at birth."

"Why is this important?"

"It could be important for JJ because US citizenship will allow her to live in either country with all the rights of each. With a little evidentiary paperwork, JJ can have a US passport."

"In essence, the government accepts him as her father and grants her rights?"

"Yes. She'll have clear and direct access to US universities and jobs in US companies or the federal government, without immigrant alien status and all its restrictions."

"That might be good for her as she gets older. It would help JJ cut a path in the world with fewer bureaucratic worries and paperwork. But will that give your parents any power to take her from me?"

"No, don't worry about that. You're her mother. However, it might help convince my mother of your commitment to reunite JJ with her and Dad." Andy shifted to a new topic. "I have more good news. My parents are having their annual Labor Day party. I told Mom and Dad about you, so you're invited as a 'pal of Jack's during his time at Glatton.' I haven't told them about JJ yet, but I have a plan. You and JJ will come on Friday. We'll introduce JJ to Mom after she's met you. How does that sound?"

"Andy, what did you tell them about me? I was certainly more than a pal of Jack's."

"I know. I'm taking it one step at a time."

"Why didn't you tell her about JJ? Wouldn't that make it easier to accept her granddaughter—if she knew about her before she meets us?"

"Maybe, but seeing is believing. She can't deny JJ or you once she sees her in the flesh. But just as importantly, I want to make sure Mom meets and accepts you first."

"All right. I guess you know best."

"Are you willing to come on Labor Day weekend? Is the plan ok with you?" asked Andy.

"Yes, I'll risk it."

"Good, I'll pick you and JJ up at Plymouth's train station on the Friday before Labor Day. It's a small town west of Detroit, directly south of White Lake. Don't forget to bring swimsuits. I'll arrange for train tickets and call you with the details once I finalize plans with Dad. Until then, I miss you. I miss the both of you."

He hung up.

***

Amahli sat staring at the phone's receiver before placing it back on the cradle. Andy's thoroughness and caring pleased her, but he was hiding something about his mother that required him to be a protector of sorts, a protection she welcomed. He was steady, never pushing, sensing her needs and asking permission. His predictability and calmness made her feel safe. She was trying to not become romantically involved with Andy, the brother of her dead lover, but it was becoming more difficult. She shuddered at the thought of what both families might do if she did. It was good that he lived in Detroit. If he were in Chicago, she feared that any kind of relationship with Andy would create tensions with Sam. Sam's impulses weren't as predictable. That made him exciting to be with, but was also a bit daunting at times.

JACK'S GIFT

216

CHAPTER 24

Andy and Joe lounged in the wooden Adirondack chairs at the end of the long dock out over the water, enjoying the evening. They wore white cotton tee shirts and loose seersucker slacks, a luxury for men used to more formal dress. A whispering breeze kept the mosquitos away but let glowing lightening bugs hover near them.

The chairs were old, as old as the cottage, but Joe and Dorothy kept them repaired and painted a forest green every two years, except for the year she wanted blue ones. No chairs could replace these two. When Joe and Dorothy sat in them, they were king and queen of their cottage realm. When Jack and Andy had sat in them, they were connected, no matter what the brothers fussed over during the day. Tonight, sitting in them, father and son were able to share closeness without words.

Night fell and a textured tiger-orange moon rose above the tree line on the other side of the lake. The tips of their cigars burned in the dark, smoke wafting lazily into the air as it was caught in the light breeze. They sipped aged Kentucky Whiskey from jelly glasses that Dorothy had hand painted with yellow and pink flowers. This was their after-dinner summer weekend ritual since Andy returned from the war. Their time together helped fill the gap of Jack's loss.

"You know, I wish Jack was still with us, but I know he can't be." Joe sighed.

Coping with his wife's roller coaster emotions over the past seven years had taken a toll on Joe. Some weeks Dorothy was highly energetic, making plans for Jack's return, convinced he was still alive. Other weeks she plunged into the depressive reality of his death, grieving the loss. In between, she was the woman both father and son knew and enjoyed. It was difficult for Joe as he tried repeatedly to assuage her pain. Her unpredictable outbursts ruptured the normalcy that he craved. Their relationship, once so utterly loving, was now one of toleration and appeasement.

"I know, Dad. I miss him too."

"But we have you. That's what's important. Never forget that," Joe said. Andy nodded. "So, tell me more about this wartime friend of Jack's who's now in Chicago. We knew BJ and Tommy, but he never mentioned others. You seemed a little evasive about the details with your mother and me at dinner."

"It's a complex story. I need to tell you before I share it with Mom." Andy flicked the ash of his cigar into the water. "What does Mom believe this week about whether Jack is alive or not?"

"This week she says he's gone. And with you around, she's more settled, even happy. My worry is when you're not here—that's when depression overtakes her. She has visions that Jack will come back to her somehow. Remember that dream she had after he was declared dead in 1945?"

Andy nodded again. "Dad, I'm sorry I can't be here with you more. The job…you know what it's like sometimes."

"Andy, I don't mean for you to feel guilty about your mother. You're not her keeper, I am. I'll always be at her side. There were so many years, full of love, caring for each other, and fun times. She sacrificed for me, taking care of all of us. She's always loved me, Jack, and you very, very much."

"I understand, but when I'm through telling you the story, you may think Mom's visions about Jack coming back are true…in a manner of speaking." Andy saw his dad's worried expression. "Dad, relax. There're no ghosts in this story. Let me start from the beginning."

Andy took a sip of his whiskey. "The friend I mentioned at dinner was not just one of Jack's pals. The friend was his fiancée, a young woman named Amahli Simmons."

Joe leaned forward in his chair, listening to what Andy was telling him.

***

When his son was finished, Joe said nothing, tossing the stub of his cigar into the lake. A sizzling sound pierced the surface of the still water. Andy watched his dad's eyes tear. "Dad, don't be sad. It'll be all right."

Joe's voice was a whisper. "These aren't sad tears. They're tears of joy. To know that Jack genuinely loved someone, and so thoroughly, is wonderful. His life, however short, was full. That's incredibly good."

"Dad, there's more." Andy braced for his reaction. "They had a little girl who was born in August 1945. I met her before Amahli left for Chicago. Her name is Jaya Jack Simmons, but her nickname is JJ. She's bright, curious, outgoing, and her smile is contagious, just like Jack's."

"Goodness. How grand! It's completely Jack. He just let it happen, never worrying about the consequences."

Tears continued to stream down Joe's face. He gulped, choking as he held his face in his hands.

"Dad, take a deep breath." Andy whipped out his handkerchief, giving it to his father. Joe wiped his eyes, drew in a breath, and sat back in his chair, gazing into the night sky.

"It's true," said Andy. "You're a grandfather. Amahli is doing a wonderful job raising JJ. The girl even has the Jackson ears, guaranteeing she's a member of this family." Andy laughed and his dad grinned. "She's tenacious, like her mother. I'd even say precocious, able to question what adults tell her."

He pulled two photos out of his wallet that he took—one of JJ and one of Amahli—and handed them to his dad with a small flashlight he took from his slacks pocket.

Joe studied them. "They're beautiful, both of them. I assume you have a plan."

"That I do, Dad. Tomorrow, instead of using our time to stake out fishing possibilities before breakfast, we'll figure out how to break the news about Amahli and JJ to Mom."

"Yes, better in the morning because I'm exhausted now. We have to be careful and learn our parts before we talk with your mother after breakfast."

As they stood and stretched, Andy glimpsed his mother watching them from the porch. She disappeared quickly into the house before he and Dad started walking down the dock.

***

Sunday at the lake was predicted to be a hot one, as was often said about late summer weather in Michigan. Dorothy was up early while it was still cool, making breakfast: fresh squeezed orange juice, fried eggs, bacon, hash browns, toast with butter and jam, and plenty of strong black coffee. It was here at the cottage where Dorothy was most happy. It reminded her of the days before the war—the days before Jack's disappearance and bad memories. Her need to keep everything aligned and in control to maintain her balance wasn't necessary at the cottage like it was at the Detroit house. The silverware and dinnerware didn't have to match. Her dress was casual, not formal. A cotton apron protected her print shirt and white cropped slacks from the spitting bacon fat.

As she managed the pans on the stove, she thought about what Andy didn't say at dinner. There was nothing new that Tommy Pitman's old letters hadn't already communicated. However, it was nice to hear once again that Jack loved his work navigating the big B-17s and that he had many good experiences and friends while he was there.

Joe and Andy came in from their ritual morning lakeside walk. With her hair out of the tight rolls she normally wore, Dorothy felt younger than her fifty years, wishing husband and son would mention how young she looked. Instead they teased her about shuffling around in her bare feet instead of wearing shoes. Dorothy laughed anyway, kicking her legs in the air to show off her agility.

"Sit down, boys." She pushed her hair behind her ears and returned to the stove. She poured coffee into the mugs, then brought the breakfast platter to the table. Everyone served themselves and got down to serious Midwest eating, as if they were farmers preparing to plow the back forty, as was often said in Dorothy's family when she was a child.

Joe put his fork down and spoke casually. "I think Andy has some great news for us."

Dorothy looked up from her plate. "What about?"

"Well, Mom, I told you about a close friend Jack had in addition to BJ and Tommy, right?"

"Yes, I know that Tommy and BJ were there at Glatton with him. Who is this other friend? Neither of them mentioned anyone special when they wrote me after Jack's plane went down. What do you know about him? I assume he was a fellow American, right? What kind of work does he do now? Maybe you can bring him around sometime so we can meet."

"Mom, don't get carried away. One step at a time. Did Jack ever write to you about a woman he met at Glatton?"

Dorothy shook her head. Her eyes narrowed. She put down her coffee, staring at Andy as he spoke.

"Well, when I was in France Jack wrote me in one of his letters about a woman. He never gave me a name, just said he was seeing someone who worked at Glatton. After his plane went down, I just forgot about it, figuring it was nothing serious."

"Well, I'm glad for that. I can believe women fawned over him. He always was the best looking of the two of you."

Andy inhaled and smiled at his mother, refusing to let the criticism touch him this time.

"Sometimes the world is full of surprises, Mom. Jack's friend I mentioned meeting at the conference is a woman, not a man. Today, she's a diplomat in the British Foreign Office. During the war, she was a communications and translation specialist at Glatton. Her name is Amahli Simmons."

Dorothy digested her son's words before speaking.

"Well, that's nice, Andy, but her name sounds foreign. What kind of mother would name her daughter Amahli? I can't believe such a person would know Jack."

"Why a name like that? Because Amahli has a mother who is Hindu and a father who is of British and Scottish heritage."

Dorothy eyed her son as he spoke.

"What reason would there be for her to lie about knowing Jack?" asked Andy, looking to his father for support.

Before Dorothy could start her questioning again, Joe put a firm hand on her shoulder. "Let Andy tell you the story." She pulled away from him, sucking in her breath, but sat down again. With her calm, Andy told the story of Amahli's parents, her upbringing, and how she became friends with Jack, BJ, and Tommy while working at Glatton.

"Well, it's all well and good that she found you at the conference, but it sounds to me like you were set up. Really, Andy, how could you fall for such a scam? What would she want with us after all these years? We have no duty to know her. She certainly doesn't need to know us. If she was important to Jack, he would've told me. And anyway, she would've contacted us sooner if she was for real. BJ and Tommy never mentioned her in their letters, so she couldn't have been anyone significant."

Her forehead wrinkled. Her fists tightened. Andy reached for his mother's hands. She attempted to pull them back, but he persisted, holding her fists in his hands, looking straight at her, less than a foot from her face.

"Mom, Jack fell in love with Amahli, and she with him. They were going to be married in November 1944. But that never happened. He died November 8th, remember?"

"How could I forget the date?!" Dorothy snapped. "I don't believe it. How do you know they were engaged? He would have written me about her. He always told me everything."

Her voice, if not her words, accused Andy of lying. Joe stepped in again. "Dorothy, you can't believe that. Jack had his secrets, believe me. All children do. Amahli was his secret. I know it's the truth because she wears his Army Air Service ring," he explained.

He took one of the photos out of his pocket—the close-up of Amahli with her left hand on her chest. The ring was in plain view.

"Look at the picture, Dorothy." She stared at the photograph, not wanting to believe what she saw.

"She's so exotic, and it's not a wedding ring. She could have stolen it from him." Dorothy looked at the men. "She can keep the ring if she wants, but there's no need for Joe and me to do anything else."

She stood up, desperately looking for confirmation from her husband. Not getting it, she started to clear the breakfast plates from the table, slamming them on the counter behind her.

"Sit down, Dorothy!" Joe commanded for the first time in many years. She sat. "I can't dismiss Amahli, nor should you. Jack must have loved her enough to give her that ring as an engagement ring. We should share our memories, our photos, and our love of Jack with her. She knows so little about us, his family, and about Jack when he was young."

"Mom, she wants to meet you and Dad." He watched his mother consider his plea.

"Why is she using you as her conduit? Why didn't she write us first, years ago?"

"She was afraid you'd just throw it away and not believe her…as you're doing right now."

Dorothy looked at her husband. Her voice was strained. "But she's so different from us, isn't she, Joe? She's not like us. We have nothing in common, do we?"

"We have Jack in common with her, Mom. Amahli has a special respect for Americans. You and Dad willingly sacrificed one of your own sons for a people you didn't know. She wants to pay her respects. You and Dad can tell her so much about Jack. She has only her memories and the ring. She wants to thank you. She wants you to know how much she cares and appreciates your sacrifice. She has a gift to share with you."

"I guess she could visit sometime." Dorothy looked at the floor.

Joe spoke. "How about we do this: we'll invite Amahli to visit here at the lake. What do you think about Labor Day? It's a long weekend, so both she and Andy can take time off from work. She can take the train from Chicago, and Andy will bring her to the lake. If all goes well, she'll stay for the holiday. If you're uncomfortable after talking with her, then we'll respect that, and Andy will drive her back to Detroit before the evening ends."

"I don't think that'll be necessary," Dorothy corrected her husband, regaining her queenly decorum. "We can put her up here. Anything else would be rude."

"Mom, I'm glad you're willing to meet her. Amahli knows this may be a shock for you and Dad. She fully understands that it may bring back memories, both sad as well as happy. It can all be overwhelming."

Dorothy stood up. She decided that if this was what her husband and son wanted, then she would be in charge of making it happen. She would impress the hell out of this Indian girl from Britain.

"I will make this woman understand what America all is about. We'll have a big cookout, like we always do on Labor Day. We'll teach her how we celebrate the hard work of America's workers. We'll share with her and she can share with us, and then she can return to Chicago—or London, or wherever she comes from—able to tell all her British family and friends how wonderful we Americans are."

***

Back home in Detroit after Joe departed for work Monday morning, Dorothy sat at the kitchen table, writing. She needed to know if this woman was a gold-digging fraud, as she still suspected.

Dear Tommy,
I hope this letter finds you, your wife, and the twins doing well. They must be old enough for school by now.

Is the farm doing well? Nebraska is nice, particularly in the summer, although I've never been there.

We're happy to have Andy home now. We see him almost every weekend. We miss Jack. His room is ready for him if he ever returns. I have such hope that he might someday.

Andy's doing well in his big corporate job. I'm so happy that the war is finally and completely over, and that America is safe.

I'm writing to ask you about a woman who calls herself Amahli Simmons. Andy met her at a conference in Detroit this summer. She claims that she was engaged to Jack, but I'm not sure. Neither you nor BJ ever wrote to me about her, and Jack never told me about her. I saw in a photo that she has his Air Service ring. I need to know who she is and whether she can be trusted.

I've lost track of BJ and have no idea where he is living. Please write back ASAP. Also, please address the letter to only me.
Sincerely, Dorothy Jackson

She walked to the post office, rather than putting the letter in the mailbox. She didn't want Joe—or anyone, for that matter—to know about it. While she waited for a response, there were preparations to take care of…if not a trap to lay.

Less than two weeks later, Dorothy opened the letter she received from Tommy.

Dear Mrs. Jackson,

So good to hear from you. My family is well, our crops are growing like crazy (as are the twins), and prices are good for at least this season, and are projected to be good for next year. So we have nothing to complain about and much to thank God for.

As to your request for information about Amahli Simmons, I can tell you that she and Jack were engaged. There is no doubt that they would have been married in November 1944 if he lived. She was devastated by his death. BJ and I helped her through the initial shock as best we could. We were all fast friends. As far as I am concerned, she is everything she says she is.

My best to you and your family, Tommy

PS: I also lost touch with BJ. Last I heard he was in London working construction to help rebuild the city and doing some theater work. I'm sure Amahli will know of his whereabouts.

After reading the letter, Dorothy relaxed her defenses some, but she still questioned why this woman waited so long before contacting them.

***

It was the Friday morning before Labor Day. "Dorothy, how are plans for the party coming?" Joe asked as he brought his empty coffee cup back into the kitchen from the cottage's porch.

"Everything's fine. I shopped yesterday. This morning I'm going to clean, then enjoy the afternoon at the dock with a large glass of iced tea and listen to the radio. There's a broadcast with Frank Sinatra I want to hear. The house suffers from summer fatigue and Jack's room needs a good airing. Andy will bring the woman up this evening and the other guests won't be arriving until Saturday afternoon."

Dorothy wasn't looking forward to putting her up in Jack's room, but it was a workable solution given that the cottage only had three bedrooms.

"I need to go out for the day, and I didn't want to leave you with a lot of work. But I see as always, you have it all under control. Hope you don't mind," he said.

"What on earth will take you away from here for the day?"

"I've got to go back to the plant for a few hours. There's been holiday shift scheduling issues and if I don't go help make peace and get things straightened out, we could have a union walkout on our hands. Not good for Labor Day celebrations, is it?" He chuckled. "It'll take a few hours to get over there, so don't expect me until late afternoon."

His words were firm and serious. Normally Dorothy never protested his working, and hopefully she wouldn't today.

"I don't understand. Couldn't you just call?" Joe shook his head. "Ok, do what you have to do. Just be sure to be here when Andy arrives. I don't want to meet the woman without you here."

"Don't worry, my dear." He bent over and gave her a kiss on the cheek. "I'll be back in plenty of time to meet Amahli with you. It's a beautiful day and I'll be out of your hair." The screen door slapped closed behind him as he walked out.

****

At Sam's insistence, he delivered Amahli and JJ to Chicago's Union Station before dawn on Friday morning. The streets were empty, yet to awaken to the day's noise and traffic.

"JJ, you have a great trip. Enjoy meeting your new Grandpa and Grandma. They're going to love you a big bunch." Sam could always reassured as well as charm a woman, no matter her age. He unloaded the luggage from the car at the curb.

"They're not new. I bet they're as old as Nani and Papa," she said, correcting Sam. "Uncle Andy is picking us up at the train station."

Sam turned to Amahli, playing his best forlorn lover role. "I'm going to miss you. Be careful not to let anyone hurt you—physically or emotionally. Don't let any of them get the best of you."

Sam kissed her. They were a couple now, seeing each other several times a week through the summer. They often went to his apartment, but Amahli never stayed overnight. She refused to let him be with her at her place because of JJ. Their lovemaking was passionate and satisfying for her. He was a robust lover, and she knew that Sam felt confident enough to ask her to marry him before she and JJ returned to London at the end of December. She discouraged such talk, still unsure if they could be happy together. The idea of being a diplomatic wife, helping her husband's career beyond what he could do by himself was, most likely, his hope, not hers. What would happen to her career? That question remained unanswered.

"Don't worry. Andy will be there, and so will his father. I'll be double protected." Amahli stared at the sidewalk.

"That's what I'm afraid of. Those men will kidnap you and JJ and never let you return to Chicago," Sam said. "I know this trip is important to you—just don't get caught up in the past. I don't want to lose you to your old lover's ghost."

Amahli was taken aback at his words but decided not to challenge them.

"I'm doing this for JJ, not for myself, remember?" Her tone chastised him. "She needs to know as much as possible about her father. It will complete the circle. That will be good for all of us."

"I hope so, my love." Sam grasped the lapels of her wool coat, pulling her closer.

She gave him a warm kiss, welcoming his embrace. "I may be back sooner than you think. I'll be lucky if his mother doesn't throw me out on the street. Don't forget that I'm the British harlot who absconded with their son, then gave birth to his illegitimate child."

As she said it, the strain that was tearing at her heart as well as her mind released. Her body seemed to melt into his.

"Really, Sam. I can take care of myself."

CHAPTER 25

The morning bloomed as Amahli's train headed south out of Chicago, farmland on one side and industry on the other, next to the shore, rushing by as the train rounded Lake Michigan. Great expanses of corn, wheat, and soybean fields, dotted with small towns, overtook the landscape as the train made its way east across Indiana and then northeast into Michigan. JJ slept, spread across the seat with her head on her mother's lap.

Amahli gazed at row after row of grain fields racing by, thinking how similar they were to the countryside she saw on her trip back to London from Glatton in April 1945—pregnant and brimming with apprehension. The anxiety of that day returned now.

Will Mrs. Jackson explode at seeing a granddaughter she doesn't know she has, like my mother did upon hearing about my pregnancy by an American GI? Will Mr. Jackson and Andy intervene or stay back, as Papa did, making me stand up for myself? What is suddenly killing my courage this morning? Why do I feel like a helpless, heartbroken young girl again?

The train ride churned up the tormenting memories of Jack's death and her struggle to accept it. Heartache ripped through her chest, taking her to that dark, lonely place she thought she had escaped. Only JJ's stirring brought her back to reality, out of her past pain, reminding her that she was the grown-up now. She must stop any tears or sobbing that could spoil this happy time for JJ. When she first told JJ about the trip to her grandparents' summer home, she was like a jack-in-the-box, jumping in every direction while she screamed with delight, then insisting they pack immediately for the trip.

Amahli dug deep into herself to find the strength to endure whatever lies ahead, live in the present, and look to the future. She prayed that Andy and Mr. Jackson stayed on her side through it all.

The train left Kalamazoo. JJ stretched as she woke, then looked at her mother.

"Mummy, we're really, really going to see Daddy's mother and father! You promised me we would, and now we are. You are amazing! You can make anything happen. Isn't that the best ever?"

JJ jumped into her mother's arms, giving her a big hug and smothering kisses. Amahli laughed and giggled with her.

At the Plymouth station, Amahli and JJ gathered their belongings and straightened their hair. Her daughter wore blue shorts, a pink pullover shirt, and a new pair of white canvas shoes. She was ready to play. Out the window Amahli spied a tall elderly man with Andy on the platform. His graying hair and glasses gave him a kindly, grandfatherly look. "He's perfect," Amahli whispered to herself. Through the window, she grinned and waved. As she stepped down onto the platform with JJ next to her and the cases just behind them, JJ screamed with delight, dashing ahead to overtake Andy.

Andy and his father were scrambling to help Amahli with the suitcases when JJ almost toppled Andy with a huge hug, then turned to her grandfather and stood silently in front of him.

"Hello, you must be JJ. I'm your Grandpa Joe." He held out his hand, squatting his sturdy six-foot body down to her level to shake her hand. Suddenly words spilled out of her mouth like milk from a bottle.

"Pleased to meet you, sir." She made a little curtsy as she shook his hand. "I was named after my daddy. Did you know that? I'm seven and I am starting second grade next week."

This girl has definitely seen too many Shirley Temple movies, Amahli thought.

"Well, I'm pleased to meet you too, JJ. Yes, your father was my son, but you know that, don't you?" Joe said, not missing a beat in the conversation.

"Yes, I do. And I know that Uncle Andy is your son, too." She looked up at this tall, distinguished-looking man, her eyes twinkling with excitement. "And I must say, I'm sure I'm your granddaughter. Just look at my ears. They're just like yours."

The little girl pulled back her hair, laughing, pointing at her ears and then his. There was silence. Amahli blushed, but before she could reprimand JJ for her rudeness, Joe whooped.

"Well, I guess that proves it!" He got teary, then composed himself. "Are you ready to visit with us up at our lake cottage for a big Labor Day party?"

"I sure am! Mummy told me that Labor Day is a time every year when Americans celebrate everyone's work." She rattled on, gulping for breath. "Can I go swimming with you? I'm not really good at it, but maybe you can teach me. Ok? Can Mummy swim, too?"

"If you brought your suits, you certainly can." Grandpa Joe belly laughed. He stood, turned to Amahli, gave her a long close embrace, and then turned back to JJ. "Come with me, JJ. I bet you're thirsty. Let's get a pop before we take the ride in the car to the lake."

She took his hand and they walked off the platform to the vending machine. "Can I have a Coca Cola? Can I put the money in the machine? How long will the ride be? What color is the car? Do we get to sit in the back seat together? How big is the lake?"

Andy and Amahli listened to this endless stream of questions as the two disappeared into the small wooden structure of a station.

"I guess they'll get along just fine," Andy said. "Seems like true to form, she's got control of the situation."

"Your father is so perfectly wonderful. Now I understand why Jack was like he was, and you are the way you are."

"Yeah, I guess so, but my mother may not agree."

Amahli gave him a quizzical look. "Well, since I haven't met her yet, I won't draw any conclusions. Before we join JJ and your dad, what is the plan for when we get to the cottage?"

***

The radio inside the house was sending Frank Sinatra's voice through the air, loud enough to cover the sound of tires crunching gravel as Andy's car pulled into the driveway behind the cottage. There was a picnic table on the edge of the gravel. Joe directed JJ to sit with him. Before she could ask questions about where Mummy and Andy were going, Joe pulled out a deck of cards and shuffled.

"Now, do you know how to play poker?" JJ shook her head. "Well, live and learn, young girl. I'm going to teach you the best game in the world, right here, in just minutes."

"Is it better than Go Fish? Because that game's so boring."

She swung her short legs through to sit. Joe shuffled and JJ began her love affair with five-card stud.

Amahli and Andy walked around the side of the cottage to the front porch, which faced the lake. Dorothy was at the end of the dock in one of the Adirondack chairs, staring out over the water, listening to the music. She lazily held a cigarette in her right hand, and a glass of iced tea sat on the dock next to the chair. Andy and Amahli started down the front steps to the dock, which suddenly seemed miles long. Their shoes thumped on its wooden slats. Dorothy turned, but did not stand. Expressionless, with her lips tight together, she beckoned Amahli to sit down and waved Andy away.

Dorothy inspected the intruder taking the seat next to her, her eyes never leaving her. "So, you're Amahli Simmons. You knew my son?" Her tone sliced through the air between them. "Tell me who you are, and what is your relationship with my Jack?"

Amahli started to speak, but Dorothy cut her off. "Tommy Pitman confirmed that you're the real thing, so I'm listening."

There was no Andy to protect her now from this lioness who radiated protective suspiciousness. Amahli took a deep breath and told her story. She talked about her background, her parents, how she met Jack, how much they loved each other, and their plans for marriage after his fatal mission. Dorothy didn't respond.

The two sat silently for several minutes. Amahli looked out over the lake, feeling oddly comforted by the water's soft lapping against the shoreline. The fir trees at the water's far edge across the lake stabbed the sun-filled sky. She turned in her chair to face Dorothy, her voice firm and strong.

"I want to know you and your husband so I can learn what made Jack the man he was. I want to hear from you about his childhood, the things he did that made you laugh and the things that made you cry. I want to see his baby pictures, his school pictures, and your family pictures. I want to see and know everything about him."

Dorothy's face softened but gave nothing away, keeping her body rigid in the chair and her eyes on the lake. Her voice was firm. "It's been seven years since the war ended and eight years since he died. Why didn't you write? Why did you wait so long, and then have Andy act as your go-between?"

"I apologize for the delay in contacting you. The truth is, I thought you'd dismiss me out of hand. My parents had difficulty accepting the idea of an American in my life. I assumed that you might have the same difficulty in accepting me, a British and Indian woman, in your son's life."

Silence again. Dorothy gazed out across the water into nothingness, waiting.

"To be brutally honest with you, Mrs. Jackson, if it were only about me, I'd never have contacted you. But there's someone else who finally drove me to connect with you, yet always made me fearful of doing so."

Dorothy turned and glared at Amahli with new respect. Amahli drew herself up as straight as possible and paused to inhale.

"You see, something happened before Jack died that changed everything. On the last night Jack and I were together, we became engaged and I became pregnant, but Jack never knew about the pregnancy." She braced herself for Dorothy's rage, disgust, and rejection, but Dorothy just sat speechless, continuing to stare out over the lake.

"On August 8, 1945, I gave birth to a little girl at home with my parents. With their love and support, I raised her while I finished my education and started my career. When I understood that she needed to know you, then I knew I had to find you."

Dorothy turned back to look at Amahli again. "You're telling me that we have a granddaughter? A seven-year-old granddaughter?"

"Yes, Mrs. Jackson. I know you really didn't need to know me. It would have been nice, but with Jack gone, my being around you would've only brought back the misery and grief you suffered, as I did. But when my daughter was born, all that changed. I knew that one day she would need to know you and your family. She was Jack's gift to me, to you...to all of us. Together, we're her family."

"What is her name?"

"Her birth name is Jaya in honor of my Hindu heritage, and her middle name is Jack. Everyone calls her JJ, including me. As I told Andy, I never want her to forget who her father was."

While Dorothy didn't move, her face paled.

"Mrs. Jackson, a child should know her family's story: both sides of her family. Only you and Mr. Jackson can give her that."

Again, silence filled the air between them.

Dorothy sighed, and then spoke. "Miss Simmons, you had no right to keep us ignorant about our granddaughter. However, I fathom why you did what you did. However, I need you to be aware of something."

Amahli waited. The air was rich with tension as the hot afternoon sun washed across their faces and glared in their eyes.

"You must understand how important your daughter is to me. She's more than my granddaughter. You see, I've always believed that someday our son would come back to us, not as a ghost but as a living person. I never gave up that hope deep inside my soul. Since we lost him, I dream about him as a boy, as a man, and as a son. But the one dream I remember most vividly, so vividly that I wrote it down, was on August 8, 1945, the day your daughter was born."

Dorothy removed a folded paper from her pocket. "On this paper I captured that dream and I carry it with me at all times, like I imagine you wear Jack's ring all the time. It is my lifeline to Jack. On that night I dreamed that he was alive, coming back to me. Not as he was, but as a child."

Amahli swooned in her chair, almost fainting, and gasped for air. Dorothy briefly waited for her to recover.

"The last thing I witnessed in that dream was his body, dressed as a soldier, transforming into a young child. I took the child into my arms, then I woke up. You've brought me that child."

Jack's mother doubled over in her chair and moaned for all the suffering she had endured. She keened, letting the sorrow spill out of her body. Amahli knelt beside her, reaching her arms around her, and cried with Dorothy for both their losses.

***

Andy paced the front porch, watching the two women engage in what he thought was a battle of nerves. When he saw them suddenly embrace and cry, he called to Joe, "Dad, bring JJ and come to the front porch! It's time." Joe and JJ trotted around the cottage as fast as they could. When they reached Andy on the porch, he pointed at the end of the dock.

"What is happening, Uncle Andy?" JJ puckered up, about to cry when she saw her mother on her knees. "Is Mummy hurt? Why is she crying with that lady?"

"No, your mother isn't hurt, JJ." Andy took her hand. "That lady is your grandmother. Looks like your mother just told her about you. Take Grandpa's hand and walk down the dock to meet her."

The tall man with bright blue eyes behind gold-rimmed glasses walked his granddaughter down the dock. Andy followed close behind. When the women heard them approaching, they quickly stood, wiping their eyes, trying to compose themselves. Joe directed JJ to Amahli, who took her daughter's hand and clearly summoned her strength.

"Mrs. Jackson, I'd like you to meet JJ, your granddaughter. For some time she's been pestering me to come meet you. It took a year to make it happen, but here she is."

Dorothy dropped to her knees and held out her arms. After her mother's nod of encouragement, JJ raced into her grandmother's arms, almost knocking her over. Dorothy embraced her and looked at Joe. "Her scent is the familiar perfume of the child…the one I've never forgotten."

Amahli looked at Joe and Andy saw him wink at her. It was good. They all were good.

Joe said, "Dorothy, you need to share this child. You look like you're molded together there on your knees!" Dorothy and JJ loosened their embrace, blushing, and giggling.

The battle was won. But was there a war yet to be fought? Andy didn't know. Dorothy, now composed, stood, retaking command of the scene.

"This calls for a celebration. It sure does." She brought her voice to full volume. "Joe, you and Andy go back to the cottage and break out the good stuff. Amahli, let's take JJ and head to the kitchen to get this young girl some of the cookies I made today, and fresh lemonade. Then we can all sit together on the porch and get to know one another."

"Yes, of course, Mrs. Jackson."

"Call me Dorothy. Everyone else does." Then she looked down at JJ, who was holding her hand. "And you, my young girl… You call me Grandma."

CHAPTER 26

Amahli and JJ visited the Jacksons often after that Labor Day reunion. On every visit, Grandma and Grandpa regaled them with tales about Jack—the good boy ones, the bad boy ones, the baby ones, and the teen ones. Photograph albums, scrapbooks full of collected memorabilia, and toy boxes were extracted from den shelves, backs of closets, and basement storage. As they shared them, Grandpa and Grandma told more stories, adding in outings and celebrations over the years with numerous relatives. Every award, ribbon, press article, medal, grade card, and saved letter was offered up with ample commentary, mostly by Dorothy. Joe sat, enjoying the happy family.

The Jacksons welcomed Amahli into the family, including her in their conversations, plans, and outings. However, as time passed, Amahli couldn't shake the strange sensation that Dorothy considered her more of an outsider rather than a family member. She couldn't put her finger on it exactly, but she sensed that although not pushing her away, Dorothy had retreated from the warmth of their first meeting and was staying emotionally distant. Amahli worked at being amiable, never contradicting nor questioning what was planned. She told her parents in her letters home how nice everyone was to her and how strongly they embraced JJ. However, in November she wrote to BJ—the last letter before the Thanksgiving holiday visit—expressing her worries.

> *Dear BJ:*
>
> *…Please don't say anything to my parents, but I have to tell someone, so it's you, my dear friend. Please forgive me. Sometimes I feel almost invisible to Dorothy, respected but not family. I believe she sees me more as JJ's guardian or nanny, rather than her mother. It's strange. Andy tells me it's only a phase she has to work through, but I'm worried about it.*
>
> *With Joe and Andy, I'm totally family. They include me, whether it's a walk in the neighborhood, an excursion to the zoo that JJ likes so much, playing cards in the recreation room, singing around the player piano, or watching TV, like the Ed Sullivan Show, or a new comedy called the Jackie Gleason Show that I particularly like. JJ loves the Roy Rogers Show so much that she wants a cowgirl outfit for Christmas! I'll try to buy one before we leave in December. I am fairly sure that it will be difficult to find in London.*
>
> *Don't misunderstand me about Joe and Dorothy. They truly do love JJ with all their hearts and are doting grandparents. But I miss you and my parents. I'm looking forward to coming home at the end of the year.*
>
> *Missing you, Amahli*

What she didn't tell BJ was that Dorothy's behavior often isolated JJ from her mother. Dorothy didn't befriend Amahli by taking time to be alone with her, doing things together that women who grow close naturally do—shopping, cooking, or cleaning up after a meal side by side. Dorothy remained polite, but never familiar.

Amahli was beginning to believe that she would always exist at the emotional edge of this woman, no matter how she attempted to gain her acceptance. Whatever Amahli did never seemed to be enough, or even matter. Dorothy showed no interest or enthusiasm for who Amahli was or what she did, nor solicit her likes, dislikes, or opinions. She never inquired as to whether Amahli approved of what was planned for their visits. She seemed to assume that Amahli would go along.

Dorothy put all her emotional and physical energy into JJ. From the time they arrived at the Jackson home until they left two or three days later, JJ was the center of their world. Grandma kept the child next to her almost every minute of the visit, whether it was to help prepare dinner, shop in town for a new treasure, or see a movie on a Saturday afternoon. Toys, books, and dolls were accumulating in the Jackson's living room— the sacred formal room, almost never used, but Dorothy encouraged JJ to amuse herself there. Grandma surprised her with new dolls and doll house furniture she purchased after the first visit. She spent hours in make believe with JJ, sometimes just watching the child create her own fantasies. At night after dinner, Grandpa, Grandma, and JJ often played poker.

Nothing came into the bedroom JJ shared with her mother except a brown teddy bear that had been Andy's. This old bear was so lovable with its amber eyes, floppy legs and paws, and scraggly brown fur. JJ and Teddy often walked with Andy on Saturday mornings so he could tell her stories about growing up with her father. She carried Teddy around with her everywhere.

If not the nanny, Amahli sometimes felt like the maid, nervously watching JJ and her grandmother while waiting for instructions. Dorothy explained that since she did all the cooking, it would be helpful if Amahli cleaned up afterward so she could have more time with JJ during their visits. Luckily Andy always came to her rescue, helping her and trying to make light of their role as scullery maids.

Grandma also made the bedtime decisions. "Well, it's time JJ got ready for bed. I'll take her in."

She helped the little girl get into her jammies and brush her teeth. Then she called in Grandpa, who sat on the edge of the bed, propped up with a pillow next to JJ, reading bedtime stories while Grandma sat in the chair at the end of the bed, knitting a new sweater or mittens or a scarf for her little girl.

Of course, JJ loved the attention, never hearing 'No' to any request she made of Grandma and Grandpa.

***

On Wednesday morning, Amahli rushed to get ready for their Thanksgiving visit to the Jackson home. As she and JJ came down in the elevator, she remembered to check for mail from the night before. She detoured to the mailroom and opened the brass box to find a letter among the magazines and advertising circulars. It was from BJ, but there was no time to read it if they were going to make the early morning train. She quickly stuffed it into her purse and returned the rest to the mailbox. She hustled JJ into the waiting taxi and headed for Union Station. Sam wanted to take them to the station as he'd been doing, but Amahli demurred this time.

Now settled on the train with JJ in her coveted window seat, sleeping, Amahli read.

Dear Amahli,

Your parents keep me posted on your success in connecting with the Jackson family. I am thrilled that you accomplished your mission.

Your mother feeds me well, and she's become my teacher in a way—I'm learning to cook Indian. I come early to dinner once a week so she can drag me into the kitchen to help. Just goes to show you how lonely she's feeling without you and JJ around. (You can stop laughing now as you imagine me standing next to your mother at the stove, me in a frilly apron.) Such warm people, your parents. You're so incredibly lucky. However, I know I'm a poor stand-in for you and JJ. That's why I am writing.

At dinner this past week, we got to talking about your coming home. I had to share your last letter with them, please forgive me. We're genuinely concerned, even though your father was stoic, saying that the adjustment to being a member of the family would take time, and that as long as you had Andy's and Joe's support, you would be fine.

Your mother was upset, to say the least. She's afraid that you'll be hurt, and decide to stay in the States longer to try to win Dorothy over. I'm afraid for you as well. Not because you won't come home, but because of the emotional toll it has taken on you already. Personally, I don't think it's healthy for you to be in such emotional conflict. Your mental health is at stake.

Your parents respect your ability to make your own decisions and would never tell you about their worries. However, I am telling you right now: Come home as soon as possible. I know what it's like to live among people who resent you because of who you are. It won't help to keep trying to please them.

Wire me the details of your return as soon as possible. I will meet you at the airport when you arrive. Don't wait until the end of the year.

Once again, we're all enormously proud of what you have accomplished on your journey over there, but it's time to come home.

Worried about you, BJ

Amahli folded the letter, putting it back in her purse. Perhaps they should go home sooner. Thanksgiving weekend is an opportune time to remind the Jacksons that she and JJ will return to London in December, perhaps before Christmas. The announcement would give everyone time to say farewells at one last visit in the first or second weekend in December. Knowing that no one wanted to talk about their leaving, her announcement would be a challenging one to deliver.

***

The Thanksgiving dinner celebration included the family and Dorothy's and Joe's friends, Louise and Lou, whose grown children lived on the West Coast. Amahli found them delightful people as they chatted at cocktails in the living room before dinner.

Dorothy called everyone to the table sharply at 4:00 p.m. As they walked into the dining room, a table fit for royalty greeted them. A white damask tablecloth was accented with matching napkins embroidered with a scripted "J" in silver napkin rings. The good dishes, as Dorothy called them, were set. Purchased right after the war, Andy told Amahli that she never told Joe that each setting cost more than $5.00—too expensive for most people. Every piece was stamped on the underside in red: "Made in Occupied Japan." Each dish was hand painted with an explosion of pale pink chrysanthemums, the plates framed by a pale green rim almost two inches deep, with gold edging. The set had become a family treasure to be handed down from generation to generation.

The crystal stemware sparkled. Sterling silverware, again engraved with a scripted "J," lay perfectly at the sides of the plates. White candles flickered, dancing around the magnificent turkey sitting on a silver platter, ready for carving. Amahli knew the traditional family side dishes of wet and dry dressing, mashed and sweet potatoes, cranberry sauce, roasted oysters, and string bean casserole were stationed in the kitchen in silver-plated serving dishes with matching engraved covers, awaiting delivery to the table.

Amahli scanned the table. "Dorothy, this is an astoundingly brilliant table."

Dorothy smiled triumphantly, standing at the head of the table, nodding like a queen holding court, and asked everyone to find their seats. Names were written on small white cards at each place setting. She watched Amahli take the seat between the two guests, not with JJ and Andy on the family side of the table.

Before Joe carved the turkey and the maid delivered the side dishes, Dorothy spoke.

"This Thanksgiving is special. It's the first of what we know will be many with our granddaughter JJ, the little girl that our son Jack, gave us. We are so blessed to have her. Please raise your glass to thank God for bringing him back to us."

Amahli seethed, wanting to run screaming from the room, but she didn't. She couldn't let Dorothy win, proving her to be a rude, emotional, illogical woman and a bad role model for her daughter. Amahli raised her glass with the others to the toast and sipped her wine. Andy, sitting across from her, did the same, but scowled at his mother as never before.

Dorothy, ignoring Andy's frown, looked out over the table she ruled. "We have a wonderful surprise. Although raised in England until now, our lovely granddaughter will tell us all about the importance of Thanksgiving."

JJ stood and told the Thanksgiving story that she learned in school. When she finished, everyone applauded; she curtseyed, then sat down. Beaming, JJ said rather loudly, because Grandpa was sitting at the other end of the table, "Grandpa, can you carve the turkey now, please? I'm starving!"

Everyone laughed and dinner proceeded without incident. Amahli held her tongue.

CHAPTER 27

The Friday morning after Thanksgiving, Amahli was browsing through the paper when she overheard an argument in hushed tones emanating from the kitchen across from the den where she sat. She stretched herself around the chair to see what was happening. She saw Dorothy standing with her back to Andy as she prepared breakfast.

"Mom, you can't do that. Amahli is JJ's mother."

"What do you mean I can't? You got the child a US passport, so she's a US citizen. Amahli was never married to our son and I have plenty of evidence that by heredity, she belongs to us."

"By heredity she belongs to Amahli as well, Mom. You won't stand a chance in court."

"How do you know that? The woman works full time to support herself and the child. Your father and I will be able to provide JJ with full-time family care, so some stranger won't have to take care of her. A mother shouldn't work."

"Mom, Amahli has her parents to help her. And it's not for you to say whether a woman should or should not work. You don't want to do this. Jack loved Amahli, and she brought JJ into this world so that makes her family."

Dorothy kept her back to Andy, silently preparing breakfast.

"Have you talked with Dad about this? What did he say about your idea?"

"Your father will do whatever I want." She poured the scrambled egg mixture in the hot pan.

"What? You haven't told him?" Andy frowned. "Don't be so sure about that. How can you be so cruel?! Your granddaughter will hate you if you do this."

"I'm doing what is best for her. She'll appreciate the life your father and I can give her here in America. Her father was an American and she'll be an American. I'm going to talk with our lawyer on Monday."

With that Andy walked out of the kitchen, slamming the back door.

Amahli suddenly realized the seriousness of her situation, now a full-blown emergency. She had to get herself and JJ out of Detroit and back to England as soon as humanly possible. She saw Andy outside, walking around the house.

She met him at the front door with coats, closing the door softly behind her. She knew JJ was fully absorbed with rearranging furniture in her doll house in the living room. Dorothy was still in the kitchen, checking the oven to see if the biscuits were done. Neither noticed her leaving.

They walked silently to the sidewalk. As they turned the corner at the end of the block, they looked at each other.

"Andy, what has happened with your mother?! She's crazed! Can she take JJ away from me?" She shook as she spoke, her face filled with desperation.

"No, she can't take her away from you. Neither Dad nor I will let her get anywhere near a lawyer or courthouse. My mother's in a panic because you'll be leaving soon. She gets harebrained ideas when she's stressed and anxious. It's at the worst when she feels like she's losing control. Relax. Let's not upset her at breakfast and let it go for now. She'll calm down."

"Upset her? What about upsetting me?!" Amahli said, near tears. "She's my child, not hers!"

"Amahli, Mom doesn't see you as JJ's mother. She sees herself as your daughter's mother because she believes that JJ is her son reincarnated."

"That only makes the whole thing worse and proves she's out of her mind!" Amahli screamed. "I come all the way here to unite two families, only to tear both of them apart. How did that happen? What can I do?"

"Amahli, don't panic. It won't help us." He took her in his arms. "I will never let anyone take JJ from you or hurt either of you. Tell them you are leaving, and then we will get through today. Can you follow my lead at breakfast? She doesn't know you heard us argue, so let's go to breakfast as if nothing has happened."

"'As if nothing has happened'? Andy, I'm so furious that I want to beat your mother to within an inch of her life." Amahli breathed in deeply then exhaled, her breath creating a cloud as it hit the cold air. "But I won't, for JJ's sake."

She started walking quickly down the sidewalk, leaving Andy standing alone. Then just as suddenly as she left, she turned and came back. She stared at the ground and took his cold hands in hers. "I'm sorry I blurted all that out. I have no option but to trust you to get us away without wounding JJ."

Andy wrapped his arms around her, then stood back and shared his plan. It made sense to Amahli and calmed her. But if the plan worked, Andy might tear his own family apart. This quiet man was braver than she ever suspected, putting her before his own mother.

She painted a smile on her face, took Andy's hand, and walked back to the house and into the kitchen after scooping up JJ from the living room floor. Breakfast was served.

***

Andy watched Amahli speak first as she pushed eggs around her plate with a triangle of toast. "Dorothy, I thank you for such a grand Thanksgiving dinner yesterday. I genuinely enjoyed talking with your friends, Louise and Lou. They're such kind people. But now I must tell you that I've been called back to London immediately, so JJ and I will be returning on the train to Chicago Saturday morning. We'll not be staying the weekend."

Everyone stopped eating except JJ, her eyes jumping from one adult to the other while she munched her toast, kicking her feet under the table. No one told her about these plans, but after looking at her mother and then Andy, she didn't ask questions.

Cutting through the silence and reading Andy's expression to see that something was afoot, Joe said, "Well, then. I am so sorry to hear that. We were so looking forward to more visits before the end of the year. But no matter. We'll take advantage of the time we have today and tonight."

Andy followed up quickly, looking at Amahli. "Mom and Dad can take JJ shopping for Christmas today so you can take presents back to your family in London."

Joe reached out, taking JJ's hand. "We'll miss you very much this Christmas, my sweet granddaughter, but we've been so blessed for the time we've had with you. You're the best granddaughter anyone could have."

Joe then turned his attention to Amahli. "I love you, for you've become a daughter to me…as much as Jack and Andy are my sons. You're family."

Dorothy glared at her husband as Andy continued. "We'll make plans for all of us visit London next year." He spoke to JJ. "Until then, I want you to take Teddy to London so you can write us about everything Teddy and you do in London. And Grandpa, Grandma, and I will write to you! We love you so much. We want to know all the exciting and wonderful things about your life and your family in London."

Dorothy scowled at Amahli. "Why didn't you tell us sooner? We have so many things to do before you leave."

Turning to her granddaughter she said, "We'll take you to Hudson's today to shop for Christmas, like Uncle Andy said. We'll have a grand lunch in its tearoom while we're shopping. Amahli, I know you'd like to come too, but it's best that you don't since we're going to buy your present, as well as the others."

Andy circled the wagons, as travelers of long ago did when faced with danger. "That's great, Mom. Then you, Dad, and JJ will enjoy the day."

He'd told Amahli he knew his mother wouldn't pull any funny business with Dad around. Amahli put her napkin on the table, following Andy's lead.

"That's kind of you, Dorothy, because JJ will love the day with you and Joe. We'll have much to do if we're going to leave before the end of next week so your shopping will save me time, and JJ would love your help selecting presents, and I do trust your taste. I'll write a short list for gifts for my parents." Andy squeezed her hand under the table.

"JJ, won't this be fun?" Dorothy's smile was definitely forced. "We'll get presents for your grandparents in London, for your mother, and one for your Uncle BJ. Then Grandpa and I will buy your presents. I know just the right outfits, and you'll get to try them on to make sure they're a perfect fit."

JJ giggled and clapped her hands while Andy stood. "Amahli, let me take you to lunch at our favorite diner here in Detroit while they shop. You know the one where we ate during the conference last June? You've never eaten what they're really famous for—thick grilled Ruben sandwiches." Filling the air with nonsense, he continued. "Although the sandwich history is murky, both a Nebraska hotel and a New York City deli claim to have invented it. It migrated to Detroit, where we love it and made it our own. Before you leave, you have to experience it. That will be my present to you."

She caught his lifeline. "What a great idea! American food amazes me." To JJ she said, "Now, run and get ready. Be sure to brush your teeth after eating all that butter and jam on your toast."

JJ jumped up and ran out of the room while Amahli went to the den to create the shopping list and the others finished their coffee. After a few minutes she returned to the kitchen, handing Dorothy the list. "Thank you again for doing this. JJ is thrilled. When you get back, I can write you a check for these."

Dorothy was no longer scowling, just frowning. "Good, but don't worry about the money. We have more than enough. Now let's all get ready for the day."

Andy and Joe sighed in relief with a battle avoided.

***

Dorothy and Joe left with JJ for the shopping excursion, leaving Andy and Amahli to clean up the breakfast mess. After the dishes were washed and the table wiped clean, the two left in Andy's car. In less than thirty minutes, they pulled onto a parking lot.

"Thought we'd make a first stop at Dad's plant so you can see close-up how American manufacturing production lines operate today. Even on a holiday weekend, men turn out cars on the assembly line."

As Andy drove down a road next to the main plant building, Amahli said, "What a great distraction. It's breathtaking—the size of it all." Once inside, they walked for over an hour, viewing how parts were added as each frame moved forward on the assembly line. At the end, a completed car, ready for engine testing, rolled off the line and was pushed into the lot.

"American engineering is something to behold. I think the only other country able to do this kind of quality mass production were the Germans, and they lost the war," she said.

"Well, let's hope we never lose a war."

"True. I'm hungry. Is it lunchtime yet?"

***

Amahli bit into her grilled corned beef, melted cheese, and sauerkraut sandwich with much gusto. The special dressing leaked out the corners of her mouth and they laughed. Andy grabbed an extra napkin, catching the drips on her chin. She wasn't able to eat all of the gooey hot sandwich, but gave it her best try. Andy congratulated her on her attempt.

It was a small, intimate moment. As she wiped her hands and mouth one more time on a second napkin, she said, "I love the way you and your dad decided so quickly on what to do this morning. When did you get a chance to tell him what happened?"

"I didn't, he just picked up on what was said at the breakfast table. It was easy for him because we are on the same wavelength, so to speak. Sometimes it's almost eerie. We blend with each other like butter on white bread." Andy said. "I'm the man of action, and Dad's the man of sensitive emotions."

"It sounds like the relationship I have with my father. I think our fathers have more in common that I thought. And you—you're just as sensitive as your dad. Don't fool yourself."

***

After lunch and back at the house, the two descended into the Jackson's treasured recreation room, a paneled knotty pine hideaway. Andy entertained Amahli with what seemed to be a zillion sing-alongs at the 1920s upright player piano. Each song was recorded on rolled paper, punched to strike the right piano keys at the right time. They sang until both were breathless and laughing at their common inability to carry a tune.

"It feels great to forget everything for a few hours. I feel like I'm back home in England. Your recreation room is so much like an English pub, especially the mirrored back panel surrounded by rows of miniature liquor bottles behind the bar. It reminds me of the pub where I met Jack."

"I'm sorry. Should I have not brought you down here?"

"Andy, it's fine. I'm enjoying being with you. Tell me about the liquor bottles."

"Dad and I always bring back mini liquors that stewardesses hand out with meals on airplanes. He visits other plants and I make calls to build vendor and manufacturing partnerships with other companies. He loves them so much that he also buys them at the local liquor store instead of the normal-sized bottles."

The atmosphere made Amahli comfortable, right down to the dartboard on the far wall. Andy saw her staring at it.

"That was in the last package Mom and Dad got from Jack in 1944. I believe it was your recommendation to purchase it, am I right?"

"Not really. I just told him not to buy clothing for your mother at that time of year." Amahli smiled. "Want to play a game or two?"

"Sure. But I have to warn you, I'm really good," teased Andy. They played and talked and drank, using several of those bottles—the Tennessee Whiskey ones. By four o'clock they were waltzing and singing as the piano automatically played.

***

Piano music greeted them when Dorothy, Joe, and JJ walked through the back door just as the sun set. JJ ran down the basement stairs to the recreation room.

"Grandpa and Grandma!" she yelled up. "Uncle Andy and Mummy are dancing." She started clapping, then joined the two of them to finish the dance.

"Come on up, everyone," Dorothy yelled down. "We need some help with the packages." The three scrambled up the stairs to assist in unloading of the car. There were presents for everyone, all wrapped.

In the spirit of family togetherness, Dorothy let Amahli help make turkey sandwiches, the Jackson's traditional day-after-Thanksgiving dinner. After the leftover side dishes were reheated, they gathered around the dining room table, now casually set with only the necessities. The remains of pumpkin and chess pie were served for dessert. It was a pleasant dinner for a change. JJ ate, but Amahli noticed that she was a bit more quiet than usual. Perhaps the day was exhausting for her, like it was for everyone else.

Amahli excused herself, taking JJ back to their room to pack. Dorothy was about to protest, but a stern look from Joe changed her mind. She went to the den to embroider. Andy and Joe got out the cribbage board and played, counting and moving pegs quietly. The house went dark before 10 p.m.

***

Early Saturday morning it was the time for Andy to drive JJ and Amahli to the train. JJ ran down the hall into her grandmother's bedroom, closing the door behind her. After five minutes, standing at the front door with Andy, Amahli called to JJ. "Come on. It's time to go. Where are you?"

"I'm here, Mummy. I'm here. Look what Grandma and Grandpa bought for me!"

She sashayed down the hall. Instead of her navy coat, she was wearing a new one. Amahli looked at Dorothy and then to JJ. "Such a pretty new coat! It looks like cashmere. The little fur collar and matching muff are brilliant. Did you thank Grandma? Where's your old one?" Amahli forced a smile.

JJ danced around the front hall, acting the princess she had become, swinging Teddy on her arm. "Grandma said I needed it. She said she was going to give my old coat to her maid for her little girl."

Dorothy flushed, embarrassed hearing her own words coming back at her. Joe and Andy watched Amahli's face tighten as she bit her tongue and smiled. "Thank you, Dorothy. That was kind of you, although unnecessary."

JJ had more to say. "And look, Mummy! Grandma and Grandpa also got me my Dale Evans outfit. It's just what I needed." She opened her coat to model her new outfit.

"Looks like Santa won't need to bring you that for Christmas, will he?" Amahli stood to her full height in front of Jack's mother. "You've made her very happy," she said with her fists clenched, stuffed into her pockets.

Dorothy nodded in acknowledgement, then bent down for a last hug and kiss from JJ and gave her one more present. She whispered, "This is a special present, just for you."

"Can I open it now?"

"Why don't you wait until you're on the train? Now go, and don't forget, we're going to see you soon."

Everyone stepped outside onto the front porch. Dorothy gave Amahli a perfunctory embrace. "You've done a good job caring for JJ. Thank you. She is the most wonderful gift Jack could have given us."

Amahli embraced her in the same manner, absorbing the words. "Dorothy, every child deserves to know her parents and grandparents. It was my commitment for you to know her and for her to know you and Joe. I'll see that my daughter writes often."

Then both women turned and went their separate ways—Dorothy back to the front steps of her home and Amahli to Andy's car.

Joe and Andy stowed the suitcases and box of presents in the trunk of Andy's navy-blue Buick coupe. JJ gave Grandpa Joe one last big hug and many sloppy kisses, then Joe helped her into the back seat on the car's passenger side. He righted the passenger side seatback.

After a long embrace with Amahli, he said, "I'm sorry your time with us is ending this way. Andy told me you won't be back, but I hope someday to see you and JJ again."

Joe turned and walked back to stand with his wife. His stride was slow and heavy, weighted down with sadness.

Andy stepped forward to help Amahli into the car. He whispered, "You did an amazing job this morning. You won't have to do that again." Amahli, her face empty of emotion, got into the car. Nothing was said as they backed out of the driveway, then headed for the station.

From the rear seat, JJ broke the silence. "Can I open my present now?"

"Of course you can. You don't have to wait until you're on the train. I bet Uncle Andy wants to know what it is as well."

Andy smiled at her in the rearview mirror as he drove. "That's a good idea, JJ. I have no idea what it might be."

The little girl ripped away the colorful patterned paper and matching ribbon, but the gift was trapped inside a cardboard box that was taped shut. JJ handed it to her mother, who slit the tape with her nail, then carefully pulled it from the box. She paled. "Andy, pull over for a minute. I have to show you this."

At the side of the road, he examined the triptych of photos—a picture of JJ's father, one of Andy, and one of Dorothy and Joe with JJ—perfectly framed in ornate brass and black lacquer. "The photograph of my brother was taken when he was commissioned to be a navigator in the summer of 1944, and the one of me is my official corporate portrait. But I've never seen the one of JJ with Grandma and Grandpa." Andy handed the triptych back to Amahli, then pulled back onto the road.

"I know where that one came from," JJ proudly proclaimed, pointing to the one she was in. "When we went to the movies, Grandma took us to get our picture taken after the movie. Isn't it nice?"

"I've never seen it before." Amahli glared at Andy, who could only shrug his shoulders.

"Oh, Mummy. It's beautiful. It's my whole new family." She grinned the smile of a satisfied child. "Did Grandma give one to you too?"

"No." Amahli lowered her head. Andy reached his right hand out and took her left one. She held his tightly and closed her eyes.

"Well, I wish you were in the picture of me with Grandma and Grandpa. Then it would be perfect."

Amahli stared straight ahead, sucking the roadway into herself, trying to make the distance between her and Dorothy grow faster.

After a quiet time, JJ asked, "Mummy, where do I belong?"

"What do you mean 'where do you belong?'" asked Amahli, displaying a furrowed brow. "Tell me what you mean."

"I mean, do I belong with you or do I belong with Grandma and Grandpa? Will I someday live with Grandpa and Grandma, or will I stay in London with you?" The child's tone was serious, as if she were asking for instructions on how to do a math problem. Andy and Amahli shared their confusion.

Turning around in her seat, Amahli faced her daughter. "Who said that you might come to Detroit to live someday?" The little girl was silent and withdrew from her mother, looking down at the floor of the car. "Come, JJ. Who told you that?" Amahli urged. "No one will get in trouble."

"It's a secret, Mummy. She made me promise not to tell."

"Was it your Grandma Dorothy? Just nod. That way you aren't really saying who."

JJ nodded. Amahli softened her voice. "JJ, I'm your mother and I love you more than all the stars in the sky. You're my daughter. We belong together and will be together always. My work here is done, and now it's time to go home to London on Friday. Nani, Papa, and BJ are waiting for us."

JJ exhaled a big sigh. "That's good, Mummy. I don't really want to live with Grandma and Grandpa because I'd miss you and Nani and Papa and Uncle BJ."

She was still Jack's daughter, the man who moved forward and accepted life as it happened. Amahli released her hand from Andy's, then banged her chest three times and swallowed her anger.

"What's good is that Grandpa and Grandma know you and you know them. You can write letters and send them pictures all the time, just like Uncle Andy said. You'll be pen pals. Won't that be fun?"

JJ clapped, reached up, kissed her mother, then returned to watching the road out the rear window.

***

At the station, after checking in the suitcases and box of presents, there was time before the train's platform and track would be posted. They sat one of the benches in the main waiting room, the wood highly polished after years of use. The noise of hustling people and train whistles ricocheted off its walls muffled their conversation. JJ was focused on a book they just bought for her. Amahli leaned into Andy.

"Your mother's behavior is intolerable," she hissed. "How could she say that to JJ? She dismisses me as irrelevant, and then uses the child as a pawn in a struggle to get possession of her!"

Andy steadied himself. "I don't think my mother realized what she was attempting to do. She lives in her own fantasy world."

"Oh, she knew, Andy. At Thanksgiving she was appalling. I just sat there and didn't respond. I didn't want to embarrass you, and I didn't want a fight right in front of JJ either. She knew how to use my politeness against me. She's a manipulative bitch, quite frankly, Andy. You're blind to it. You're too forgiving because you love her, like any son. What she didn't calculate is that I'm much stronger than she thinks I am. She will never see her granddaughter again. She sabotaged any possible relationship with her beyond letters and photos. I will not forgive her, ever. I'll not be ignored. I'll not let her pit JJ against me."

Andy put his elbows on his knees, turning his hat over again and again, searching for words, afraid he had lost her forever.

"Please, Amahli, don't abandon me and Dad. We'll fix it. Mom's very insecure. That's why all the fancy dinners, clothes, and even maids. And she's always been obsessed with my brother. Your daughter is his reincarnation, like I told you before. I just didn't think she would go so far as to get between JJ and you."

"You can't fix her—can't you see that? Your mother is not right in the mind. You can't defend her any longer because she's abusive, telling JJ to keep secrets like that. What makes her so obsessive?"

"After Jack was killed, her pain over the loss festered. Time helped Dad and me accept it, but not Mom. She started idolizing him, believing that he could do no wrong and that he loved her, his mother, more than anyone else." Andy searched for words. "She always believed that Jack would come back from the dead because of that dream. To her, your daughter is her son, and therefore belongs to her."

"But where does that leave you, Andy? You're her first son. Aren't you supposed to be the favorite? The one the younger one looks up to?"

"That would have been great, but wasn't that way. She was extremely strict with me. I spent all my time trying to be the good boy, wanting her approval. I did everything she asked—went to college, came home a hero from the war, and then became the corporate exec she wished my dad was. Jack refused to seek her approval. She was lenient with him and he refused to follow her dictated path, yet somehow he got her approval anyway. How he treated her, how he mesmerized her, I'll never understand."

"Andy, I am so sorry. To me you always seemed so invulnerable, so adult, so in command."

"Wouldn't that be grand? Inside I'm just a kid sometimes. But enough of me." Andy paused, then continued to talk about his mother. "So, you enter the picture. She couldn't believe you because Jack didn't tell her about you. Therefore, you couldn't exist." Andy lowered his head, staring at the ground while he spoke. "It wasn't Jack's fault, but he wasn't perfect either. I just don't know what else to say."

"Well, isn't that a big kettle of fish?" Amahli laughed, putting her arm around him. "She rejects us both because neither of us fit into her fantasy or measure up."

They sat on the bench, close enough to hear each other breathing but not saying another word until the train's platform and track were posted. They stood, gathered up JJ and her belongings, then walked to the platform to their train.

"I'll send your parents a note. I've upset your family's stability."

"You really haven't upset anything that wasn't on the brink of collapse anyway." He embraced her. "Mom's reality, like I said before, is confused with her dreams. It's more apparent each day as she gets older. I just don't want to lose you because of her."

"You haven't lost me, Andy. In fact, I am seeing that your brother changed my life in ways I am only beginning to understand."

"Amahli, I'm not Jack, nor will I ever be. I'm not the charming romantic guy. I'll never sweep you off your feet, but I'll be there for you when you want me…and need me. I'm not sure I can be the lover he was to you. I have no idea if you can ever love me, but it does not matter. I want you in my life, in any relationship you can handle. You and JJ have become essential to me and any happiness I may have." He kissed her softly on the forehead. She pulled his lips to her mouth. The kiss was soft and long.

JJ pulled at her mother's skirt, breaking the spell. "Mummy, it's time to go!"

Nothing else was said. They boarded the train, Amahli looking back at Andy with tears in her eyes but a smile on her face.

The same night after Amahli and JJ returned to their Chicago apartment, she wrote to Andy's parents.

Dear Joe and Dorothy,

Thank you for letting JJ and I come into your lives.
Thank you for sharing your son Jack with me. I feel
I've completed the circle for all of us. JJ now knows who

her father was in so many new ways. She knows and loves you, and I appreciate your love for her.

We won't be able to visit again, so please do write JJ as often as you can. She'll want to hear from you and write to you. I'll be sure to send photos and updates to you on a regular basis.

Thank you again for your hospitality and kindness. Sincerely, Amahli

CHAPTER 28

First thing Monday morning, before she left for the consulate office, Amahli called London. "Sir Williams, I have good news."

"I have to meet a colleague soon, but I always like to hear that. What is it?"

"I'm pleased to report that my work has wrapped up sooner than expected, so I need a favor. Instead of spending December here, I would prefer to leave immediately. Any loose ends or reports can be finished from London. Could you please authorize us to fly home at the end of this week?" Amahli's voice was strong.

"Is something wrong, Amahli? Is your daughter all right?"

"She's fine, sir. But I've been away for almost nine months and we miss home. I must confess that long-term overseas assignments are not my cuppa tea."

"I'm sorry to hear that. I know the Chicago consulate is very satisfied with your work. The last time I spoke with Sam, he sounded like you might stay permanently."

"Sam was mistaken, sir. I don't know why he would say that to you and I'm sorry if there was some misunderstanding, because I had no intention of staying in the States permanently. I'm proud of what I was able to accomplish here, and now that it's done, I want to come home to my family, you, and the London office."

"Of course you can leave right away. In fact, I'm pleased. I do need you here, but was willing to wait to talk with you about your next assignment until the first of the year. There's plenty of work for you in London, including several senior-level NATO assignments I think you are ready for."

"Thank you, sir. This makes me incredibly happy. I can't wait to talk with you about them. Could you please have your secretary cable the travel authorization to Miss Kress in the Chicago consulate so I can get the flight arrangements changed today?"

"Yes, of course. We'll see you here next Monday or Tuesday, then. I'll let Charlie know you're coming. We'll celebrate your return and get your next assignment underway. Must go. Goodbye for now."

***

Amahli arrived at the consulate office a bit before ten, walking immediately to Sam's office to confront him, but he was already in a meeting. It was just as well. No need for a public scene. She left a note on his desk.

Sam—Will meet you for dinner at the Italian place at 6 p.m. If you can't make it, let me know. I'm tied up until then. We must talk.—Amahli

Next she met with Miss Kress to find out if there were any open project action items that had to be closed out this week before she left. She also asked her to work with the consulate's local travel agency to get the tickets, already scheduled for the end of December, changed to Friday.

Amahli returned to her desk to review her diary for December appointments that had to be canceled and to write notes to the lawyers she'd been working with during the partnership negotiations since July. She also made appointments to meet with the Chicago senior consulate officer and his deputy. They were great to work with, and she wanted them to know how much that meant to her.

About 2:00 p.m., Miss Kress delivered the new tickets. Amahli wired BJ the flight information and arrival time. She made an appointment with JJ's school to get her last assignments and school transcript paperwork so she could register her for school back in London after their return.

Amahli left the office about 4:00 p.m. and walked home. There she talked with her rental agent, Mrs. Abernathy. She'd been on a month-to-month lease, and since she'd already paid the December rent, there were no issues about leaving early. She contacted the furniture rental company to see Mrs. Abernathy for the furniture pickup after she left. Lastly, she arranged for her sitter to stay with JJ until she returned from dinner that night.

****

Sam was at the table when Amahli arrived at the restaurant. He stood and reached for her across the table, creating a handsome but formidable presence.

"How was your Thanksgiving in Detroit? It was your first, wasn't it?"

"We came back early. It was a disaster, Sam. But that's not what I want to talk about. Sit down."

Her voice growled. Sam sat like an obedient dog. "Ok, what on earth is happening, Amahli?"

"I spoke with Sir Williams this morning. You should be ashamed, Sam. Why did you imply that I would be working in Chicago permanently the last time you spoke with him? That's my business, Sam, not yours."

"Well, I just assumed that you'd want to after having so much success here. Everyone is just amazed at your work."

"What? Because I'm a woman?"

"No, I didn't mean that, Amahli. Look, I'm sorry, but I thought you'd be happy that everyone loves your work and would want to continue here."

"The satisfaction with my work is not the issue, Sam. You cannot speak for me to my superiors or anyone for that matter. What's gotten into you?"

"Nothing. I just want you to stay."

"That is not for you to arrange. Are you trying to manipulate me? The work I was asked to do here is done. I told you I was going home in December. That's all I ever committed to. Just so you know, JJ and I are leaving for London on Friday. This is my last week in Chicago."

Sam sat in shock, seemingly almost at a loss for words…but not quite.

"Don't leave Chicago, Amahli," he pleaded. "You know I love you, so marry me. You'll never have to worry about anything again. We'll become the most dynamic diplomatic couple the UK can send around the world and JJ can grow up as you did, immersed in different cultures, able to have the most enriched education available. Let's spend the rest of our lives together, the perfect couple."

"Sam…" She sighed. "We would make a handsome couple, but I told you before that I would not commit to you, or to Chicago. These months in the US have taught me that I don't want the life my parents had when I was young. I want something more settled. I want to be in London with my family and have a job that will let me be close to them. I can't live in the States. My heart is not here. JJ and I belong in London with the people who helped me make my way in this upside-down life I found myself in."

"But I thought you loved me! We don't have to get married right away. I told you before, I'll wait." His voice strained, loud, again pleading. "I did everything I could for you. Don't you understand?"

Amahli sat silently. Not a word came from her sealed lips.

"Why do you think you were asked to stay on after the conference? It was a way that we could be together."

"How dare you try to control me like that?" Fury spit from her mouth. "You didn't ask me if that was what I wanted. You assumed you knew what was best for me, or maybe best for you. I don't want to be taken care of. I don't want anyone to think for me or to make decisions for me. I'm not that kind of woman!" Amahli caught her breath, trying to calm herself.

Other people in the restaurant were staring at them. Embarrassed, she lowered her voice and tried to smile, looking him straight in the eyes.

"Look, Sam. This weekend I learned what I want and made the decision to return to London now. I'm sorry it isn't the decision you were hoping for, but it's the right decision for me and JJ, and I believe it's the right decision for you." She reached for his hands across the table to keep his attention.

"Look, we were great together. You're a completely charming, sexy, cultured, and savvy man. You made me laugh and be comfortable in letting go of my past. But that's not what I want in a husband. I want a man who loves me because of my soul, not because of my packaging. Even if I relented and we married, both of us would be unhappy in time. You'd be unhappy because I can never be the subordinate diplomatic wife to your lead. You're astoundingly good at what you do, and you must have the right woman at your side to do it. I would be unhappy because I won't be your sidekick, as Americans call it. And I don't want to be away from my family in London. I must be near them."

"What if I commit to going back with you to live in London? I know you're the right woman for me. From the day I met you, I was in love with you. I thought spending our nights together meant that you loved me too."

"I never told you I loved you, Sam. There were always feelings between us because you offered me the charm, romance, and sexual experience that Jack gave me. I missed it more than I realized. And you're the most handsome man around, you know that." Amahli smiled. "Sex is luscious in the short run, but not enough for me in the long run, I'm afraid."

A spell swirled around them as time passed in silence. Sam eventually spoke.

"Look, you may be right that you aren't the right person for me. But then again, maybe you are. I think you'll regret this decision someday." He paused, looking at the expression on her face. "But that does not matter, does it?"

"No, it doesn't, Sam. Leaving is the right decision for me. And staying is the right decision for you."

"Charlie warned me that you always did exactly what you wanted and got what you wanted."

"Sam, I'm sorry."

"You're breaking my heart, Amahli." Sam pulled his hands to his heart and leaned toward her.

She laughed. "My dear friend, you're a bit melodramatic."

Sam pouted. "Well, then, kiss me goodbye and let me go lick my wounds."

Amahli looked at him sympathetically. "Your wounds aren't fatal. You just need some time to heal." They stood and put on their coats. Amahli wrapped her arms around him, kissed him on the cheek, then whispered in his ear, "You know I care about you. You'll always have a warm place in my heart. Now you go take care of yourself, you handsome devil."

She pinched his ear, threw her head back, and walked out of the restaurant, waving to him behind her. She believed Sam would get over it. He just needed some time and a new girlfriend…the right girlfriend.

***

Amahli arrived home to find JJ sitting at the dining room table, coloring. She paid the sitter, who thanked her, praised JJ, and wished them well on their journey. Amahli turned to her daughter. "Well, my young girl.

Have you written Grandma and Grandpa a goodbye letter?"

JJ stopped coloring and looked up at her mother. "Not yet. Is Sam taking us to the airport on Friday?"

"No, I won't be seeing Sam anymore."

"Too bad. I liked Sam."

"Me too, sweetheart. But what's more important is that we get home to Nani and Papa. London is where we belong."

JJ smiled, then dictated her goodbye letter, her mother carefully recording the words.

Dear Grandma and Grandpa,

Thank you for being my grandma and grandpa. I loved visiting you. I loved all the toys you gave me, especially the doll house and all the furniture. Too bad I couldn't take it home. The three pictures in the fancy frame are nice. I can't wait to show my new family to Papa and Nani.

Tell Uncle Andy that Teddy is excited about his first airplane ride. I'll make sure he's a good bear on the trip and eats his vegetables. I hope you have a very Happy Christmas. I'll write to you often.
Love and many hugs, JJ

Amahli reread the letter, soaking up her daughter's innocence. Then she helped JJ address the envelope and put a stamp on it. They would mail it in the morning before the rest of the week flew by. Meeting with the teacher, a last visit to the Chicago Zoo, a day to pack, and a last day in the office for meetings and goodbyes with staff.

JJ was excited because she was going to work with her mother. She'd never done that before.

JACK'S GIFT

CHAPTER 29

The phone on his nightstand rang, jarring Andy awake. He grabbed the receiver. "Hello?"

"Andy, this is Dad. I need you to come over as soon as you can." His voice was almost a stutter, shaky.

"Dad, what's happened? Why the emergency? It's the middle of the night."

"It's your mother. She's not herself, and I need help calming her down. She's been chasing me around the house, screaming about our lost son, telling me it's all my fault. She got hold of a kitchen knife."

"Dad, where are you now? Are you safe?"

"I've locked myself in the den. It's where I'm calling you from. Lucky we added that line last spring…"

"Stay where you are. Did you call the police?"

"No! I can't do that to her. She doesn't mean it—she's just having another episode."

"Another what? Dad, what's going on? What's she doing right now?"

"She's in the hall, walking up and down, crying and laughing at the same time. She's incoherent. Just come as soon as you can."

"If she tries to get into the den, call the police, Dad. I know you don't want to, but don't hesitate if she threatens your life or her own."

***

Andy arrived at his parents' house in less than an hour. *Why didn't Dad tell me about the other incidents?* It was May now, five months after Mom had the breakdown in December after Amahli and JJ left. He pulled out his house key as he jogged to the front door. With no front step light and the streetlight out, only the moon lit his path. He knocked. He didn't want to surprise or frighten his mother and wanted to alert his father.

He yelled through the door, "Mom, are you awake? It's Andy. I'm going to let myself in." He got no reply. Cautiously, he unlocked the front door and entered.

The hall light was on. His mother slouched on the floor with her back against the den's door. Her arms hung down by her sides, hands on the floor, palms up. A kitchen knife lay by her right hand and her chin rested on her chest. She had wet herself.

She was breathing, but she appeared unaware that Andy was at her side. It was a sight he would never erase from his memory. He heard water running. He called through the door, "Dad, I'm here. I'll be right back. I have turn off the faucets in the bathroom."

When he returned, Joe said, "I can't slide the den pocket door open. It's stuck."

"That's because Mom's leaning against the door, Dad. I'm going to call the police and an ambulance. They'll know how to move her and get her to the hospital."

"Do you have to? She'll be so embarrassed when she finds out."

"Dad, I don't care. She looks like she's in some kind of trance. My training says not to move her. When did she go quiet?"

"About fifteen minutes ago. I was afraid she was dead. Thank God she's breathing."

Andy could still hear tremors in his dad's voice. "Sit tight, Dad. Take deep breaths. I'm going to call the doctor as well." Andy picked up the knife and put it in the kitchen, safe from his mother's reach. Using the front hall phone, Andy called the police and then the family doctor, Dr. Pitts, who cared for his mother and father for years.

"Tell the police I'll meet the ambulance at St. Mary's," said the doctor. "I'll call you as soon as I can check her condition if you don't get to the hospital before then. I'm glad you're there with your father."

Andy squatted by his mother. She was conscious now. "Mom, what happened?"

"I don't know." Dorothy's voice was scratchy. "I don't remember anything. I feel awful. I must have done something. Is your father all right?" Dorothy's eyes filled with tears, her tone with remorse.

"Dad's in the den. Dr. Pitts will meet you at the hospital, and the ambulance medics will get you there. They and the police are on their way. We'll get there as soon as we can."

Dorothy started to protest, trying to get up, but couldn't. She fell back against the door. The ambulance arrived and the technicians moved her onto a gurney. Dad quickly opened the den door and emerged. Together father and son followed. With a lost look on her face, she was loaded into the ambulance. Sirens blared and lights flashed as it left the driveway for the hospital.

With two policemen now at their sides, Andy and his dad returned to the house. He looked at his father to see a broken man, a man who had lost everything. Andy suggested they go to the den. Gently, the police helped Joe into his wingback chair. Andy brought a glass of water, then sat at his dad's side listening as the story of the last months unfolded. How foolish of me, Andy thought, not to have seen the cracks in my mother's behavior grow wider until she collapsed upon herself.

Joe sat in his chair, his hands in his lap, twisting over each other as he spoke. "I tried to keep you out of it, Andy, thinking that your mother would get better. I just didn't see how bad it could get."

"Mr. Jackson, please tell us as best you can from the beginning what happened."

Joe turned toward the two uniformed policemen. The younger stood, ready to take notes, and the other, an older man, sat on the ottoman across from Joe.

"Ever since we received the letter from Amahli, our granddaughter's mother, after last Thanksgiving, it's been difficult. She wrote that they wouldn't visit again after they returned to London and Dorothy's bouts of depression and excited anger worsened. She'd become emotionally unstable after we lost our youngest son Jack in 1944."

He pulled the letter from the end table drawer next to his chair and gave it to the policeman. Joe stopped talking. He looked at Andy, and then back at the floor by his feet.

"She ranted about how JJ, our granddaughter, was kidnapped from us. About how evil Amahli was— what a whore she was, and that she had no right to have been with our son. I tried to calm her, talk with her to help her regain reality. Sometimes that worked and she returned to her normal self, writing JJ letters and taking good care of me and the house.

"At other times, such talk only made her more upset. She ran screaming through the house, scooping up all the dolls, books, and toys we gave our granddaughter, moving them from one room to another. Last week she dumped them all—except the dollhouse and its furniture, which I hid from her—into an old oil drum in the backyard by the garage and burned them. She watched the blaze, looking like a bum huddling over a fire to keep warm. I thought the neighbors would hear her, but she quieted. Finally, as the fire died, I was able to talk her back into the house. She went straight to the bedroom, collapsed on the bed, and slept for twelve hours."

"Mr. Jackson, why didn't you call us then? Didn't you realize she could have hurt herself, or you?"

"I honestly believed she wouldn't hurt herself. I thought she was grieving over the loss of the grandchild. You see, she really thought this child was not just our granddaughter, but the actual reincarnation of our youngest son. Our granddaughter was born the same day Dorothy dreamed that Jack would come back to her as a child."

Andy reached for his dad's hand and held it.

"What happened next?" The policeman's voice was uncommonly gentle.

"The next morning after she burned the toys, she woke up, got dressed, and fixed coffee and breakfast. I told her what happened. She laughed like it was all a joke, saying I must've had a bad dream. I asked her to see our doctor, but she insisted that the episode never happened, that it was a figment of my imagination. She was completely rational, thanked me for giving away JJ's toys as she requested, and continued a regular correspondence with her granddaughter just as Amahli suggested in her letter. She wrote every week, and we received many letters and photos back over the past months."

The policemen looked at Andy, who shrugged his shoulders. "Dad never told me about any of this. When I visited, she seemed fine."

"I didn't want to worry you, so I made sure your mom was in a normal cycle before I invited you over. You know how private your mother is about things. She would've been mad at me, and I didn't want that. I just wanted our quiet life back. Everything seemed ok."

"What happened then?" The policeman interviewing Joe shifted his weight. Andy noticed. "Can I get you something to drink?"

"No, no thank you. I think we should continue if your dad is ready." Joe nodded that he was.

"Well, it was about three or four weeks ago when I noticed that money was disappearing from my wallet. Not much, just a few dollars now and then. I asked her if she knew what might be happening. She blamed our maid and promised to fire her. I thought no more about it, but after Dorothy fired the maid, money started disappearing again. In an effort to figure out what was going on, I left for work as usual one morning, but parked around the corner and walked back to the house. I was going to tell her I had a flat tire and needed to call the gas station to come change it. As I walked through the kitchen, I heard a shuffling in the den. I found her there with a small wad of dollar bills in her hand. She was trying to stuff it into the crevice of the chair seat, under the cushion. I asked her what she was doing. She said, 'Saving for a rainy day.' I asked why. 'Because you're going to leave me, and I'll need money to live on.'

"I took her in my arms, asking why she would think such a thing. I told her I would never, ever do such a thing, that there was no reason for such thoughts. But she pushed me away, saying I was just like the others. 'What others?' She said, 'The people who told me that you were going to leave me, and that I have to take care of myself.'

"She told me to get out of the house, to go to work, and that it was none of my business. So I did, but I also called Dr. Pitts. He promised to stop by to talk with her, but when he did that afternoon, Dorothy was fine. She laughed about me misunderstanding that she found the money that the maid stole. She somehow convinced him that it was just a big mistake, explaining that she was just stressed from having to do all the housework because the maid was gone. Dr. Pitts gave her a sedative and left a prescription to get filled. I didn't connect this episode with the ones earlier in the year, so the doctor didn't know about them.

"I played dumb with her, helping her hunt. We found over $100. She must have been stashing it way before I realized that money was missing. She was probably hiding her housekeeping allowance, as well as cash from my wallet."

Joe sighed and looked plaintively at Andy. "Son, I'm so sorry. I believed her." Andy gave his hand squeeze.

"So, did anything else happen between when you found the money and tonight?" the policeman asked, encouraging Joe to continue.

"Nothing more than the usual nitpicking and criticism. But now that I think of it, in the last month I noticed she wasn't playing bridge with her girlfriends, nor were we invited out for dinner. I was fine with it because our social life was starting to tire me. Dorothy is very social."

"What sparked this incident, do you think?"

"I was coming home late because I had to meet with the union about some work rules. My early afternoon calls to her went unanswered. When I finally got home, about two hours late, every pot, pan, and piece of cooking equipment were out of the cupboards, scattered on the floor and countertops. She was inspecting them. She immediately started yelling at me about how she couldn't make dinner because she didn't have the proper pan to cook a decent meal, that the house was falling apart, and that she had to go clean it again and again because I fired the maid.

"I tried to remind her that she let the maid go. She screamed, 'You're lying! You're lying, like all the others!' Then she started marching through the house, turning the faucets on in the bathrooms and kitchen, letting the water run. I ran around after her, turning them off, trying to get her to sit down so I could reason with her. She did sit, finally. I was exhausted, but she was just getting started, it seems. She ran into the kitchen and pulled out the kitchen drawers. Silverware, knives, and other utensils crashed to the floor. We had another screaming match. None of it made any sense.

"Anyway, she suddenly stooped down to the floor, picked up a knife, and then lunged at me so fast that I couldn't get it away from her. I ran into the guest bedroom—the closest to the kitchen—closed the door, and locked it from the inside, only to find myself without a telephone to call Andy for help. I listened to her moaning and marching and screaming at me, 'I'm going to find you! You can't get away!'

"After about an hour, she quieted. I heard her walk to the far end of the hall and into our bathroom. She turned on the water again, but instead of trying to stop her, I threw open the door, ran into the den, slid the den door closed, and locked it. That's when I heard her coming down the hall, ranting, and that's when I called Andy."

The older policeman and Andy walked outside while the younger one reassured Joe that they would be in touch, and not to worry.

"Look, I'm not a psychiatrist, but I think your mother is seriously ill and needs help. I'll send the report over to Dr. Pitts tomorrow. I suggest you get your dad out of this place for a while to somewhere calm and protected."

"I'll do what I can, but this is his home. He'll be safe, and as comfortable here as anywhere else, as long as my mother doesn't come home. Once we talk to the doctor, we can make decisions. I'll take some time off to see him through this." The men shook hands.

Andy helped his dad clean the place up, fixed sandwiches that they picked at, then drove to the hospital.

***

Dr. Pitts arrived at the hospital as Dorothy was rolled into the Emergency Room. He listened to her incoherent speech and ramblings about the voices, examined her glazed-over eyes and weak physical condition, then immediately called the on-duty psychiatrist. She was admitted to the psychiatric ward for further tests. When Andy and Joe arrived, Dr. Pitts filled them in on her condition.

Joe signed commitment papers and saw that she was as comfortable as possible in the ward. As Dr. Pitts approached her bed, he observed Joe and Andy holding her hands and kissing her goodbye, but she was nearly asleep by then from the sedatives he'd prescribed.

Although it seldom occurred in older adults, Dr. Pitts explained that it appeared that Dorothy may have experienced a schizophrenic breakdown. He, the cardiologist, and the psychiatrist also speculated that some form of atherosclerosis, a hardening of the arteries that restricts blood flow to the brain and other parts of the body, could have triggered the increasingly severe episodes. They decided that she should be transferred to a nursing home with a secure area for elderly residents with dementia and other behavioral issues. There were few drugs that could calm her, beyond sedatives, so a place to keep her sheltered and safe from herself and others was critical.

***

Joe asked Andy to write JJ explaining that Grandma was ill. He didn't have the words. To Amahli, Andy wrote to explain what happened. He didn't know how, but he would help his dad, if his dad would let him.

Amahli wrote back and sent a small package with it. Andy shared the letter with his father.

My dearest Andy,

How did you ever find the words to tell JJ what happened to Grandma? It was the most beautiful letter, a story from the heart, the best that ever was written, as far as I am concerned. JJ will cherish your words forever, as will I. She looks forward to getting letters from Grandpa.

I know you'll find your way through this tragedy, and your dad will get reestablished with your support.

I hope you receive a package I sent soon. Please give it to your dad. It's my way of saying thank you for being so wonderfully kind to me to make me a part of his family.

Thank you for staying connected over the past months. Through your letters, my parents and BJ have come to know you and understand why I care for you so much.

I continue to miss you since our return to London. Leaving you and your dad was the one thing I regret. Please continue to write. Now that I'm home, I see that I need you in my life, as you told me before I left London. You were able to support me without making me feel dependent on you. That makes you a treasure. If you ever decide to make a big change, a real change, come to London. I will be here.

With much affection, Amahli

"Andy, she's in love with you. Are you in love with her?"

"Maybe. I thought I was, but now I don't know. I can't think about her right now, Dad." Andy blushed, put Amahli's letter in his wallet, and then said, "Here's the package she sent."

Joe pulled off the string and brown paper to open a small box. In it was Jack's Air Service ring and a letter from JJ. Inside the locket was, not Amahli and Jack's picture, but a photo of Dorothy and Jack. They sat silently for a few minutes. Then Joe read JJ's letter aloud.

Dear Grandpa,

I am sorry that Grandma is sick. Tell her to get well soon and that I love her. I'm sorry I won't be able to see you both again. I miss the card games and I wish you were here to teach Mummy, Papa, and Nani to play five-card stud. Every time I try to teach them, they end up laughing. I'm not sure they will ever learn. I tried to get Uncle BJ to help me, but he says he only knows how to play bridge. I don't believe him.
XOXOXO, JJ

***

Over the weeks that followed, Andy and Joe watched Dorothy slip more deeply into her fantasy world. She was a child again who enjoyed playing with dolls. She talked to them endlessly, finding solace in their companionship. She couldn't be cared for at home, so she stayed in a nursing home near enough so Joe could visit regularly.

He continued to work. It provided balance to his life, a counterbalance to caring for Dorothy and the sadness it brought upon him. He told Andy that on the weekends, he visited for several hours. Several times during the week he stopped by as well.

Dorothy rarely recognized who Joe was. Somedays she ignored him, and some days she welcomed him as if he were a new neighbor from down the hall. Through his visits, he became friends with the nursing home staff, all of whom appreciated his kindness and attentiveness to his wife. His consistent attention ensured that Dorothy was well taken care of. He promised Andy, and Dorothy, that as long as she lived, he would be there for her.

After the first month, Andy stopped visiting his mother. His frustration and anger with her for tearing their family apart became more than he could bear. The only thing that seemed to give Andy any solace was helping his father.

Joe's body had been growing weak from a lack of exercise, so Andy helped him develop a walking routine. He also hired a part-time housekeeper to cook and clean, and his father slowly rebuilt his life through the summer and fall. Joe began seeing old friends again to play cards or go out for dinner. Andy checked in on him twice a week and grew confident that his dad was going to be ok.

The coming Christmas holiday would be a sad one for his dad, but not a depressive disaster. They would make it through together. To witness his remarkable ability to adjust to new circumstances was a lesson that Andy would not forget.

***

Over time, Andy continued to find it difficult to cope with conflicting emotions about his mother—his sorrow over her current state, his bitterness over what she did to her husband and Amahli. His work, once engaging and purposeful, became meaningless. What good is corporate success if your family is broken?

The emptiness led to depressive thoughts that frightened him. Such thinking had never occurred before, not even during the war, and he knew he had to do something about it soon, before it got the better of him.

Andy spent many restless nights, tossing and turning, trying to figure out what he should do. No matter how hard he tried, he kept coming back to the belief that his mother's condition was a just reward for her past behavior. Her years of manipulation, arrogance, and putting herself above others was hurtful and bigoted. Now she was a woman who had lost connection with reality, abandoning those she cared about and all who cared about her.

Andy knew this thinking was wrong. The physical disease, not her moral character, were at the root of his mother's behavior. He tried to focus on the mother he loved as a child. The smart and clever woman, caring for him and Jack for so many years, generous with her time, providing them with an abundance of small pleasures—help with homework, special pancake breakfasts, surprise after-school walks through the woods, cheering for them at school sports events, and bragging to her friends about their successes. Andy remembered the sparkling Christmas mornings when he and his brother unwrapped their presents to find exactly what they wished for, and the many nights when his mother read bedtime fairytale stories and poems that made their imaginations dance with delight. But he was still lost.

***

After a quiet dinner with his father, Andy confessed. "Dad, I'm frustrated with my life. I don't like my work anymore—it has no purpose. I'm angry with Mom for breaking our family up. I don't know what to do."

"Andy, you're too young to drown yourself like this. You can't be responsible for what you can't control or you'll end up a bitter, lonely man. Give yourself a break, son, and don't let your mother be your responsibility. She's my responsibility. She took care of our family, making sure we had the best life we could, no matter what our circumstances, but she wasn't perfect, God knows. I know you got shorted sometimes and I am so sorry for that, but we must forgive her…and forgive ourselves for not being able to fix her."

The men sat silently together.

"I guess you're right, but I'm so very worried about you. You're going to need help. We're in this together, aren't we? You're only fifty-two, Dad. That's too young to spend the rest of your life alone."

"Don't worry about me because each day is better. I'm confident my loneliness and sadness will subside eventually. You're the best son a father could have, but you will not be my keeper. It's time for you, as well as me, to rebuild our lives."

"Maybe you're right." Andy sighed. "There's something else. I've tried to keep my distance with Amahli. You know we met as work colleagues and I wanted to keep it that way after she told me about Jack. Hell, I didn't want anyone thinking that I was going to steal her from my dead brother. But I have to tell you, I love her. I've been fighting it since I met her and I can't stop how I feel. Isn't it wrong for me to love my brother's woman? Isn't that warped in some way?"

Joe smiled. "Really? Your brother's been dead for almost nine years. Amahli's been, in essence, a widow all that time. I don't know what your problem is now. Both of you recognize what you feel for each other. She loves you, she said it in her letter. And you've finally admitted what I've known since I saw you two together the first time you brought her to the lake house. Take the woman at her word. She wouldn't say she loves you and invite you to cross an ocean if she didn't feel the same way."

Andy blushed. Silence filled the room for several minutes. "Well, Andy, what are you going to do?"

"I guess I'm going to London. I'll either get a transfer, or quit and find a job when I get there."

Joe smiled. They toasted to the future with their favorite Tennessee Whiskey.

***

Father and son spent a quiet Christmas together. They pulled out the many photos of Jack that Dorothy showed but didn't give to Amahli and her daughter. Andy selected the ones that made his dad and him the happiest and pasted them into an album, writing the story of each photo. Then, Andy wrote in the inside cover:

To Amahli and JJ,
These are Dad's and my favorite memories of Jack, who brought us together through his love.
Andy

Andy scheduled his departure to arrive in London on New Year's Eve, a year after Amahli left the States.

***

A knock at the door went unheard by Amahli and Papa, who were deep in the kitchen cooking. Maa was in her study finishing a review of a student's research article while JJ fiddled with her first electric train set that she put together in the front room, an unexpected request to Santa Claus. Again, a knock at the door.

JJ jumped up, ran to the door, and opened it to find Uncle Andy standing in front of her. "Mummy told me you were coming to London." She fell into his arms, screaming, "He's here! He's here! What a grand New Year's party we're going to have!"

EPILOGUE

Joe didn't attend the wedding in 1954, less than a year after Andy arrived in London. He wrote that he couldn't, expressing his need to stay by Dorothy, but his words conveyed both disappointment and unhappiness. Unwilling to let the father of the groom live in such state of frustration, Amita wrote how much she admired the commitment to his wife, then put him in the middle of the prewedding festivities by adding volumes about the wedding plans. She secretly slipped in a photo of Amahli in what would become her wedding dress, promising that it would be supplemented with a special album of wedding pictures soon after the wedding. Additionally, Amita arranged for a telephone connection with Joe so he could participate in the joyous ceremony from Detroit.

Amita was jubilant about the marriage. Her daughter was marrying a man who met all her criteria, and her daughter was happy and at peace. Amita insisted on a formal wedding, blending Hindu and British traditions. Amahli wore her mother's favorite yellow and gold sari. Andy donned his first proper English cutaway suit, complete with striped pants, black morning coat, and gray vest.

Unlike large Hindu weddings that could include over 1,000 guests, with dancing and parties for a week, this wedding was small, celebrated in the Simmons' home with close friends and family. Sir Williams and Charlie Sachs were best men. Amahli's maid of honor was JJ, sporting her first sari. Sam Toller sent a slightly ostentatious bouquet that dwarfed the Simmons' entry hall table, with a note wishing them the absolute best and announcing his engagement to Miss Jennifer Wadsby of Chicago. Amahli laughed, explaining to her mother that all Sam needed was time to get over their breakup and find a new girl—someone who actually met his criteria for the perfect diplomatic wife.

As planned, Joe was on the phone when the couple said their vows. It was worth every farthing as he cheered and cried in celebration. He sent the couple Dorothy's sterling silverware and "Made in Occupied Japan" china as his wedding gift, confident that Dorothy would have wanted it to stay in the family. For JJ, he sent the doll house and all its furniture.

***

Amahli and Andy took JJ with them to Detroit for Dorothy's funeral less than five years after the wedding. It was a long-awaited reunion with Joe, but it was also a sad time. Andy comforted his dad over his wrenching decision to not allow the doctors to insert a feeding tube. He knew that his wife would never have wanted to live, unable to speak or eat while bedridden in diapers as her body disintegrated, finally catching up with her already starved brain.

A year passed before Joe could contemplate a future. But in the spring of 1959, he knew it was time. With Andy's encouragement he sold the house, moving into a roomy, bright modern apartment. He kept a few things beyond the essentials: the rec room dartboard, his wingback chair from the den, and the family photos and memorabilia, along with the letter box Dorothy stored in the cedar chest at the end of their bed.

The sale of the home provided Joe with a tidy sum, which he invested wisely in the stock market, again with Andy's advice. He considered an early retirement because he also became fully qualified for his pension at age sixty, and the law changed in 1961, allowing him to collect social security at age 62. He always treasured a quiet and predictable life, but now he surprised even himself—much less Andy and Amahli—when he declared he itched to do something new. Maybe travel. Certainly he was going to London. His friends at the plant thought it a tempting idea, but cautioned him about engaging with the Socialists who seemed to be running everything "over there" now. He laughed and declared that nothing would suit him better.

***

JJ wasn't an only child for long. Emily was eight now. JJ spoiled her baby sister, bequeathing onto Emily the title of Family Princess, and a princess she was, a girl loving frilly fashion. JJ gave her the sacred dollhouse and its furniture as soon as she was old enough not to attempt eating the furniture instead of decorating the dollhouse with it.

JJ morphed into a tomboy, loving sports, the out-of-doors, and all things mechanical. By age nine, she was fixing her bicycle and tightening her own skates. By age fifteen, she cajoled Andy into teaching her how to change their car's tires and oil. She was driving at sixteen, disappearing into the countryside on weekend excursions with friends for country hikes and camping.

Her passion for soccer meant Arsenal season tickets with Papa. Although a mediocre team in the 1950s, he and JJ were loyal because of its Scottish ownership in the late 1800s and factory worker roots. When Amahli asked why she liked sports so much, JJ replied, "Don't you remember, Mum? The baseball games Sam took us to were so much more interesting than the museums…except, of course, the Museum of Science and Industry. Since I can't watch baseball here, football is the best option."

Her mother sighed. Her oldest daughter was becoming more like Jack every year.

***

Snow fell on London during the Christmas week of 1962, igniting the air with a holiday scene worthy of Currier & Ives. Streets glistened, and lights decorated the city. Amahli and Andy took special care in decorating this year because their home was the central location for the Simmons-Jackson Family Christmas Celebration, just a ten-minute walk from the Simmons' home.

Amita and Thomas insisted that Joe stay with them the first two weeks of his month in London. Having never traveled outside of the States, they were concerned he would need a quiet place to rest and a guide to tour the wonders of London and it surrounds. But Joe surprised them. After some initial help with maps, tips for places to see, and ways of getting around, combined with only one day of touring with them, he left the next morning, declaring, "I'm going out and about on my own." It was a huge success, repeated many times during his visit.

He was particularly enthused with riding the double-decker buses, navigating the Tube with hordes of people, and taking lunch in pubs, where he engaged in lively chats with the locals. He met JJ, now seventeen, after school, and she took him to all her favorite haunts. He loved her schoolmates, and they completely enjoyed hearing his stories about living in the States. Dinner was with Amahli and Andy and the kids, JJ and Emily. He thought it all joyous and wonderful.

Emily met Grandpa Jackson on this first Christmas visit and immediately fell in love with him. He was one of the few things JJ and she totally agreed on. To the girls, Grandpa and Papa seemed remarkably similar because they both ran interference for them with the other adults.

In almost everything else, there was a tension between the girls. Disputes about messes ended in a line of tape separating their spaces in their shared bedroom. JJ teased Emily unmercifully, dominating her younger sister. Andy and Amahli worked hard to keep a balance between the two girls, and to pull them apart at times. Like the time after Andy formally adopted JJ, Emily came screaming and crying to them.

When asked what was wrong, the four-year-old bellowed, "JJ says she's luckier than me because Daddy's her uncle, too." Discussions with JJ about getting along with her sister became the norm, not the exception.

As a teenager, JJ wanted to attend university in the States to study computer engineering, a new technology field that was just coming to university curriculums. She was brilliant at math and sciences in school and wrote Grandpa about her interest in coming to the US for college. He suggested the University of Michigan, only thirty miles from him. Joe encouraged her interests, believing that she inherited both his and Jack's engineering genes. Women were a rarity in the programs, but her high school teachers encouraged her to apply anyway. Like all parents, Amahli and Andy were concerned about her being so far from home, but did not say no.

***

Amahli continued in her diplomatic work, taking positions with increasing responsibility. She traveled occasionally, but was never absent from home for more than two or three weeks at a time. Andy arrived in London with a job. GM was more than happy to assign him to a London-based corporate strategy group that was formed after the signing of their partnership with a British parts manufacturer and an auto assembly production facility. The work focused on the future, looking at potential markets, technology innovation, and futuristic automobile designs to meet the growing need of the young people dubbed Baby Boomers. He found purpose in his work, as well as having brought his family back together.

Their marriage was the partnership Amahli needed. Andy grew into it most comfortably, always joking that it was easy for him because back in 1953 in Detroit, he was always left to clean up after meals with Amahli when she and JJ first visited. The experience taught him what he needed to know. He laughingly blamed it on his mother for driving him to it. That and Amita's cooking classes—designed especially for him now that BJ came to visit less often—and his gentleness with their children made him a near-perfect partner.

When asked about her husband by colleagues or acquaintances, Amahli would smile slyly. With a twinkle in her eye she would say, "No man is perfect, but Andy is damn close."

***

On Christmas Eve the extended Simmons-Jackson family came together. People gathered at Amahli and Andy's home a bit after seven. Cocktails were served in the front room as new arrivals were introduced. The couple observed the action in the room, smiling and listening.

Amita was in charge. "Joe, I want to introduce you to a dear friend of mine, Chanda Khatri. She and I have been close since before the war. Chanda, this is Mr. Joe Jackson, Andy's father from Michigan. I've seated you next to each other so you might have time to chat."

She smiled at both of them, then moved on after refreshing their drinks. Joe and Chanda looked at each other, laughing a bit awkwardly, realizing they'd been set up. Andy and Amahli took bets on how long it would be before her mother would have them out on a date.

Amita spied BJ and his friend. He gave Amita a knowing smile, then Amita gathered everyone together To BJ inn front of everyone, she said, "We're so glad you could join us tonight. I know you've been terribly busy lately. I miss you in the kitchen, as well as at our dinner table. Andy's had to take over for you, and he's certainly not as good a cook as you are!"

They laughed. Amita then said to BJ in a formal manner, "Please introduce your friend to everyone while I freshen your drinks."

"Of course!" said BJ, his voice filled with pleasure. "I want everyone to meet my partner, Jeremy Jones. He's been the one keeping me busy."

Jeremy gave him a "What in the hell are you doing?" look. BJ smiled, put his arm around Jeremy's waist, and began introductions.

"This is Amahli. We served together at Glatton with JJ's biological father, Jack. He was my best friend. This is Andy, the husband of Amahli, adopted father of JJ, and Jack's brother. We agree that I reminded Jack of Andy. Amahli and Jack were the first two people to accept me as I am.

"This is Joe, the father of Andy and Jack. This is Chanda, Amita's best friend. Amita has plans for her and Joe." He paused for a minute while everyone was giggled like schoolchildren.

To quiet the room, BJ raised his voice. "Can I have your attention, please! These are JJ and Emily, my nieces. I've been Uncle BJ since the day I showed up at Amita and Thomas's doorstep in 1945." Amita returned with fresh drinks. "And as you already know, this is the lovely Amita and Thomas, my second set of parents. They're the ones who saved me from insanity when I first moved to London."

BJ turned to Jeremy and said, "This is my family. I know it all sounds confusing, if not a bit incestuous, Jeremy, but if you join me, they will be yours as well as mine."

The room exploded in shouts of "Here! Here!" and glasses were raised to toast the couple.

JJ shouted over the chattering adults, "Come on, everyone. Let's eat! Emily and I are sitting with BJ and Jeremy so we can hear all the news about what's really happening in London."

It was the best Christmas ever.

JACK'S GIFT

ACKNOWLEDGEMENTS

I've been a blogger and business writer for many years, but never attempted long form storytelling. I come to fiction later in life. With the encouragement of my family, friends, and a persistent editor, I am on my way.

My beta readers—Diana Mayes, Carol Binkowski, Pat Littell, Sandy Mears, Dottie Soelke, and Holly Myers—provided invaluable feedback to enrich Amahli's story that, I hope, resulted in a memorable read for all who love tales about families, connections and freedom.

Many thanks go to my editor, Susan Uttendorfsky, owner of Adirondack Editing, who helped me repair my many first-time author blunders to bring this revised edition to readers.

ABOUT THE AUTHOR

Dorine developed her storytelling voice by blogging about living in Memphis, Tennessee in Memphis Diaries; approaching her golden years in Sixties Shorties; revealing the ups and downs of owning, captaining, and living aboard a 46' sailboat in Raghauler Journal, and accounting for retired life in Dare I.

After a consulting career of over thirty years, co-authoring two business books and many industry articles, she earned her doctorate in communications design (DCD) in 2000 from the University of Baltimore. She taught at Georgetown University in its Communications, Culture, and Technology graduate program and at the University of Baltimore in the Yale Gordon College of Arts and Sciences. She was also the chief information officer for the Peace Corps from 2010 to 2015. Dorine lives in northern Virginia.

Visit her website, dorineandrews.com

QUESTIONS FOR DISCUSSION

1. This story takes place over 75 years ago. What relevance does it have for today's younger readers?

2. Dorothy Jackson and Amita Simmons are both strong and dominant women. How do each meet—or not—meet the challenges created by events and changes to their families?

3. Both Dorothy and Amita have cultural biases about people different from themselves. Are they able to move beyond their racism? Why?

4. Is Amahli manipulative in her struggle to establish her career? How does her experience shape her career decisions?

5. In the 1950s, few women had careers such as Amahli's. How relevant is her career struggle for today's women? Have such struggles disappeared, or have they just shape-shifted? What do they look like now?

6. What is the symbolism of the yellow sari? How do Amahli and her mother address their conflicts with traditional and modern methods?

7. Why do Jack, Sam, and Andy fall in love with Amahli? Would Amahli have stayed with Jack for life if he lived?

8. In the end, why does Amahli choose Andy? Why does she decide not to stay single, as she declares at the beginning of the book?

9. Why does Joe change the way he wants to live after Dorothy's death?

10. What is the essence of Andy and Joe's relationship? What are its strengths and weaknesses? What does that portend for our own lives?

11. Does Amahli do the right thing when she refuses to let JJ visit Dorothy again after the disastrous Thanksgiving gathering? What else might she do?

12. What do BJ and Tommy contribute to the story? Are they important characters? Why?

13. What issues might JJ encounter when Andy becomes her adopted father, as well as her uncle?

14. Jack's gift to Amahli is JJ. What are Jack's other gifts? Why might they be considered gifts?